HOLD ME CLOSE

SHANNYN SCHROEDER

To all the survivors

Shane Callahan drove the loop around O'Hare again. He could've parked in the cell phone lot, or if he'd been smart he would've waited for Maggie to call him when she landed. But excitement overtook him. She was coming home.

Finally. For good.

He stayed in the left lane, moving like a snail, hoping he'd see Maggie emerge from the airport. Instead, another cab cut him off. He bypassed the terminals and curved left for another trip around. His cell phone buzzed. He glanced at the screen and saw the message from Maggie.

I'm here! Have my luggage. Be out in a few minutes.

His heart raced. He took a slow breath. He felt like a kid on Christmas morning. At least the weather made that believable. The city had been hit with another snowstorm last night. The nasty weather made February feel like the longest month instead of the shortest.

Shane shifted into the center lane until he pulled up at the international terminal. Maggie stood at the curb, stomping her feet. Her short jacket barely met her waist. And she had no gloves. Her cheeks were pink as the wind whipped her hair around.

She was a sight for sore eyes.

He stopped the truck and had nearly forgotten to put it in park before opening his door. His big smile stretched his cheeks in a way they hadn't been in forever. He rounded the back of the truck, and Maggie ran and jumped at him.

His first thought was that she'd lost weight again. She was nothing in his arms. But as she wrapped her arms around his neck and he breathed in her scent, he couldn't think of anything but Maggie. She was home.

"It's so good to see you," she said, muffled against his shoulder.

Even though he didn't want to, he released her and set her back on the curb. Looking at the suitcase at her feet, he asked, "Is that all you have?"

"Yeah. I shipped back boxes that'll arrive in a few days. I hope. I didn't want to worry about customs. I just wanted to get home."

He grabbed the suitcase and put it on the narrow back-seat of the truck and offered Maggie a hand to step up into the vehicle. "Everything okay with your mom?"

"Yeah, I guess. Not that I would take her word for it. Ryan said the doctor has said she's doing well, and as long as she continues to eat right and take her meds, she can bounce back from the heart attack."

He closed her door and got behind the wheel.

"I wanted to be back here weeks ago, but I felt bad for my boss. I didn't want to leave him with no help, and then there was all the packing. I didn't realize how much stuff I'd accumulated over the last year and a half."

She rubbed her hands together in front of the vent, so he turned the heater up full blast.

"Not that I'm complaining about you finally coming

home, but are you here just because of your mom?" He flicked a glance in her direction when she didn't answer.

"Not really," she finally said. "I mean, that was a big thing. But as much as I loved traveling and meeting new people, it started to feel like I was still running away."

As Shane pulled out of the airport and onto the Kennedy Expressway, he smiled at the snarl of traffic. Rush hour would give him more time alone with Maggie. Her family would occupy her every minute as soon as they found out she was home.

"Running from what?"

"Everything." She turned the heater down. "I need to get my life back."

An uneasy sensation pricked the back of his neck. Whenever Maggie spoke with that kind of conviction, it usually meant she planned to do something other people wouldn't like. "How do you mean?"

She stared out the passenger window. "Let's stop for some coffee."

Shane made his way to the right lane and the nearest exit. He got off at Harlem and drove down the street until he came to the mall. Slush coated the street and mountains of snow were piled on the curbs. Shane pulled into the parking lot and found a spot.

Maggie jumped from the truck and didn't wait for him as she headed into the mall, her hands tucked tightly into her jacket pockets. Her hair was longer than he remembered. The dark strands flowed behind her. He smelled perfume in her wake as he caught up with her.

The mall wasn't crowded, and they found a coffee shop, ordered, and sat at a small table. Shane draped his jacket over the back of his chair, but Maggie kept hers on. The girl was always cold.

"Spill it, Magpie."

Her gaze shot up to meet his at the use of her nickname. Although her siblings had given her the name because she'd been so loud as a kid, she'd become quieter over the last few years.

"When I left Chicago, Ryan was pissed. He accused me of running away."

"Big brothers can be like that." He'd lock his sisters up if they even thought about running halfway around the world alone.

"But he thought I was running from him. You know how he is. And in my mind, that might've been it too. But after traveling around and settling in with my cousins, I realized I was still missing out on life." She sipped her coffee. "Ever since Todd…" She paused, and Shane knew she did it to gather her strength because she hated talking about him.

Shane reached out and held her hand.

"He took so much from me, Shane. It's been almost five years since he raped me, and I've never stepped back in O'Leary's. It's my family's bar. I grew up there, and he took that from me. And my first apartment. I'm supposed to have great memories about my first apartment, but that's ruined."

"I know," he whispered. Guilt tugged at him.

Her fingers tightened on his. "I'm taking it all back."

"How?"

"I'm going to talk to Ryan and start working at the bar. And if there's an apartment available above the bar, I'm going to move in there."

Shane's lungs froze. Yeah, it had been nearly five years, but he remembered all the times where something would trigger a bad reaction in Maggie. She couldn't go some places or see things or smell things without falling apart. She had good reason to have stayed away from O'Leary's. No one expected her to go back.

He forced oxygen into his body. "Are you sure that's a good idea?"

"Something needs to happen. I'm better, Shane. I really am, but I'm still not myself."

He stroked his thumb along her knuckles. There was a time that even this small contact had been too much for her. She *was* better. He saw it all the time. But still. "Have you talked to Dr. Janzen about this?"

Maggie sipped her coffee again and shook her head. "I have an appointment later this week."

Great. So she dumped this on him before her family, before her therapist. How the fuck was he supposed to know what to say?

"Rushing into something like this isn't a good idea. You need to think about it and talk to Dr. Janzen. She's always steered you right."

"I'm not rushing. I've been thinking about it for a long time. I miss being part of the family business. Everyone tiptoes around me when it comes to the bar. They're all still afraid to even talk about the business in front of me. It's ridiculous."

"But living above the bar?"

"I don't want to live with my mom forever."

He could definitely sympathize with that idea. "I'm looking for a new place, too. Why don't we go rent something together?"

"What happened with Joe?"

"His brother needs an apartment, so Joe asked me to move out."

"That sucks."

"So what do you say?"

She bit down on her bottom lip. "I need to live above O'Leary's. To know that I can."

Thoughts raced through his mind. "At least wait to talk to Ryan until after you see Dr. Janzen."

"She won't change my mind."

He already knew that. But it would buy him some time. "She'll talk to you about how to approach it, though."

Maggie nodded and smiled.

The knot of tension in his neck and the flurry of thoughts in his head disappeared. He'd seen her smile every time they FaceTimed or Skyped, but nothing could compare to the real thing.

"That's why I wanted to see you before I told my family I was coming home. I knew I could count on you to listen and not tell me I'm dumb."

"You're never dumb."

"Yeah, well, sometimes I do dumb things. And my family likes to point it out to me all the time." She finished her coffee, and he realized he hadn't even touched his.

He wanted to talk her out of this. It was a bad idea and had a ton of potential to set her back. He couldn't bear to see her go back. He couldn't imagine not seeing her gorgeous smile again.

"Thanks for the coffee. I think I'm ready to see my family now." She stood, breaking contact with him.

When he stood, she wrapped her arms around his waist and settled her head on his chest.

"I'm glad you came to pick me up. I needed this."

"Me too." He'd missed her something fierce over the months.

MAGGIE STARED OUT THE WINDOW AS SHANE TOOK STREETS through the city to get her to her mom's house. Asking him to pick her up had been a good choice. She could've asked

Moira, but her sister would try to talk her out of her plan. Shane was the best listener she'd ever known. He'd proven it again today. The guy even remembered the name of her therapist. Who did that?

Shane. Always Shane. He'd been there for her through the good and the really, really bad. Even when it was hard, and she'd tried to push him away because she didn't think she could be around any guy after being raped, he stayed. Not in an obnoxious *I know what's best for you* way, but in an *I care about you* way. Without him, she probably never would have had the guts to travel.

After he pulled up in front of her mom's house, he put the truck in park but didn't turn off the ignition.

"Coming in?"

He let out a small chuckle. "You decided to come home without telling your family. Then you had me pick you up from the airport. They're going to have plenty to say, and I don't want to be caught in the crossfire. I think I'll head home."

"Chicken."

"Smart."

"Whatever." She yanked on the handle and jumped from the cab.

Shane met her and grabbed her suitcase. After setting it on the curb at her feet, he held her hand. "I'm glad you're finally home."

"You're gonna get sick of me."

"Never." He slammed the door. "Give me a call if you want to get together later."

"My family will probably fill my night. And then some. I'll call when I need to escape." She hefted the bag and stared at the front door. Although she knew Shane had gotten back behind the wheel, the truck didn't move.

Of course he'd wait for her to go inside. She waved at

Shane and walked up the steps. The last time she'd made this trip, she entered a living room filled with her siblings all crying. Their mother had had a heart attack and was in the hospital. The whole episode made Maggie realize how much she was missing. Not just for herself, but with her family.

As the youngest, she'd always been able to count on having her family there. It had never occurred to her that at some point they might not be. She turned the knob on the door and found resistance. She fished out her keys and let herself in.

With the door closed at her back she paused and took a slow inhale. No dinner smells. And quiet. She couldn't remember a time when home was quiet.

"Mom?" she called, hoping her mom was there.

"What? Who is it?"

A relieved sigh joined the smile on her face. "It's me, Maggie."

She turned the corner and walked through the living room and dining room. Her mother stood at the door to the kitchen. The teacup in her hand shook. Maybe a surprise homecoming wasn't the best idea.

"What's wrong?" Eileen asked.

"Nothing. I'm home. For good."

Her mom set her tea on the table. "When did this come about? And without so much as a phone call."

Maggie hugged her mom and breathed in the scents of Jean Naté cologne and Estée Lauder makeup. Mom gave her a quick pat on the back.

"How do you feel?" she asked Eileen.

"Fine. Same as I have been every time you've asked. I've had enough of the coddling." She took up her cup again and sipped before sitting at the dining room table.

Yeah, Mom was back to herself. Even with regular reports from her siblings about Mom being fine, nothing could replace experiencing it. She sat adjacent to Eileen. "Is it okay if I move back in for a while? It'll only be for a little bit until I figure out what I'm doing next."

"Of course. I have this big house all to myself."

"Thanks."

Her mom stared at her with narrowed eyes. "What's wrong?"

"Nothing."

"Then why are you home?"

"It was time."

"*Psh.* You came back because of my trip to the doctor."

"That was part of it. I'm worried about you, Mom."

"I told you, no need." She pressed her lips so tightly, the pink line of lipstick disappeared.

"I needed to come home. I had a great time in Ireland, but it's time to move on. I need to start making a life for myself. Figure out who I am and what I want."

Her mother gave her one sharp nod in response.

"I'm going to go unpack."

"I'll make dinner."

Maggie tried not to roll her eyes. She knew her mom would be on the phone as soon as Maggie's foot hit the bottom step to go up to her old bedroom. "Can you tell them to give me a day before they descend?"

Her mom didn't answer, and Maggie knew she didn't have a chance. She lugged her suitcase upstairs and stood in the middle of her bedroom, the same bedroom she'd shared with Moira for years. Many of her things were still there, but there was no sign of Moira.

She tossed her bag on the bed and sat beside it. Would she want to live alone? Sure, she'd done it briefly. But even that hadn't been really living alone. She'd lived in an apartment above the bar. Her brothers worked downstairs. She always had family around.

Was that a good thing? Or bad? She made a mental note to add that to the list of questions to talk to Dr. Janzen about. She got up and started putting away her clothes. Everything was exactly where she'd left it. It was as if no one had stepped foot in the room since she left a year and half ago.

As much as things didn't change here, so many others had. At Christmas, she'd been surrounded by her brothers and sister who had all fallen in love. She felt as if she'd missed out on something. It felt like waking from a dream, feeling like she was the same person but she'd time traveled. Everyone else was different.

It was another reason she was glad she'd seen Shane first. He was the same old Shane he'd always been. She liked being able to count on some things.

Just like when she heard a loud noise downstairs, she knew her big sister had come over. Knowing Moira, she beat everyone else there. Moments later, pounding on steps let her know Moira was too impatient to wait for her to come down.

"Maggie!" she screamed from the doorway. She squeezed her in a tight hug. When she let go, Moira tried for an angry look, but Maggie wasn't buying it. "Why didn't you tell us you were coming home?"

"Because I didn't want anyone making a big deal out of it."

Moira crossed her arms, which pushed her big boobs up, emphasizing them even more. Maggie wished she had a little more in that department. Moira had gotten more than her fair share. "So why are you home?"

"Why is everyone so suspicious? I've been gone for over a year. I figured you'd all be happy I came back."

"We are. But you always seemed happy when we talked. Did something happen?"

"No. Except Mom having a heart attack. That was a

wake-up call. She's not going to be here forever." Maggie paused and debated how much she should tell Moira.

Moira threw her arms around Maggie again. "I'm so glad you're home. I missed you and I don't really care why you decided to come back as long as you're happy."

"I'm getting there. I'm at least trying."

"I'm here if you want to talk."

"Not yet. But soon." Maggie pulled away. "So how long do I have until everyone else shows up?"

Moira wrinkled up her nose. "Ryan and Quinn are on their way. So are Colin and Liam."

Maggie rolled her eyes. So much for having a day.

Moira nudged her shoulder. "At least Michael's on at the fire house, so he won't be coming."

"Whatever. You know this means Mom's cooking for everyone. You can do the dishes."

Hooking her arm though Maggie's, Moira turned them toward the stairs. "Only if you help."

As much as she wanted to be irritated, Maggie couldn't be. It felt too good to be home. Knowing that it was real, not just a brief holiday visit, but really digging back in at home with her family was nice. Traveling had been a great adventure, but it couldn't top the stability of her family.

She followed Moira down the narrow, winding steps and wondered how many trips she'd made up and down this staircase. The scarred wood and smudged wall looked the same as it had her entire life.

They reflected how she felt. Damaged, but comfortable.

Two days later, Shane walked into O'Leary's Pub. Unlike Maggie, he'd been to the bar since her rape. He'd worked there for a few months after, but he'd felt like such a failure that he couldn't continue. He just hoped Ryan wouldn't hold it against him.

He didn't recognize the woman behind the bar; it wasn't Mary, who'd been the manager for years. He waited to get her attention. "Is Ryan here?"

"Yep. He's in his office. Want me to get him?"

"No. I know the way. We're friends." Calling Ryan a friend was a bit of a stretch, but it kept things simple. He walked through the main bar, where a few people were eating lunch. Just past the back room, he entered the dark hallway that led to the office and the bathrooms. As he raised his hand to knock on the office door, he eyed the metal door at the end of the hall. It led to the alley and the back stairs to the apartments above the bar. The apartment where Maggie had been raped.

He couldn't afford to think about that right now. He knocked and waited for Ryan to call out.

"Come in."

Shane opened the door and strode through before closing it behind him. "Hey, Ryan."

At the sound of his voice, Ryan's head shot up from where he'd been staring at his computer screen. For a moment, Shane thought Ryan didn't remember him, but they'd seen each other briefly at Christmas.

"Shane? What are you doing here?"

He walked forward and pointed to the chair in front of the desk. Ryan nodded and Shane sat. "I need to talk to you about Maggie. Have you talked to her yet?"

"I saw her the other night, caught up about the usual stuff. Why?"

He let out a little sigh, grateful that Maggie had kept her word and waited to talk to Ryan. The question now became whether he should tell Ryan what Maggie's plans were or if he should just ask for a job. He scrubbed a hand over his head.

"I'm going to tell you something about Maggie, but you can't say anything to her. She plans to talk to you, but…shit. I'd like my job back."

"You want to be a bouncer again? I thought you were working with your dad."

"I am. I'd like to work nights."

"I don't have a spot right now. What does that have to do with Maggie?"

Damn. He had no idea how to keep Maggie's secret and still get what he wanted. "Maggie is going to ask you to hire her. To work here."

Ryan froze. "What? Why?"

Shane shoved out of the chair. "I don't really understand. Something about facing her fears and getting her life back." He spoke to the wall instead of facing Ryan. "I want my job back so I can be here for her."

Ryan didn't respond. Shane turned back and looked at Maggie's brother. The news he'd delivered seemed to age the man. For as much guilt as Shane carried because of what had happened to Maggie, he knew Ryan felt it deeper. Maggie was his baby sister, and it had happened in his bar.

"I'll have to hire her, won't I?"

"I don't think she'll take no for an answer. You know Maggie. When she gets an idea in her head…"

"Fuck. There has to be a way to talk her out of this." Ryan rubbed the back of his neck. "I don't have an opening for a bouncer."

Shane dug in his pocket and pulled out a twenty. "Then I'd like to buy a couple of O'Leary's T-shirts. I'll be here every night she works. I'd prefer if she believes I'm working instead of watching her."

"You're serious. You're going to give up all of your free time to pretend to work for me? For free?"

"She thinks this will be easy. I don't want her doing it alone."

"Put your money away. I'll give you the shirts. If I have an opening, the spot's yours."

Shane shoved the bill back into his pocket. "One more thing."

Ryan's eyebrows rose.

"Do you have any apartments free upstairs?"

"One. Why?"

"Crap. Maggie's going to want it."

Ryan paled. The man looked like he might throw up.

Shane's heart stuttered. "Fuck. Please tell me it's not the one she had before."

"No."

Maybe it would've been better if it had been. No way would she ask for that apartment. "What is it then?"

Ryan scrubbed his face with both hands, looking wearier than a man in his thirties. "I'm going to tell you something, but you can't say anything to Maggie. I haven't told her yet."

More secrets? He wasn't built for this. He nodded.

"Just after the holidays, a letter came to my mom's house to notify Maggie that Todd is getting out of jail."

"What?"

"He served his time."

"Why the hell haven't you told her? It's been months."

"She was still worried about our mom. And she was in Ireland. He wouldn't be able to touch her there. Since she's been back, I haven't found the right time." His face was pinched, like he knew he'd screwed up.

"You need to find the time, right or not."

"What the hell is she thinking?" Ryan asked. "Why here?"

"I'll let her explain it to you. I tried to convince her that we should get a place together as roommates, but she wasn't interested." Shane sank back into the chair, feeling as nauseated as Ryan looked. "I'm afraid for her," he admitted quietly. "Especially now that I know Todd is getting out."

"You're looking for a new apartment?"

Shane nodded.

"I have another apartment. It hasn't been remodeled yet. I got sidetracked with having a baby. If you don't mind living on a job site, it's yours."

"How much work does it need?"

"It's gutted. The bathroom is mostly done."

"How much for rent?"

"You do the remaining work while you're living there, you can have it free. We'll revisit rent when you finish. Besides, I'll feel better with you here in case Todd contacts her. This would be the first place he'd look."

Shane thought about it. How much time would he have to handle a remodel between working with his dad and pretending to work at the bar? But he'd be close to Maggie. Nothing else mattered. "Deal." He extended his hand to Ryan. They shook, and Shane stood to leave. His lunch hour was almost over and his dad would be looking for him.

As he opened the door to leave, Shane turned back. "This is just between us, right? The reason for me being here. You know she'll go apeshit if she knows."

"Yeah, I know. When will you move in?"

"In a day or two. I should be here before she moves in."

Ryan rose and came around the desk. "If you have a couple of minutes, I'll grab the keys for you now. Then you can move in whenever you want."

Shane checked the time. "Sure." While Ryan opened a drawer in a long credenza, Shane sent a text to his dad letting him know he'd be back soon.

Ryan pulled out a ring of keys and flipped through them. He found the right ones and handed them to Shane.

"Thanks," Shane said as he pocketed the key.

"Thank you. For everything. It means a lot that you look out for her."

Shane nodded and left. Of course he looked out for Maggie. He'd failed her once. He wouldn't let anything happen to her again.

CHAPTER 2

Shane managed to finish the rest of his workday without spending too much time thinking about Maggie. He'd already talked to his roommate, Joe, to let him know that he'd found a place. Grateful that things aligned in his favor for a change, Shane packed up his tools and looked at his dad. He'd need to tell him what was going on.

"Hey, Dad. Buy you a beer?"

"I wouldn't turn one down. Where to?"

"Mulligan's is right down the street," Shane said, knowing the bar often had blue-collar workers filling the place in the late afternoon.

"Meet you there."

Shane lugged his bucket of tools out of the apartment complex they were remodeling. At least this job prepared him for living above O'Leary's. More of the same day in and day out. Unfortunately, now there would be no escape.

He beat his dad to the bar, so he grabbed a table and ordered a couple of beers. His dad found him before he was halfway done with his draft. Without saying a word, Dad took a big gulp of the brew.

"So what's the occasion?"

"Maggie's home."

"Good. Bet that makes you happy." Another drink.

"The thing is, she's got this idea that she wants to work at O'Leary's and live above the bar."

"Isn't that where—"

"Yeah," Shane answered. "It's complicated. During lunch today, I went to see Ryan O'Leary to ask him about working there again."

His dad's eyebrows slammed down, but Shane continued. "I'll still work with you, but I'll be at O'Leary's on the nights she works. And I'm moving in above the bar. They have one more apartment that needs to be fixed up. I live rent free if I do the work."

"Why are you doing this to yourself?" His father's voice was low and stiff.

"Because I need to know she's okay. She won't lean on her family when she freaks out. And I'm fairly certain she will. She'll need someone to be there for her." He finally took another drink of beer to wet his quickly drying throat. He'd never spoken to his dad about his feelings for Maggie. Everyone knew they were best friends, and he'd always left it at that.

His dad shook his head.

"It's the right thing to do, Dad."

"And what happens when the police department calls you up?"

Shane hadn't even thought about that. He'd taken the test over a year ago and hadn't been called for training. He shrugged. "I'll cross that bridge when it comes. If it happens. Right now, this is what I need."

"How does she feel about you playing bodyguard?"

Shane laughed. "She doesn't know."

His dad shook his head again. "Don't you think she'll get suspicious when you keep popping up wherever she is?"

"Don't care."

"You're playing with fire with that one, kid. I remember her temper."

Shane smiled. His dad had known Maggie for years, and his assessment was accurate. "I'll take my chances."

His dad sobered. "No joke. What will you do if she doesn't want to have anything to do with you?"

"That's not possible. She's my best friend. She knows I wouldn't do anything to hurt her." He drained his glass. He knew Maggie. There was very little he could do that would send Maggie running from him. They'd been through too much together, knew each other too well.

"I hope you're right."

Maggie walked into Dr. Janzen's outer office as she had hundreds of times. She had no idea how hard it would be to come home. She'd assumed she'd be able to slide right back into her life like nothing had changed. Even now, she wasn't sure what changed or how they changed.

She bit her lip against a smile. That was why she needed to see Dr. Janzen.

Dr. Janzen's door was closed, but no In Session sign hung, so Maggie knocked. No one answered, so she took a seat to wait.

Moments later, Dr. Janzen came in through the office carrying a cup of coffee.

The woman didn't appear to age. Her short brown hair was still cut in a cute bob. Today she wore a gray skirt and white blouse. Maggie had always imagined Dr. Janzen's closet as a severely organized space, with each skirt paired with an appropriate blouse. Maggie had seen this exact outfit many times. She was pretty sure she was familiar with the doc's entire wardrobe.

"Maggie, how are you?"

Maggie stood and shook Dr. Janzen's hand. "I'm pretty good, thanks."

She walked ahead of Dr. Janzen into the office and waited while she flipped the IN SESSION sign outside the door before closing it. Maggie sank onto the dark brown suede couch. "New furniture."

Dr. Janzen nodded as she took a seat and set her coffee on the table beside her. "How are you really doing?"

"I'm good. I'm back home now."

"And how were your travels?"

"Fabulous. I saw so much and made friends."

"I bet your family is happy to have you back."

"Yeah, I think so."

Dr. Janzen didn't say anything. Maggie knew she was allowing time for Maggie to gather her thoughts and figure out what to say.

"I feel like a fraud," she finally blurted.

"How do you mean?"

Maggie looked out the window and clasped her hands in her lap. "I told Ryan I wanted to travel because I felt like I was missing out on life. It was partly true, but I felt suffocated here." She took a deep breath. "The thing is, a lot of that followed me."

Dr. Janzen still didn't speak.

"I had a great time traveling. But I'm still missing out. I came back because I'm worried about my mom. After her heart attack, all I could think about was that she could die and I wouldn't be here. Plus, my siblings are all moving on, getting married, having kids. I'm still missing out."

"How does that make you feel like a fraud?"

Maggie licked her lips. "I dated while I was in Ireland."

Dr. Janzen nodded and waited.

"I couldn't have sex, though. Even when I wanted to, I couldn't follow through." She thought of Ian and how much she'd wanted to have sex with him.

"Maggie, we talked about recovery. Everyone moves at a different pace."

"But I felt ready. I liked this guy. And I miss being with someone, you know, really being with them."

"Feeling ready is good."

"Then I kind of froze, like a wave of fear washed over me."

"And then?"

"I stopped." Maggie leaned forward with her elbows on her knees and held her head. "Ian didn't take it well."

Dr. Janzen scooted forward in her seat. "How did you feel?"

"Like a failure." She shook her head. "I wanted to, but couldn't do it. And Ian stood there, looking at me like I was a freak."

"Did he know you'd been raped?"

Again, Maggie shook her head.

"That is a vital conversation, Maggie. Anyone you plan to be intimate with has to be aware."

"It's not something you toss out over dinner, you know? I don't even know what to say."

"It needs to be said. What if you're with a man you really care about and he does something that triggers panic and fear in you? If he doesn't know about your past, he won't know how to help you."

"I just wanted to be a normal girlfriend."

"This is your normal."

"Doesn't mean I have to like it."

Dr. Janzen smiled. "No, you don't. Any other memories or

triggers?"

Maggie lifted a shoulder. "I've avoided things that could be triggers." Leaning back on the couch, she added, "But I'm going to talk to Ryan about working at the bar and getting an apartment above the bar."

"Why?"

She looked at her doctor's impassable face. "Because I haven't stepped foot in the bar in almost five years. It's my family's business, and I feel like I've lost part of my life because of it."

Dr. Janzen tilted her head, readying whatever her next thought was, but Maggie cut her off.

"You taught me exposure might be good. Face down my triggers. It might help me get over it."

"Maggie, this isn't something to get over. And when we talk about exposure, it's controlled, not overwhelming yourself with possible triggers."

"It's been almost five years. I shouldn't be living the life of a nun. I want to be a normal twenty-six year old. I want to have boyfriends and go out drinking with friends. I'm tired of this weight hanging around me."

"I understand. It sounds like you've made up your mind." She sipped her coffee.

Maggie smiled. The woman did know her pretty well. "I promised Shane I would talk to you before speaking to Ryan. I think he hoped you would talk me out of it."

"I think I know you well enough to know when you'll listen."

Maggie twirled the ring on her right hand. "Do you think it'll work?"

"It depends on what your goal is. Do I think working and living at your family's bar will make having sex any easier? No. It might help you deal with that location and the memories there, though. I would suggest that instead of jumping into a job, you just go to the bar. Have dinner, spend some time, and see how you feel."

She could do that. It had actually been her plan. She needed to know she could be in the bar before she could work there.

"What about sex? I feel ready to move on."

"If you're truly ready to move on and have a sexual relationship, you'll be able to have that conversation with the man. If you're not comfortable enough with him to share your past, then you aren't going to be comfortable having sex with him."

Maggie sat there, a little stunned. She felt as if like her therapist just told her to grow up. She'd tried to tell Ian about her rape, but it never quite came out right. He was a constant distraction, making her smile and laugh. They'd never been serious together. It was part of why she'd liked him so much.

SHANE RAN TAPE OVER THE BOX AS HE PACKED THE LAST OF HIS things before moving in over O'Leary's. He hated moving. His phone buzzed with a text.

Help! Need an escape. Family driving me crazy.

Nothing like a little Maggie melodrama to break his boredom. On my way.

He didn't know what they were doing to make her crazy, but he didn't care much either. He knew a lot of what she disliked was stuff she brought on herself. It was a little of the crazy she dished out coming back at her.

By the time he parked down the block from her mom's house, the sun was long gone and the streetlights had clicked on. Most families were huddled in their homes having dinner. He walked toward the house, studying the neighborhood. He'd been here plenty over the years and it was comfortable, a home away from home. These neighbors were a little nosier than his, though.

Suddenly, something pelted his shoulder. Barely more than a sting, but enough to get his attention. He looked around for whatever kid had thrown the snowball, but saw no one. Then he heard the snicker and knew it had been Maggie. He bent over, scooped some snow, and formed it into a tight ball. Walking a few more steps, he listened for her.

She popped around from behind a tree, sailing a snowball past his head.

"Nice try." Then he threw his, nailing her thigh.

Unfortunately, she had a small arsenal by the tree trunk. She must've been waiting outside for him for a while. She turned and then fired again, swinging wildly with double-fisted ammunition. He began throwing half-formed balls to slow her assault as he rushed her position.

When she saw him coming, she squealed and ran, abandoning her post and her cache. He took her spot and began using her own snowballs against her. As each one pinged off her back, she yelped. Two houses down, she raised her hands in surrender.

"Okay, you win." She huffed and bent over, bracing her hands on her knees. "I quit."

He approached with a wide smile. He liked winning. When he came up to her, he patted her back. "It's okay, Magpie. Not everyone can be an athlete."

In a blink, she rose up and shoved a handful of snow down the front of his shirt. Damn, it was cold. It immediately melted against his warm skin and dripped a cool river that pooled at his waistband.

She took off running again. This time, her laughter echoed in her wake. It was such a good sound to hear that he stood for a moment and just absorbed it, allowed it to captivate his entire being.

But her taunt pulled him out of his bubble of enjoyment. "Sucker!"

He knew he was, but he'd never admit it to her. He ran after her again, quickly gaining ground. Her harsh "Oh, fuck" whooshed out just before he tackled her in the snow. He grabbed a handful of snow and rubbed it on her face. She yelped and squealed.

Shane kept her pinned to the ground but gave her a minute to catch her breath. She blinked rapidly, knocking snowflakes from her lids and lashes. Instead of being pissed, she smiled up at him. "Okay, you win."

"Nice try."

"What do you mean?" Her eyes went wide as if she were some innocent kid.

He held up another ball of snow and reached for her shirt. Her hand slapped down on her collar. "You wouldn't."

"Of course I would. Fair's fair."

"But I said you won. I give up."

"And I know better."

With her other hand, she shoved at his torso. "Get up, you're squishing me."

In truth, he probably was, but he didn't want to give her an inch. Maggie was the type of girl who'd run away with a mile if he did. She finally flopped her arms out wide in surrender. "I give up. You win. For real this time."

Watching her capitulate stirred some unwelcome feelings. He jumped off her and held out a hand to help her up. She eyed him through narrow slits. "What's your game?"

"Nothing. Truce."

She placed her hand in his, which felt natural, and tugged at those same unwelcome desires. He yanked her to standing. Her face was lit with a smile. Unfortunately for her, she was a little too smug. He scooped her shirt open at the top and dumped in a handful of snow. Her sharp intake of breath gave him great satisfaction.

"Never underestimate your opponent," he said, and then turned to take off.

He'd only gotten a few steps when Maggie launched herself onto his back. She squeezed his neck tightly and wrapped her legs around his hips. "You called a truce!"

"Yeah, and you fell for it. Now we're even."

Instead of another jab, she rubbed the top of his head. "I've missed this."

The friendly gesture settled him back to where he should be.

"Me too." He continued to walk back toward his truck with her on his back. "You want to tell me what your family did now?"

As he unlocked his truck, she slid off his back. "Just the usual."

"You've been in Ireland for over a year. How is anything usual?"

She climbed into the cab of the truck and waited for him to get behind the steering wheel. "They treat me like a little kid. They fawn all over me like I've just recovered from a terminal illness, but then they tiptoe around me. It's annoying."

He started the truck and asked, "Where to?"

"Anywhere but here." She stared out the windshield. Her cheeks were red from the cold and the snow. Her laughter was gone, and he wanted it back.

"Dinner?"

"Sure."

Because she didn't offer an opinion about where to go, Shane just drove. She had something on her mind, something more than her family hovering. When he pulled into the parking lot of their favorite hot dog stand, she sighed.

"How'd you know?"

"Everyone knows you can't get a decent hot dog outside Chicago. Plus, you look like you could use some fries and a chocolate shake."

Her smile returned for a flash. As he reached to open his door, she grabbed his arm. "Wait."

He stopped.

"Todd's getting out."

His entire body hardened. He despised hearing that asshole's name on her lips. He said nothing because he didn't want to lie about Ryan already telling him.

"Ryan got the letter informing me while I was gone." The muscle in her jaw twitched, and she nodded as if to answer some thought in her head.

"Are you okay?"

"I guess. It's not like I thought he'd be in jail forever. I knew this day would come. What really annoyed me is that Ryan knew —shit, my whole family probably knew—and no one told me. They're all so afraid I'm going to break. I'm stronger than that."

"Mags, I'm sure—"

She shook her head. "Please don't defend them."

How could she not know how difficult it was for all of them? Todd *had* broken her. He'd stolen a piece of her. "They worry about you, but they don't think you're going to break."

"Yeah, they do. They all take this placating tone with me. Damn, my mother still can't say that I was raped. Like saying the word itself gives it more power or something." She squeezed his hand. "That's why I needed to see you. You make me feel normal. We're just regular friends hanging out."

Even though a bit of guilt sat on his chest, he squeezed her hand in return. "I'm up for a snowball fight anytime."

CHAPTER 3

*M*aggie spent the next two days visiting old friends and trying to figure out how to talk to Ryan. If she had a choice, she'd ask another sibling, but Ryan still ran the bar. Colin could probably hire her, but if they went behind Ryan's back, it would cause more tension between Colin and Ryan. The two of them finally seemed to have worked things out, and she didn't want to be the cause of fresh problems. So it had to be Ryan.

Her friend from the neighborhood, Olivia, offered to meet her for lunch at the bar. Maggie figured having a friend with her would be a good buffer.

She sat in her car in the parking lot of O'Leary's and stared at the oak doors. She took a deep breath and felt the inside of her car cooling off since she'd cut the engine. The air outside was bitter cold, icing over all the piles of snow. Maybe she should've waited until spring to come home.

Spring in Chicago was happy and warm and fun. Winter? Not so much.

She took another deep breath. If she couldn't even do this much, how could she expect to work here?

It's just a door. Just a bar, like any other bar. She'd been to plenty of pubs while in Ireland. She could do this. She opened the door of her car and almost crept back in her seat when a blast of frigid air hit her.

A sudden knock on the window her made her jump. Olivia.

Maggie looked through the open door, and Olivia asked, "You okay?"

She nodded and climbed out of the car.

"Come on. It's freezing out here." She slipped her arm around Maggie's elbow and tugged her toward the bar. "I missed you so much. I want to hear all about Europe. I'm sure the pictures you sent didn't do anything justice."

Before she knew it, Olivia was swinging them through the heavy wood doors and into the bar. The interior was dimmer than she remembered, but the sounds and the smells reminded her of her childhood. The lunch crowd filled much of the bar space, but the conversation remained quiet.

Maggie took a moment and stared at the surrounding dark wood and waited for the bad feelings to wash over her, for something to trigger the panic. But it didn't.

Olivia ran her hand up and down Maggie's arm. "Good?" she whispered.

Maggie nodded and said, "Yeah, I think so." She walked to the bar and sat on a stool. The woman behind the counter wasn't someone she recognized, not that she should since she hadn't been there in so long, but she hoped to see Mary, the manager. This woman's name tag said Jenna.

Jenna faced Maggie and Olivia. "Hi. What can I get you?"

"Hi. I'm Maggie O'Leary. Is my brother Ryan here?"

Jenna's eyebrows wrinkled. "Uh...yeah. I'll go get him." She backed away from the bar and went to get Ryan.

"What was that about?" Olivia asked.

"She probably didn't know Ryan had another sister. If

she's been here any length of time she's probably met all the O'Learys. Except me." She took off her jacket and hung it on the back of her stool.

Olivia reached a little farther down the bar and picked up a menu. "So what's good?"

Maggie leaned closer. "To tell you the truth, I have no idea. Even when I worked here, I hardly ate anything. We'll ask Ryan."

While Olivia scanned the menu, Maggie looked around, trying to see what had changed. She saw nothing different. Was it possible that nothing had changed in five years?

"Maggie?"

At the sound of Ryan's voice, she spun in her chair. "Hey."

His face filled with worry. "You're here."

"Yeah. I thought it was about time."

His mouth opened and then closed. "Are you okay?"

She hopped off her stool. "I'm good. I thought it would be harder, but it's kind of like walking into any other bar. Except this one has some great memories."

"And some not great ones."

"You know, I still don't remember much from that night. I thought walking in here might trigger something, but as I'm sitting here, I'm remembering good times." She turned and pointed toward the back room. "Like the time Shane played darts with Michael after work and they'd both had too much to drink. Shane's dart flew across the room and nailed Michael in the arm."

Remembering that night made Maggie smile. Michael had been cursing a blue streak, and Shane had doubled over laughing. Maggie had to yank the dart from Michael's arm. She remembered it wobbling as Michael yelled at Shane for his poor aim.

Then she turned to the end of the bar. "Or the time Shane and I played beer pong and busted the mirror."

Ryan crossed his arms. "When exactly did that happen?"

Maggie smiled and kissed his cheek. "Sorry. Thought you knew."

"So what brings you here? Other than to tell me all the juvenile things you've done in my bar."

"Olivia and I came for lunch. What's good?"

"Everything's good, of course."

"Spoken like a true business owner." She sat back on the stool.

Ryan nodded to Olivia. "Hi, Olivia. How are you? I don't think I've seen you since the block party."

"I'm good. Finally moved out and into my own apartment. Still bring my laundry home, though."

"Well, I have work to do, but you two enjoy lunch on me." He bent over and kissed Maggie's head. "Come find me if you need me."

"I'll be okay." She watched Ryan walk away. Jenna returned to take their order.

"Can I start you off with a drink?"

"Just a Coke for me," Maggie said.

"Me too," Olivia added.

When Jenna left to pour their drinks, Olivia asked, "So you're really okay?"

"Yeah. It's weird because I feel totally normal. Like I keep waiting for it to hit, but nothing. Like I told Ryan, I'm just remembering the good times."

Jenna returned with their Cokes, and both Maggie and Olivia ordered burgers. For the next couple of hours, Maggie sat in her family's bar and hung out with an old friend. They laughed and shared stories and caught up.

By the time they were ready to put on their coats and brave the cold again, Maggie finally felt as if she had come home. Only the nagging feelings about why she'd stayed away remained.

~

SHANE WALKED THROUGH HIS NEW APARTMENT. NOT THAT IT really qualified as a living space. Every wall had been gutted. At least they'd gotten around to insulating. Otherwise he'd be able to see his breath. He walked to the nearest radiator and touched. No heat, which wasn't a huge surprise. The pipes would probably need to be bled. That would be the top priority.

A stack of drywall sat in the corner waiting to be hung. He flipped a switch and a bare bulb in the ceiling lit. In the bathroom, he found all new fixtures installed. He turned the tap and water flowed. As long as the plumbing and electric were complete, the rest would be easy for him.

He'd have to talk to Ryan about the kitchen and what he wanted done there, and when Ryan would be able to order the materials. His dad could probably use his contractor's discount to get Ryan a deal. He didn't know why Ryan hadn't asked his dad to come in and do the work.

Then again, the only time he saw Ryan was while he was with Maggie, and in those cases, Ryan would never bring up the bar, much less the apartments upstairs.

He turned and sat on the stack of drywall. What the hell had he gotten himself into? This would be like juggling a third job. College had been hard enough when he had to go to class and work nights here. Now he'd have to work with his dad, work at the bar, and squeeze in time to finish this place.

His best hope was that Ryan would schedule Maggie for only a couple of nights a week. He watched the remaining bit of his social life slip away.

But Maggie was home and she was safe.

As he had the thought his phone rang, and without

looking at the screen he knew it was Maggie. He pulled the phone from his pocket. He was right. "Hey."

"I did it."

He heard the smile in her voice. "Did what?"

"I went to O'Leary's for lunch today with Olivia."

Shane's muscles tensed.

"I talked with Dr. Janzen, and she suggested what I planned anyway. Just go to the bar to see if I would have any reaction. And you know what? Nothing. At least nothing bad. I sat there and remembered nothing but good times."

He smiled. "I'm glad. Did you talk to Ryan about coming to work?"

"Not yet. I'm going to wait until Sunday dinner with the family."

Good. He had time to get moved in and settled. Hopefully with walls. Looked like he knew what he'd be doing this weekend. He stood.

"What are you doing tonight? I want to celebrate."

He glanced at the bare room again. He closed his eyes. "Nothing. Where do you want to go?"

"How about Sorrentino's? I've missed their pizza."

"Sounds good. Pick you up at seven?"

"Fabulous."

He disconnected and turned off the meager light in the room. Before locking up, he shot a quick text to Ryan to ask about the radiators. After work tomorrow, he'd get his dad to help him move his bed in. The majority of the rest of his things would go into storage. The less he had to work around in here, the smoother it would go.

SHANE SPENT THE NEXT FEW HOURS PACKING THE LAST OF HIS stuff. He'd lived with Joe for the past three years, but he hadn't accumulated much in the way of possessions. He had a dresser, bed, and nightstand. The living room furniture was all Joe's. Except the TV. That was his, but he wasn't sure he'd bother trying to hook it up until he finished the living room. At least football season had ended.

He showered, changed, and left to pick up Maggie. When he arrived at her house, he knocked and waited.

Mrs. O'Leary opened the door. He towered over her as always, but she looked good. If he hadn't known she had suffered a heart attack a few months back, he'd never have guessed it.

"Shane. Come in. It's good to see you." She opened the door wider.

He bent over and kissed her cheek as he pulled her into a hug. He'd learned over the years that Mrs. O'Leary would never initiate a hug, but she'd welcome it from him. She squeezed him back.

"I've missed seeing you. What have you been up to?" she asked as she locked up.

"Working with my dad. Waiting for the police department to call. The same things I've been doing."

"You should talk to Jimmy. Maybe he could help with the police."

"Jimmy?"

"Jimmy O'Malley. Moira's fiancé. He's a detective, you know. Worked on a big case for the mayor last summer." She ushered him into the living room and sat on her chair.

He moved to the couch. Jimmy O'Malley had never crossed his mind. He knew of him, maybe even had met him a few times over the years. He knew Jimmy and Liam were friends.

"Maggie'll be down in a minute." A quiet smile stole across the woman's face.

"I'm glad she finally came home."

"We all are." Her gaze shot over his shoulder to the stairs

that led to Maggie's room. "Ryan told me what Maggie plans."

Shit. He'd asked Ryan not to tell anyone.

"Thank you for looking after my girl."

"I'd do anything for her."

"You're a good boy."

Thundering feet on the steps drew his attention. That was a sound he would always associate with Maggie and the O'Leary house. For such a small woman, she had the feet of an elephant.

"Sorry I'm late," she said with a smile.

"That's something I can count on."

"I'm not *always* late."

"You keep telling yourself that." He kept the joking going to distract himself from how beautiful she looked.

She wore nothing special. It wasn't like this was a date. Although he hadn't seen Maggie dress up for a date in years, he remembered what it did to him. He tried not to stare as she bent over to tug on her boots.

Her jeans were snug on her slight curves. The plaid shirt she wore open over a tight-fitting tank slipped off one shoulder exposing her smooth skin. She might as well be dressed to go to a painting party, but he was getting turned on. She shouldn't still have this effect on him.

As she straightened, she flipped her hair over her shoulder. "Ready?"

"Yep."

"See you later, Mom. Don't wait up." She gave her mom a quick kiss on the cheek.

Mrs. O'Leary looked at him. "You be careful driving, now. The roads are still slick."

"I'll bring her back safely."

When they arrived at the restaurant, the warmth of Sorrentino's wrapped around them. The interior could only be described as cozy. Low lights, candles flickering on the tables. Although the setting could be romantic, it was still very much a family restaurant.

Maggie inhaled deeply. "Oh, man. That smells so good. You have no idea how much I've missed Chicago pizza."

"I think I do. I remember when we FaceTimed while I was eating leftovers."

She looked over her shoulder with her blue eyes narrowing. "That was just mean. You did it to make me envious."

He smirked. "I wanted you to know what you were missing."

The hostess led them to a corner booth. It was the same booth where he'd planned to ask Maggie out a year and a half ago and instead she'd told him she was leaving Chicago. He'd planned a perfect night and thought he'd had the right words to convince her they would be good together. Her announcement told him how wrong he'd been.

He waited until she slid in, and he sat across from her. The hostess left menus on the table and returned moments later with glasses of water and a basket of bread.

Maggie snatched a piece of bread and slathered it with butter.

"Tell me about going to the bar. Does your family know?"

She nodded. "Ryan was there." She chewed and swallowed. "I don't know what I was so worried about. It was nothing."

"That's not true, Maggie. Going there was a huge deal."

She shook her head. "Maybe years ago it would've been momentous. It wasn't, though. It kind of pisses me off. I stayed away for years out of fear. But you know what hit me when I sat there eating a cheeseburger? Good memories."

"I'm glad." The tension in his muscles eased a fraction. A lot of times, Maggie would cover what happened so her family wouldn't worry, but she didn't keep things from him. She wasn't just painting a pretty picture here.

"Remember the time you nailed Michael with a dart?"

"How could I forget?" Michael had made him do extra work for the next week, claiming his arm was too injured. In addition to his duties as bouncer, Shane had lugged up cases of beer and alcohol from the basement to "help" Michael. The help ended when he caught Michael doing one-armed push-ups to impress a chick.

Shane took a gulp of water and asked the question he wasn't sure if she'd answer. "So you didn't have any flashbacks or think about..."

"Todd? No. He didn't come to mind at all, except when I started to get mad at myself for staying away."

Hearing her say that asshole's name turned his stomach. He hated giving him any space in their conversation.

The waitress arrived and took their pizza order. After she left, Maggie looked like she was somewhere else.

"What are you thinking?"

She began pulling the crust off the bread and making a small pile on her plate. Not a good sign.

He reached across the table and covered her hands with his, stilling them. With a smile, he said, "Come on, Magpie, you can tell me anything."

CHAPTER 4

Maggie stared at Shane's big hands on top of hers. His words reassured her. She'd always been able to tell him anything. Things she could never tell her family. Her fears, her nightmares, her hopes, her dreams—Shane had heard them all. Why hold back now?

"Part of why today made me angry was that I thought this was something I needed to get over. Something I needed to accomplish in order to fix myself. I'm mad because as it turns out, this wasn't holding me back." She itched to move, but Shane held her hands fast. She swung her legs out under the table instead.

"Holding you back from what?" He looked directly into her eyes.

She loved that he did that. Like he could see every piece of her. Except for the pieces she couldn't show anyone.

She leaned forward on the table and spoke quietly. "I feel like myself. Mostly. Like before Todd raped me. I don't walk around in fear all the time. I feel like I can live life again."

"That's good, Mags." Shane's thumb stroked her hand.

"But I can't…I've tried…." Why the hell couldn't she just say it?

"Can't what?"

"Have sex."

His thumb froze, and for a flicker she saw his muscles twitch before he covered with a smile. "Uh…"

"We don't have to talk about this. It's okay." Sex was one thing she had never talked to Shane about. They'd both had relationships over the years, and they respected that, but they didn't get into the nitty-gritty details.

"We can talk about whatever you need to talk about. I'm just not sure what going to O'Leary's has to do with sex. Other than the obvious, of course."

She slid her hands away from him and sank back in the booth. The cool, red vinyl was smooth under her palm. "While I was in Ireland, I dated a few guys. There was one guy, Ian, and I liked him a lot. We had a great time together. But when I wanted to have sex with him, I couldn't follow through."

Shane's hand curled into a fist. "Please tell me he didn't—"

"Oh, God, no. I mean, he wasn't happy I called it quits, but he was a good guy." She took a sip of water. "I thought that I couldn't sleep with him because of my unresolved issues here. And if I didn't have an issue at the bar, then there's still something wrong with me."

He ran a hand over his head. "Christ, Maggie. There's nothing wrong with you. It'll happen when you're ready. You're just not ready. And if some guy can't be patient and wait, then he doesn't deserve you."

Her cheeks warmed. Shane always made her feel better. Not because of the words, although they were nice to hear, but because he meant them. "Thanks. That's pretty much what Dr. Janzen said. I'm just frustrated."

"Let's put that away for now. Tonight is supposed to be

about celebrating. You did accomplish something. Just because it wasn't hard doesn't take away from it." He raised his glass in a toast. "To new beginnings."

She tilted her glass toward his. "To great friends."

While having lunch with Olivia had been good, a meal with Shane was always better. She relaxed around him, even after blurting out her issue with sex. She still couldn't believe she'd done that. He was so cute with pink cheeks. She couldn't recall ever seeing him blush before. Who'd've thought talking about *not* having sex would make Shane Callahan blush?

∾

As she lay in bed that night rehashing her day, she couldn't stop thinking about Shane and what he'd said. *If some guy can't be patient and wait, then he doesn't deserve you.* The words were lovely, and she wished she could believe them. Instead, she still felt like a freak.

Putting sex out of her mind, at least as far back as she could push it for a girl who hadn't had any in so long, she focused on figuring out how to approach Ryan about a job. Sunday dinner was coming up fast and she needed a plan.

Hours later, Maggie woke, tangled in her sheets, her heart thumping. She froze for a minute and tried to figure out what woke her. She stared at the bedroom door, narrowing her eyes to see the knob. Still locked.

Her body was on full alert, and she waited for the memory of a nightmare to hit her, but it didn't. She breathed a quiet sigh and closed her eyes again.

That's when bits of the dream came back to her. Her nerves tingled, sending an erotic message all over her body. Her nipples were stiff peaks beneath her T-shirt. She didn't know what was more frustrating—a useless nightmare or an unfulfilled sex dream. So much for putting sex out of her mind.

She thought of reaching over into the drawer to pull out her vibrator, but she was tired. She relaxed a little more as she moved her hand down over her stomach and into her pajama bottoms.

She was already wet. She wished she could remember the dream that had gotten her so horny. She stroked her clit in small circles. Her other hand went up her shirt and rolled her nipple between her thumb and forefinger. Her hips wiggled and thrust in their own rhythm. She plunged two fingers inside herself, feeling the slippery desire coating her.

As she rocked herself to orgasm, she glimpsed brief images of large hands caressing her. The guy in her fantasy was big but gentle. And faceless. She imagined his broad shoulders looming over her, his hands taking the place of hers. She tilted her head back and trained her mind's eye to seek out his face. But it was too dark.

He moved slowly, carefully, bringing her to the peak of orgasm and holding her there. Her hips jutted up off the bed and her muscles shook. She rode the orgasm through the shuddering and then rolled over.

Masturbation took the edge off, but she knew it would be better with a partner. Being in control of her own orgasm limited her pleasure. She needed to be able to let go, but she didn't know how. If only the guy in her dream became reality. Instinct told her he was someone she could trust to take her to new heights and hold her close as she came down.

She dozed back to sleep wondering if she'd ever find that guy.

SUNDAY DINNER WITH THE O'LEARYS WAS GETTING TOO BIG TO

fit in their family dining room. Maggie set the table and recounted the chairs. Brianna and Michael weren't going to make it, but Colin had convinced Elizabeth she needed to come now that they were engaged. With Ryan and Quinn and Liam and Carmen, they should be fine. She had no idea what they were going to do when they all started having kids and needed more space. They'd made do at Christmas, but it had been crowded.

The front door swung open and Liam and Carmen came in. Guilt tugged at Maggie. She'd met Carmen at Christmas and had been pretty rude to her. Nothing about her family seemed to faze Carmen, but if they were going to be seeing each other often, Maggie knew she needed to do more than pretend.

She looked at Liam. "Did you remember dessert?"

Carmen held up a plate. "I made flan."

"Interesting," Maggie said, and eyed the dish. "Liam normally doesn't let anyone mess with his dessert day. Mom might be disappointed it's not cheesecake."

Carmen's face fell and Liam shot her a look. "Rude" was all he said as he brushed past holding Carmen's hand.

Well, shit. She hadn't been trying to be rude.

Carmen's brown eyes iced over. Looked like Maggie had an apology to make. Again. "Carmen, wait," she called out to Carmen's back.

To her credit, Carmen released Liam's hand and nodded for him to continue to the kitchen without her. She still held the dessert plate in front of her like a barrier.

"I didn't mean to insult you. I'm sure the flan is delicious. Mom is set in her ways. When it's Moira's turn, we have brownies. When it's any of the guys except Liam, they stop at Blackstone's bakery. Although now that Ryan has Quinn, there are cookies and sometimes chocolate cake. Mom counts on Liam for cheesecake."

"I guess that's par for the course for me."

Maggie took a deep breath. "I suck at this. I want to apologize for the way I treated you at Christmas."

One of Carmen's eyebrows rose.

Not only had Maggie been mean to Carmen, she'd been borderline racist. It wasn't until much after the fact that she reconsidered her words and actions and how they appeared to Carmen. "I know you heard what I said to Liam then, and I'm sorry. I was out of line and bitchy. I don't want to make excuses, but I was overwhelmed, and it was easy to strike out at an outsider. I really didn't mean anything by it."

"I wish I could believe that."

"I would tell you it won't happen again, but it would be a lie. I don't always think before opening my mouth. Take the comment about flan, for example." Maggie had no other way to explain that she had nothing against Carmen. It wasn't personal. She just didn't like change, but for her big brother, she'd suck it up.

"I get it, Maggie. It's been tough, but I'm not going anywhere and I'm having a hard-enough time winning your mom over. I don't need your crap."

"I'm turning over a new leaf. No crap." She tilted her head toward the kitchen. "Let's go say hi and put this in the fridge. So you and Liam are serious, huh?"

"Yeah." Carmen's face broke into a huge smile, one that expressed the love she had for Liam.

Jealousy surged through Maggie.

In the kitchen, she watched as Carmen awkwardly greeted Eileen and whatever jealousy existed faded. Her mom was…cordial. Lame, but it was the best word Maggie could think to fit. She felt bad for Carmen, and the guilt returned.

Noise from the living room caught her attention, and Eileen rushed past them all because Ryan and Quinn arrived with the baby. No one could steal Eileen's attention like baby Patrick. While she was gone, Liam took over the stove, which was another change. Mom never let anyone, even Liam, a trained chef, cook Sunday dinner.

Carmen moved beside Liam, so Maggie left the room. At the other end of the house, the rest of her siblings had congregated. Colin and Elizabeth must've come in right after Ryan. Everyone greeted her, but Maggie still felt out of place. How was it that these new women appeared more at ease with her family than she did? Everyone settled in and chatted while they waited for dinner.

Maggie debated the best time to approach Ryan. Before dinner so he had time to cool off while they ate? Or after dinner because he'd be full and happy? She wished she could predict how he'd react. Forget it. She needed to get it out of the way.

"Hey, Ry, can I talk to you for a minute?"

"Sure." He rose from his spot on the couch and followed her into the kitchen.

Liam and Carmen looked at them, and Carmen tugged Liam's elbow. "Let's go see everyone else."

"What's up?" Ryan asked once they had left.

"I want to come back to work at the bar."

"What?"

"I want to waitress. I need a job while I figure out what I'm going to do with my life." One more thing on her list of getting herself unfucked.

"I can probably get you a spot at Twilight. Or Colin might need help at the bowling alley."

She didn't want to work at Ryan's other bar or at Colin's place. "I want to work at O'Leary's."

"Why?" Worry filled his face. She knew that look, lived with it for far too long.

She released a slow breath. "Because I want to know I can."

"I'm not looking for extra help right now."

"Bullshit. Every time Michael has needed extra money, you've found shifts for him. When Colin came back, you made a spot for him, too. I need to do this."

He raked a hand through his hair. "What makes you think you'll be okay? Because you managed to eat a meal there?"

"The truth is, I don't know, but I need to find out. I need to get on with my life."

He shook his head and let out a low chuckle. "I thought that's what you were doing when you took off to Europe."

Her arms flailed. "I don't know what I'm doing. But I do know I'm tired of being afraid of something that should be part of my life. I'm an O'Leary, damn it, and I have a right to be part of the business."

"But after everything with Todd…"

And there it was, the tiptoe effect. "I'm fine. I need to do this."

His jaw twitched. "I'll get you a few shifts. When do you want to start?"

"As soon as possible. Thanks." She wrapped her arms around his waist and hugged him tightly. "One more thing," she said against his chest.

"With you there always is."

"Can I have an apartment above the bar?"

He sighed, which was a much better reaction than the yelling she'd expected.

"I need to have my own space, figure things out. It's hard to do that living with Mom." She pulled back and looked up at him. "I don't want my old apartment. I don't think I'm that brave. But I don't want to keep living with Mom. I love her and all, but it's time for me to grow up."

"There's only one apartment available—my old one since

Colin and Elizabeth moved in together."

"Perfect." She stepped out of his arms. With the other three apartments occupied, she'd make new friends.

"You'll have to walk past your old apartment every day. Are you going to be okay with that?"

She swallowed. "I'll have to be."

"Did you tell Mom about this?"

She shook her head slowly. "Nope. I was kind of hoping you'd help with that."

He stepped farther away. "Hell, no."

"Come on, Ryan." She batted her eyes at him in the way she had for as long as she could remember. It worked on all of her siblings, except Moira.

"Nope. You want to grow up, you deal with Mom."

She crossed her arms. "Fine."

Back in the living room, she joined everyone and played with her baby nephew. She felt like she'd missed so much while she'd been gone. But being back caused conflicting emotions. She was happy to be with her family, yet disconnected because she had no idea what she was doing.

As much as she wanted to be with them, she itched to get away, escape the sidelong glances, worried brows, and hushed whispers about her.

SHANE HEFTED ANOTHER SHEET OF DRYWALL AND SCREWED IT in place. He'd worked all day Saturday and into Sunday afternoon, so most of the drywall in the apartment was hung. A couple of guys from work helped him for a few hours on Saturday. Knowing they were working above a bar acted as an incentive, because Shane bought them plenty to drink when they called it a night.

Ryan had gotten the radiators working and now the

temperature in his place ran the other extreme. Sweat snaked down his back and dripped off his face. The damn things couldn't be regulated, and he didn't have the time or inclination to determine which ones to turn off to make himself more comfortable. Instead, he'd been walking around in nothing but his boxers except when he was working.

He looked at the time and wondered how Maggie's conversation with Ryan went. He hoped Ryan was smart enough to pretend not to know she was going to ask. Wiping the sweat from his brow, he debated how much more work he wanted to do. Bottom line, he was exhausted, but he wanted to get as much done before he had to start shadowing Maggie.

He pulled a beer from the fridge and popped the top. He gulped down half and decided he could work a while longer. Moving to the small kitchen window, he cracked it open and a rush of cold air blew in. He definitely needed to get the temperature balanced. Maybe he'd stop by and see how his neighbors handled it. Ryan had said all of the apartments were full, but he'd yet to meet anyone.

With the radio to keep him company, he cut the next sheet of drywall and installed it. By the time he finished his bottle of beer, he had the drywall completely hung and his stomach growled. He stripped off his sweaty shirt, but before he made it to the bathroom, his phone rang.

When he saw Maggie's face on the screen, he smiled and answered. "Hey."

"Hi. Busy?"

"Not right at the moment. You have good timing. I'm quitting for the night." He used his shirt to wipe his head.

"Quitting? I thought your dad never worked on Sundays."

"He doesn't, but I have some work to do on my new apartment." He hoped leading with the information might look less suspicious.

"New apartment? When did you move?"

"I just moved into an apartment above O'Leary's. I was going to talk to you about it to make sure you'd be okay with it, but you seem to be doing good. Besides, Ryan made me an offer I couldn't refuse. I do the work, I live rent-free."

"Really? We're going to be neighbors?"

"I guess your talk with Ryan went well, then?"

"Yeah, he handled it way better than I expected. Which makes more sense now that I know you're living there. Why didn't he tell me?"

"I don't know."

"What made you look for an apartment there?"

"I wasn't looking. I asked Ryan for my old job back. Cara's decided that she definitely wants law school, so I figured I'd work a few extra hours to help pay for it." He hoped the minor lies about his sister wouldn't come back to bite him in the ass. Cara was headed to law school, but Maggie didn't need to know she had scholarship money. He'd helped pay for Alyson's tuition, so Maggie would believe he'd do the same for his other sister. "When I talked to him about the job, he offered the apartment."

"So you're working at the bar too." Her voice was quiet as if she was processing the whole situation.

"Yeah." He waited, not sure what tactic to take next.

"Son of a bitch." It was a quiet curse, not her calling him names. "Why would he do this?"

"What?"

"He just can't trust me. I know what I'm doing. I don't need a fucking babysitter because Todd is out."

"It's not like that." He was losing ground fast.

"What? You couldn't find *any* other bar to work at?"

"I didn't try. And I asked before I knew anything about Todd." That nugget of truth might be the only thing to save him here. "You said you were going to work here and I thought it would be like old times. When you talked about the time I hit Michael with a dart, it brought back happy memories for me too."

"But I'm sure Ryan had an ulterior motive. He always does. He doesn't think I can take care of myself."

"I can't speak for Ryan, but I figured if I'm going to be stuck working extra hours, I might as well enjoy myself. I've missed you."

"That's all there is to it?"

"Of course." He felt as if he'd won her over. She'd be furious if she found out he really was there to watch over her.

She huffed a small laugh. "Yeah, we had some fun. No beer pong. I'm too out of practice. You'll kick my ass."

"I always kick ass at beer pong." He released a sigh of relief. Everything was going according to plan. "Remember the time you tried to get us all to do that line dance thing?"

"What?"

"You have to remember. Your dad was there and you put it on the jukebox and started grabbing everyone."

"Oh, my God. The Cupid Shuffle." She broke off in a fit of laughter and the sound made his heart swell.

He didn't say another word. He simply listened until she caught her breath.

"I think that's the last happy memory I have of my dad. He couldn't follow a beat to save his life. And if I recall, you weren't much better."

"Hey, I wasn't that bad."

"Sure you weren't."

"Maybe you need to give me some more lessons."

She laughed again and in that moment everything was right in his world. He felt like he'd dodged a bullet. He just hoped he was out of range if she ever found out the truth.

CHAPTER 5

$\mathcal{M}$aggie eased into working at the bar by waitressing during a few lunch shifts. The menu hadn't changed much over the years, so she just needed to learn the new computerized register system.

When she'd worked here before, everything was old school because that was the way their dad liked it. Sometime after she stopped working, Ryan had upgraded. She met a few of her coworkers, and Jenna and Mary were her go-to people when she had questions. Although Mary had been the manager for years, Jenna had been waitressing and bartending long enough that she knew pretty much everything.

The lunch shift kept her busy mostly because she helped prep for dinner, but the tips were meager. She needed some later shifts in order to be able to pay bills. It was bad enough some waitresses assumed that because her last name was O'Leary she didn't really work. Having her mother or her brother have to pay her cell phone bill would be humiliating. Been there, done that.

After finishing her shift, she filled her car with the boxes that had arrived from Ireland, along with her suitcase. She didn't have any furniture other than her twin-sized bed she'd had since she was a kid.

Ryan had said that Colin had left the couch behind, so she planned to sleep on that until she had a new bed delivered.

As she pulled up behind O'Leary's, she paused. Her heart beat faster. Maybe she should've done a walk-through first like she had at the bar, just to make sure she could do this. She stared at the wooden steps that led to the apartments. Then she closed her eyes and waited for some memory to hit her from that night. She had to have stumbled up those stairs, but she had no recollection.

She swallowed hard and parked illegally as close to the stairs as she could. It was still cold out and she'd have to make about ten trips to get her stuff inside. The smart move would've been to call some of her siblings to help. Instead, she'd thought it'd be a good idea to do this alone.

Sometimes she could kick herself.

Balancing one box in her arms, she juggled the keys to get inside. Getting through the first door was bad enough that she set the box down next to her door. She glanced at the other apartments and wondered which one was Shane's. Rolling her eyes at herself, she unlocked the door to her apartment. She kicked the box through the doorway.

The apartments all had similar layouts: a short hallway that led to a small kitchen on the left and the living room opening to the right. Hook a left past the kitchen to get to the bathroom and the bedroom. In her old apartment, the layout had been the opposite.

Ryan's black leather couch sat in the middle of the living room. The single piece of furniture looked lonely in front of the empty entertainment center. She needed to go shopping.

But first, boxes. After one more quick glance, she locked up and went back to her car.

When she got outside, she saw Shane leaning into her car. Although looking at just his ass shouldn't have been enough of a clue, she knew it was him. He straightened from the car holding two stacked boxes.

Maggie walked up behind him. "You know, stealing is illegal."

He looked at her over the top of the boxes. "Like you have any crap I'd want to steal."

"You don't have to help me."

"I know you don't need my help. I want to help. Would it kill you to just accept it?"

"Thank you."

He walked past her and up the stairs, making her boxes look like they were empty. She grabbed her suitcase and backpack and followed him. Inside the hall, she paused in front of the door to her old apartment. Just beyond that door, her ex-boyfriend had raped her while she'd been drunk and drugged.

It was just a door to an apartment. She didn't even have actual memories, just vague feelings. Suddenly, Shane was in front of her.

"You okay?"

"Yep."

He took the suitcase from her and led the way back to her new apartment and waited while she unlocked the door. He carried the suitcase to the couch and set it down. Then he scooted a box in front of the door to keep it propped open.

As she followed him back out into the hall, her stomach clenched, and she swallowed down bile. She didn't know if she could leave her door wide open and go outside. Anyone could get in.

But if she kept locking it on every trip, Shane would

know what a freak she was. She swallowed again. Besides, Shane was with her. He would never let anything bad happen.

They worked in silence until her car was empty. She moved her car to a legitimate parking space, and when she went back upstairs Shane was standing in the hall, leaning against the door to the adjacent apartment.

She didn't know what to say to him. How could he not know that she needed to do this? "Thanks for the help."

"Anytime."

She walked past him toward her door.

"So that's the way it's going to be from now on? We're nothing more than neighbors?"

His words held a hint of edginess, which was unlike Shane, especially when directed at her.

"For now, yeah. I'm still pissed that Ryan has you spying on me."

"I told you that's not the case."

She spread her arms wide. "Yet here you are on the day I move in, when I didn't tell anyone my plan."

"That's coincidence. I live here."

She crossed her arms and rolled her eyes.

"Ryan is worried. He can't help it. He needs to know you're safe."

"Well, I am. Thanks for your concern."

He shook his head and went inside his apartment.

Her heart sank. She should enjoy having her best friend live next door. She had someone to hang out with whenever she got lonely. Who wouldn't love to live near her best friend? She couldn't quite put her finger on why the whole situation irritated her, but it did. None of it should've surprised her. This was normal behavior from her big brother.

~

Maggie spent the next few hours unpacking her stuff. It was kind of difficult since she didn't have a dresser for her clothes or shelves for her books. In the bedroom, her brothers had left a trunk she pulled into the living room to use as a table. Too bad the entertainment center they left didn't come with a TV.

She unpacked what she could and broke up the boxes. The remaining boxes she shoved against the wall. She set up her computer and started looking for something to stream online. Just as she settled on *Downton Abbey*, there was a knock on her door. She rolled her eyes but went to the door. Without opening it, she called, "Go away, Shane."

"It's not Shane."

Moira. She swung the door open. "What are you doing here?"

"I stopped by the house and Mom said you were moving in today, so I thought I'd stop by. Shane let me in as he was leaving. He's living here, too?"

"Don't remind me. Come on in."

Moira held up a pan. "I brought housewarming gifts: brownies and a six-pack of beer. I know you don't drink and beer doesn't go with brownies anyway, but it's always nice to have drinks to offer guests."

Maggie smiled. She should've asked Moira to help her move. Her sister was always fun. "I'll make a pot of coffee. You cut the brownies."

"Excellent. I think we have much sisterly catching up to do."

They settled on the couch with coffee and chocolate and talked. And talked some more. The whole time, Maggie knew Moira hedged around something, which wasn't like her at all.

"What do you want to know, Moira? You're dancing around like I don't know you."

Moira set her cup on the table. "Why are you really living here?" She held up a hand. "Before you answer, don't give me the same bullshit lines you've given everyone else. If you were just looking to get away from Mom to move on and make a life, it wouldn't need to be here."

Maggie pulled her legs up and wrapped her arms around them. Of course, Moira would know there was more to it. "Something's holding me back from being normal, being myself. At least the self I used to be. I'm trying to figure out what it is."

"First, you have to know you'll probably never be the same person. Hell, most of us aren't the same people we were five years ago, and we didn't experience anything traumatic. Second, holding you back from what?"

"Guys. Relationships. Sex."

"Hmmm…I might need a beer for this." But she didn't move. Instead, she settled back on the couch and waited for Maggie to continue.

"I'm missing out on things. Like having a boyfriend. And when I'm at the house and I see all you guys in love and getting married and stuff, it's hard. I know I shouldn't be jealous, but I am."

"You'll find a guy when you're ready."

"Shut up. Now who's throwing out lame lines like everyone else?"

"What about that guy Ian you were dating in Ireland? What happened with him?"

"I liked him. A lot. But I couldn't have sex with him. I wanted to, but then, when it came time, I froze."

"Wait a minute." Moira shifted closer. "Are you saying you haven't had sex at all since you were raped?"

"That's what I'm saying. I fly solo often enough, but it's not the same, you know?"

"Yeah, I know. I had no idea. You started dating again, so I thought things were better for you. Why didn't you tell me?"

"What good would that have done? It's not like you could do anything for me."

"What does your therapist say?"

"That when I'm ready it'll happen. But what the fuck? It's been almost five years. I feel ready. I want to have a relation-ship, and Christ, do I want sex. I miss being intimate with a guy." She hugged her legs closer. Saying this to Moira was easier than expected, but as sisters, they'd often shared all the details of their lives.

"I understand."

Maggie shot her a look.

"Okay, I don't totally understand. Five years is a long time. But what does working and living at the bar have to do with that?"

"I don't know. Maybe nothing. But like I said, I feel ready. I've had dates with some good guys. I'm not afraid to go out. Todd doesn't occupy my thoughts anymore. The only thing I haven't confronted in all this time is the bar." She sighed and laid her head on her knees. "And if it's not this, I don't have any other ideas."

"We'll figure it out. Maybe you just need to relax and date without worrying about the sex. How can you enjoy yourself and get to know a guy if you're all stressed about screwing him?" She picked up her coffee again and drank.

"I know. But it's hard. And Dr. Janzen said I absolutely have to tell the guy about the rape, but that's a hard conver-sation to have."

"So start with dating."

"I am. Olivia has me set up for a blind date tomorrow.

Coffee in the afternoon. She showed me his picture. He's cute."

"Cool. That's a start."

"But I'm nervous. I feel like I'm wearing a huge flashing sign that says 'I haven't gotten laid in five years.'"

Moira snorted. "I happen to know lots of guys would line up to help you remedy that."

"If only it were that easy." She sighed. "Enough about me. Tell me about you and Jimmy. Is he as hot as I imagine him?"

"Eww…don't tell me you fantasize about my fiancé."

"I don't. But come on. I have eyes." She relaxed again and stretched out her legs until her feet rested on the trunk.

"Yes. He is."

Maggie looked at her sister, whose cheeks were flaming. "Details, please."

"You really want details?"

"Yeah."

"You know how Jimmy's always been bossy? Yeah, that carries over into bed. He wants to be in charge all the time, but it's sexy because it's not all about him. That man has some singular focus, let me tell you."

Maggie smiled. "Maybe you shouldn't tell me *everything*. I'll never be able to look at Jimmy again." She thought about what it would be like to have a relationship like that. To be with a man who would take control but not frighten her. Her mind went back to her recurring fantasy of the big dude with the gentle touch.

Moira poked her leg. "Where did you just go? Please say you weren't fantasizing about my man."

"No." Maggie debated telling her. *Why not? This is Moira.* "I was thinking about a fantasy I've been having when I'm alone. It's the same guy, but he's faceless. He's a big guy with great arms. His hands are huge. He kind of dwarfs me. But he's gentle, knows exactly what to do. Listening to you talk about Jimmy made me think of him."

"I guess I have a mission now. I have to find a guy to match your mystery man. Any other clues as to what he looks like?"

"He's imaginary, sis. There is no finding him."

"We'll see." She stood. "I'm going to go home now. Let me know if you need any more help getting settled."

"Are you free tomorrow? I have shopping to do. I need furniture."

"Sure. Give me a call." She shrugged into her coat and headed to the door.

Maggie followed to lock up. As Moira opened the door, Shane stood there with his fist poised to knock.

Moira patted his shoulder. "Hi, again. Actually, good-bye, again. One of these times we'll both be heading in the same direction at the same time."

"I had some leftover pizza. Thought you girls might be hungry."

"Sorry, can't stay." Moira brushed past him, but then made some crazy gestures.

Maggie stared at her until she understood. Moira stood there, waving her arms and mouthing, "He's a big guy." Then she snorted a laugh.

Shane turned, and Moira waved before ducking out the exterior door. Heat rose to Maggie's cheeks. Moira knew that wasn't her relationship with Shane. But then she turned her attention back to him, needing to crane her neck to meet his eyes. Yes, he was definitely big.

"You think pizza is supposed to fix everything?"

"It was worth a shot." He held out the small box.

She sighed. "You're in luck. I didn't eat dinner, unless you count the brownie I had with Moira." She took the box and he stepped back. "You can come in."

He smirked. Damn man knew she wouldn't be able to stay mad. She took the pizza to the living room and plopped on the couch.

"You don't have a TV?"

"Not yet." She glanced at him as she bit into the not-quite-warm pizza. "Wait a minute. Did you bring pizza as an excuse to get access to my apartment because you thought I had a TV?"

"No. I brought you pizza because you like it. I hoped I could score an invite to watch TV. My apartment is a job site." He strode across the room and sat beside her.

"You helped me bring my stuff in. You didn't see a TV then."

He shrugged.

"I have my computer ready. I was going to watch a show when Moira showed up."

He looked at the laptop on the table. "It's not a very big screen."

"We'll make do." She scooted closer to him and pulled the computer onto her lap to scroll through movies and TV shows. Her knee bumped his and she was suddenly hyper-aware of him. He smelled fresh from a shower and warmth rolled off his skin. She was *not* supposed to notice these things. Damn Moira.

THIS WAS WHAT LIFE WAS SUPPOSED TO BE. SHANE SETTLED back into the couch with Maggie curled up next to him to watch TV like they had hundreds of times over the years. For the past few days, he'd been torn up knowing she was angry. Knowing they were in the same city without talking every day felt weird. They'd talked almost every day when she was halfway around the world.

He probably should've felt bad for throwing Ryan under the bus, but he didn't. If Maggie knew this was all Shane's idea, she might figure out how to stay mad. He needed to be in her corner, and she wouldn't believe that if she knew the truth.

Maggie finished a second piece of pizza and stood. "You want something? Moira brought beer."

He twitched. Although he drank, he never did with Maggie. He always figured that if she wasn't drinking, it made her uncomfortable. "You sure?"

"Yeah, I'm sure she brought it. I put it in the fridge myself." She looked at him like he was crazy.

"Are you sure it won't bother you?"

"Why would it?"

He shifted forward and put the laptop back on the table. "Because you don't drink."

She continued to stare at him and her head tilted. "I choose not to drink because I don't like to feel out of control." She bit down on her bottom lip. "The last time I lost control like that, it didn't end well. But it doesn't bother me to be around people who drink. Shit. My whole family drinks. I work at a *bar*."

Her eyes popped wide and she sank back to the couch. "You never drink around me. Why did I not realize that before?"

"Because it's not important."

"Yeah, it is." She reached out and stroked his jaw. "You gave up drinking so I wouldn't get upset. You're the best kind of friend."

With her hand on his face like that, he had a hard time keeping his thoughts friendly. "Don't go overboard. I didn't give up drinking altogether, just in front of you."

"It's still sweet." She rose and went to the kitchen. When she came back, she held out a bottle of beer.

He accepted and said, "Thanks," as he twisted off the cap.

Maggie sat and watched as he drank from the bottle.

"Ready for another show?"

She nodded and snuggled beside him again. If this was all he'd get out of life, he'd be happy. Maggie was safe and with him. At some point he might even be able to make a move to change their relationship. Every time he considered it, something stood in his way. At first, it was other guys. As a teen, she was rarely without a boyfriend. Then she'd been raped, and his greatest fear was that he would lose her, that she wouldn't want to be near him because he hadn't stopped it from happening. And then just as they seemed to be moving in that direction, she took off to Europe.

Part of him wanted to grab her and kiss her and tell her she'd always be safe with him.

But it would freak her out. She was still battling her demons. So he would wait until she was ready. He would have only one shot and he couldn't afford to blow it.

Maggie was shoving at his shoulder, and he squinted at her. Damn. He'd fallen asleep.

"I would let you stay asleep, but this is my bed."

He pushed forward. "What?" He rubbed his eyes.

"I don't have a bed yet. I'm going shopping tomorrow. Until then, this is my bed." She pointed at the couch.

"Why did you move if you don't have furniture?"

She lifted a shoulder. "Eager, I guess."

He stood and stretched. "Sorry I fell asleep. Guess I was more tired than I thought." He took his empty beer bottle to the kitchen. "Trash can?"

"On the shopping list for tomorrow."

He shook his head. The girl hadn't planned for anything. "I have a queen-sized bed. You're welcome to share it with me."

She chewed her lip again. "No, that's okay. I'll be fine here."

He rolled his shoulders. They'd often crashed together, always fully clothed, a safe distance between them. The first time, they'd still been in high school, and he'd thought for sure the O'Learys were going to skin him. He and Maggie had studied late for finals and fell asleep. After that, it had been normal.

In fact, the one thing that told him they were okay after the rape was that she'd asked him to stay with her one night.

"You know where to find me if you change your mind." He let himself out of her place and walked next door. As he unlocked his apartment, the door behind him opened. He turned to see his neighbor.

A woman about his age stood in the doorway wearing skimpy shorts and a tank top. Obviously her sleep clothes since it was barely twenty degrees outside. "Hi, I'm Janet."

"Hi, Janet. I'm Shane. I just moved in." He hitched a thumb over his shoulder to his apartment.

"I thought that apartment wasn't ready."

"It's not. I'm doing the work while I live there."

The corner of her mouth lifted. "So you're a handy kind of guy."

"I'm a carpenter."

"Hmmm. I guess that means you don't know what to do about the heat."

Ahh. Now his tired brain clicked. She was having the same temperature issues he was. "No, sorry."

"Okay. Thanks anyway. Good night." She slipped back behind her door.

As he let himself into his apartment, he realized Maggie's place had been totally comfortable. How the hell did that happen? He was too tired to focus. He'd deal with it tomorrow. He strode through the apartment, straight to his bed, tossing off clothes as he went. He cracked the bedroom window open a little to keep from getting sweaty.

All in all, it hadn't been a bad day. He had gotten work done on his apartment and made up with Maggie. With any luck, tomorrow she'd go buy a big-ass TV so they could watch it while his place was under construction.

He fell back asleep feeling the imaginary press of Maggie's body against him. The desire for that to become reality held just enough edge to annoy him. Waiting didn't come easy.

CHAPTER 6

Maggie was exhausted and the idea of canceling her coffee date tempted her, but it would've been unfair to Bill, Olivia's coworker. Moira had insisted on going all over the city looking for furniture, and although Maggie had hated it, she was glad because she was done. She had a slew of deliveries all coming tomorrow.

Driving through the slush-covered streets, she looked for a place to park near the coffee shop. When a spot opened, she pulled in. She took a minute to check herself in the mirror. While she wasn't fully made up for a night on the town, she still wanted to make a good impression. This guy might turn out to be great boyfriend material.

She swiped on some lip gloss and grabbed her purse. Inside the shop, she looked around, trying to see Bill. It wasn't too crowded, but it had an odd configuration, so she couldn't see the whole place from the door. Hopefully, Olivia had shown Bill a picture of her too, so he could keep an eye out for her.

At the counter, she ordered a hot chocolate with extra whipped cream, and while she waited for her order she continued to look around. Grabbing her cup, she debated whether she should get a table or wait here, making her easy to spot.

From behind her, a deep voice said, "Maggie?"

She spun to see Bill standing beside her. "Yes."

"Sorry I'm late. My shift at the hospital ran over a bit." He looked at her cup. "I would've bought your drink."

"That's fine."

"Let me order and we'll grab a table."

She waited while he placed his order. He was taller than her, but that wasn't saying much. He was probably five-ten or so. As he paid for his coffee, she looked at his hands. Definitely not the big guy from her dreams.

She shook her head. Damn Moira. Maggie knew the guy didn't actually exist; he was a figment of her overactive imagination. The guy in front of her deserved a real chance.

With his coffee in hand, he pointed to a free table. He waited for her to sit before taking the chair across from her.

"So Olivia tells me you've been traveling. Where have you been?"

"I went to London and then to France and Spain for a few weeks. But once I hit Ireland, I kind of settled in. I have cousins there, so it was a lot of fun to be with extended family." She sipped her hot chocolate and hoped she wouldn't get a whipped cream mustache to make her look ridiculous.

"I've always wanted to travel. It's one of those things I keep telling myself I'll do, but then I get caught up in the day-to-day stuff of life."

"I know you work at the hospital with Olivia, but she didn't tell me what you do."

"I'm a nurse." He paused like he was expecting her to make a comment.

The problem was, she had no idea what to say. "Cool."

That sounded lame as soon as it left her mouth. How could she be this out of practice for being on a date?

Bill smiled. "Sorry. I was expecting some of the usual comments like *A guy nurse?* Or *Why not a doctor?* I find that someone's reaction to my job says a lot about them."

And hers probably said she had the vocabulary of a sixth grader. "Did I pass?"

He let out a low chuckle. "Yeah."

"Do you like being a nurse?"

He jerked his head back a little. "Why would I do it if I didn't like it?"

"I don't know. A lot of people go into a career thinking it's going to be one way, and then it's not, but they're already in it, so it's hard to walk away. You have the degree, the experience, the job security, so you suck it up even if you don't enjoy it."

"Spoken like a woman who hates her job."

She laughed. Her words probably did carry that message. "Nah. I'm waitressing right now for that exact reason. I'm not sure what I want to do, and I don't want to land somewhere I'll regret."

"Makes sense." He drank his coffee, but the expression on his face was a little too serious. "Any ideas?"

"For a career? Too many. I almost feel like a five-year-old. One minute I want to be a writer, then I want to be a social worker, then I think maybe just a regular office job, something that won't ever have to come home with me." She took a long drink, feeling like she was failing a test.

"What did you major in?"

"I never got around to declaring a major. When I started college, I thought I'd get into marketing, so I have a few business classes under my belt, but mostly I experimented."

"So you haven't graduated." The statement could've been simple observation, but Maggie felt the judgment behind it.

She shook her head. Yeah, this date had taken a wrong turn. Who wanted to be out with a guy who'd make her feel like a failure? He didn't follow with another question or comment, choosing to stare at his coffee instead. "You know, I have a shift at the bar tonight. I better get going. It was nice to meet you."

Glad she had thought up the slight fib, she stood and looked around for a trash can for her cup. He stood. "It was nice to meet you."

They were obviously on the same page, since he didn't bother to ask for her number. "You too." She gave him a quick wave and dashed out the door. First blind date failure? Check. She wasn't sure she could stomach a long line of these before finding success.

The whole conversation with Bill had blindsided her. She'd been so concerned with appearing normal instead of like a victim that she hadn't considered other ways she might be a turnoff. So the blind date failed because she was failing at life. It stung.

She drove back to her apartment with her few purchases and thought about her options for the evening. She almost wished she did have a shift at the bar. At least she'd have plans. After parking her car behind the bar, she grabbed her bags and ran up the stairs. As soon as she walked through the first door, Shane's door opened.

He looked at the bags she carried. "None of those look big enough for a TV."

"You know, for someone who's so concerned about a TV, maybe you should just invest in one."

"I have one. It's in storage. I don't want it to get ruined on this job site I'm living in. Besides, if I watch TV at your place, you might cook me dinner."

"Fat chance. More like I'll order food from downstairs."

He pointed at her bags. "I thought you were buying furniture."

"I did. It's all being delivered tomorrow."

"I would've picked it up for you."

"Really?"

"Yeah, why not?"

She thought about her lack of a TV. It would be nice to watch something bigger than her laptop. "Are you free now?"

He looked down at his dusty jeans and sweaty T-shirt. "Yeah."

"A TV was one thing I didn't buy today. I was busy picking out a bed and mattress and stuff like that. Will you go with me to get one?"

"Give me a few minutes to clean up."

"Thanks. You're the best." She went on tiptoe and kissed his cheek. She tasted his salty sweat and dust. There was something to be said for the scent of a hardworking guy. "Then will you be so kind as to hook it up when we get back? I'll buy you dinner."

She winked at him. So dinner wouldn't actually cost her anything if she got it downstairs. Shane wouldn't care.

"I'll be ready in ten."

"Okay."

Somehow, shopping with Shane was less crazy than shopping with Moira. Of course, they only had one purchase to make and Maggie pretty much let Shane pick out the TV. As the guy from the store helped Shane load the flat screen into his truck, she asked, "How are we gonna get this into my apartment?"

"I'll get one of the guys in the bar to help. Maybe Ryan or Colin will be around."

"I doubt it."

"We'll figure it out. Have you met any of our neighbors yet?"

"No, but I haven't been looking either."

"There's Janet across the hall from me. I was hoping a guy might be across from you."

Maggie shrugged. "No idea."

As they drove home, Maggie asked, "Do you think it's weird that I don't have a career picked out yet?"

Shane was quiet, but then he usually did get quiet while in thought. He was not a speak-before-you-think kind of guy. She should take lessons.

"Not weird. A little unusual, maybe. Why do you ask?"

"I went on a date this afternoon, and the guy seemed put off by the fact that I hadn't finished college and I'm taking my time figuring out my life."

"A date?"

She asked about her career and he homes in on the date. Such a guy. "Coffee. A blind date. Olivia fixed me up with a guy from work. A nurse."

Shane snorted.

"What was that for?"

"A nurse?"

"What's wrong with a guy being a nurse?"

"It's girly."

"It is not. Not like it matters, though. We won't be seeing each other again." Back to the drawing board. Maybe she should ask Ryan to do a speed dating thing again. He'd done it once for Quinn.

"Uh-oh. You have that scheming look again."

"I do not. I'm just thinking about ways to find decent dates. You know anyone who would be good for me?"

"No." His answer was quick and sharp.

"Something wrong?"

"No."

She let it drop. Maybe she was being overly sensitive after her messed-up date. When they got back to the bar, Maggie offered to help carry the TV, but Shane didn't think she could handle it, so he knocked on a neighbor's door. A tall guy came out, and Shane introduced them and asked for help. His name was Alex, and between them it took less than five minutes to carry it upstairs.

"Thanks, Alex. Can I offer you a beer?" she asked once they set the box in her living room.

"No, thanks. I'm actually on my way to work. I'm a night shift security guard."

"Interesting."

He shook his head. "Not really, but I get some studying done because it's quiet. Then I have classes during the day when I'm not asleep."

"Busy. I guess we won't be seeing much of each other."

"Probably not, but it was nice to meet you."

After Alex left, she helped Shane unpackage the TV and he set about hooking it up.

"Are you sure you can tap into the cable for the bar?"

"I did it when I lived here before."

"Don't they have satellite now?"

"Crap. I figured I'd piggyback like last time." She should've talked to Ryan first. Maybe he could get her added to the bar's access. "I can use the Internet to at least stream some stuff until I figure it out." She didn't need Shane's help for that.

He'd gone to the kitchen and helped himself to one of the beers Moira brought. Looked like Moira was right. She should be able to offer guests a drink.

She played with the remote to access the Internet.

Shane asked, "What's this?"

"What?" She glanced over her shoulder where he was scrolling through pictures on her laptop. "Pictures I took."

"They're good. Since when are you a photographer?"

"I'm not really. I play around with it as a hobby."

Although if she were being honest, she'd admit that she enjoyed being behind the camera more than almost anything.

"When did this start?"

"When I was in Europe. I took a free class and bought a camera. I wanted to document my journey with more than some blurry, rushed shots."

He didn't comment but continued to scroll through her computer, so she returned her attention to the TV. She figured it out without too much trouble and then asked what he wanted for dinner.

"Are you cooking?"

"If by cooking you mean going to the kitchen downstairs, then yes."

"A burger will be good."

"Be back in a few. Pick out something to watch."

SHANE SETTLED BACK ON MAGGIE'S COUCH. HE BEGAN TO wonder what else he didn't know about her. Their too brief visits over the holidays had been about catching up and having fun. Their phone calls while she was away were about connection and missing each other. Discovering that she had a hobby he knew nothing about, one she was clearly good at, felt strange. Worse was hearing her talk about trying to find dates.

Part of him had become accustomed to Maggie being a homebody after her rape. She'd started going out again and seeing friends, but she hadn't really dated. At least not until she'd gone halfway around the world. He should've expected her to continue once she got home.

But he wanted a chance with her. He just didn't know when or if to make a move. She hadn't given him any indication she felt the same, and he didn't want to risk making their friendship awkward.

So he sat in her living room, drinking her beer, and watching TV like he would with any other friend.

But she would never be just a friend.

She'd always be special.

He set his beer on the table and focused on the photos on her laptop. He didn't know what he was searching for. But then he found it. A picture of Maggie, smiling as she looked out to the water. He had no idea who had taken the photo, but it was perfect. Her face was lit with enjoyment—Maggie always loved being near water—but a shadow still hovered over her. That was what she wanted to shake off.

Why couldn't he see that shadow when they were together?

He continued to study her pictures until she returned with food. She set the Styrofoam containers down in front of him. "You're going to make me feel self-conscious if you keep staring at my pictures."

"Why? They're great."

She smiled slowly and a hint of pink rose in her cheeks. "Like I said, it's just a hobby. It feels weird to have it scrutinized."

"I'm not scrutinizing. I have no idea how to criticize them since I don't know anything about taking pictures, but I know they look good."

And so did she, standing in front of him, a little shy about her work but proud at the same time.

CHAPTER 7

Maggie was dog tired. She had no idea why she set the delivery of all of her stuff for the same day she was scheduled to work her first late shift at the bar. If she wanted to make good tips, she needed to be friendly, so a nap was a no-brainer. But it hadn't been enough. After staying up late watching TV with Shane again, and then spending her entire day rearranging furniture as it came in, she was beat. The hour-long nap would've stretched into three if she hadn't set her alarm.

Now she guzzled coffee to wake herself up. Her stomach tumbled with nerves. Although she'd been working at O'Leary's without issue, at night the vibe was different. During the day, guys would come in on their lunch break or the old men who had nothing better to do would sit around.

At night, people came in to get drunk, party, pick up people. She hadn't been part of that atmosphere in a long time. Even when she worked other waitressing jobs or spent time in pubs in Ireland, it was never the party scene.

But it was a Tuesday night, so the bar probably wouldn't

be insane. She blew out a heavy breath. She could do this. She *would* do this.

She applied makeup and played with her hair, unable to decide if she should try to put it up or leave it down. She gathered the sides and swept them up away from her face but left the rest down. With her O'Leary's Pub T-shirt on over her most comfortable pair of jeans, she left her apartment.

The best part of living above the bar was her commute. As she locked her apartment, Shane's door opened. He stepped into the hall wearing a bar shirt.

"What are you doing?"

"Heading down to work."

"You're serious? You're really working at the bar?"

"I told you I was. Law school is expensive."

She eyed him, an uneasiness crawling through her. "Why haven't I seen you go to work yet?"

"I wasn't scheduled." He raised an eyebrow, waiting for more questions.

She hoped Cara knew how lucky she was to have a brother like Shane. Although, when she thought about it, Maggie had the same thing in her brothers. They would all do anything for her.

She walked through the exterior door and down the back steps with Shane on her heels. She hadn't worn a coat, since she was just going downstairs, but a blast of wind zipped through her, icing her skin, even through her T-shirt.

She popped in the back door of the bar nearest the kitchen without holding it for Shane. The door slammed shut and then reopened a second later.

"Thanks," Shane mumbled as he walked past her to the front of the bar.

"Sorry," she called out as she rubbed her hands together over the flat grill. Once her skin was warm and she was sure her nipples weren't poking through her shirt to give everyone a show, she went to the front.

Enough tables were filled with dinner guests to keep her busy, but she knew that as the night wore on, she'd be selling less food and more alcohol. That part still made her nervous.

As she walked through and introduced herself to the guests at her tables, she was keenly aware of Shane's eyes on her. His gaze tracked her every move. Although it didn't feel creepy, she wasn't his job. He was supposed to watch the drunks. She rolled her shoulders and made her rounds, taking over for Kelly, the waitress who'd worked the earlier shift.

As Kelly sat at the bar and closed out her tickets, she kept looking at Shane, who didn't seem to notice. Maggie wondered when Shane last went on a date. He hadn't mentioned anyone in a long time. Usually, he shared stories when they hung out, but now that she considered it, she couldn't remember when he'd talked about anyone new.

That was a piece to file away for prodding later.

The first shift of dinner guests came and went, and Maggie had gotten her second wind. The time of day hadn't had an impact on her ability to do her job at all. As she cleared a table, a man stopped her.

"I'm meeting a bunch of friends. Would it be possible for us to push a couple of tables together here?"

"Sure. Give me a minute to get this cleaned off." When she returned and started shoving the tables, the guy grabbed an end.

"Let me get this. We can get them put together. We didn't want to mess with your stations." He was a big guy, biceps stretching the sleeves of his shirt. He could obviously handle pushing a table.

"Thanks," she said with a smile, and helped arrange the tables for him and his friends. "Will you need menus?"

"We might get some appetizers later. Will you be our waitress?"

"Yes, I will. I'm Maggie. Can I get you started with something while you wait for your friends?"

"I'm Greg and I'd love a Heineken in a bottle."

"I'll be right back."

At the bar, she put in the order. Shane leaned against the wood, looking nonchalant to anyone who didn't know him. "Making friends?"

"You know it. I want big tips."

He nodded and offered her a smile, but it was the kind of smile he'd send to any customer walking through the door.

As Jenna handed her the bottle of beer, Maggie said to Shane, "You know, I saw Kelly checking you out before she left."

"Kelly who?"

"The waitress I relieved? I think she might've had to wipe some drool off her tips."

He snorted and took a stroll through the bar. She delivered the beer to Greg, who now had three friends with him. She smiled brightly at the prospect of the tips coming her way.

BUSINESS PICKED UP AS THE NIGHT PROGRESSED. ALTHOUGH HE wasn't officially on staff, Shane couldn't help but do the job. He watched for people being overserved and for anyone who looked ready to start a fight. For the most part, it was a quiet evening, except for the table of Marines who took a solid interest in Maggie.

It seemed like every few minutes they were calling her over to ask a question or place another order. Mostly, they just wanted to talk to her and earn one of her smiles. He knew the feeling. Ever since he left his apartment, he'd felt like she was giving him the cold shoulder.

He stood at the bar and drank another glass of water and eavesdropped on Maggie's conversation with the table full of guys.

"Hey, Maggie. We need another round. This time add a shot of Jack Daniels for everyone, and my friend Drew over there is going to pay for this one since he doesn't have his challenge coin."

"Challenge coin?" she asked.

Every man at the table pulled out a coin and slapped it on the table. "We all have them. When out with your buddies, if someone calls for it, you have to produce the coin. If you don't have it, you have to pay for the round."

Maggie slid her tray under her arm and picked up one of the coins. She held it up and twirled it around. "So if you all know Drew doesn't have his coin, can't you just pull this every time you want a drink? He'd have to pay your tab all night."

"Hush, now," Drew said.

Maggie smiled brightly and handed the first guy his coin. "Sorry," she said, letting everyone know she wasn't really sorry at all.

She stood next to Shane at the bar while she waited for the shots.

"You look like you're having fun."

"I am." She laid a hand on his forearm. "I know you're worried, but I'm good. Even more, I'm enjoying myself."

He felt better hearing it from her instead of trying to make an assessment based on her body language, but he still couldn't relax. He wondered if the urge to take care of her would ever subside. His dad was right. He couldn't put his life on hold for Maggie.

She strode back to the table with a tray full of shots looking confident in everything she did.

Maybe he wasn't needed here after all. He sure as hell could find better ways to spend his night than standing around drinking water. If nothing else, he had an apartment that needed renovations.

For the next few hours, he roamed around the bar and flirted with a few girls who were out celebrating a job promotion. As much as he should've been enjoying himself, though, he wasn't. He was tired and really wanted to go to bed. The bartender reminded everyone it was last call, and Shane sighed.

Bed was close.

The group of guys who had taken Maggie's attention all night were getting ready to leave. The leader, the one who had arrived first, stood and stepped close to Maggie. Although it wasn't a threatening move, Shane didn't like it. Maggie didn't seem scared, but then her color changed. She forced a smile, but her face had gone pale, and as soon as the guy turned to put on his jacket, she darted toward the back.

Torn between punching the guy for upsetting Maggie and finding out why she was upset, Shane had to decide. He opted to follow Maggie.

By the time he got to the back of the bar, she was nowhere to be seen. He knocked on the women's bathroom door but didn't get an answer, so he opened it and called, "Maggie?"

"Yeah."

"Can I come in?"

"No." Her words were weak and he didn't want to fight her, so he stood in the dark hallway with his hands in his pockets.

A few minutes later, she came out of the bathroom. He stared at her and tried to assess what to do. She was beyond upset. Her hands were shaking and her eyes red and watery. In his pockets, his hands clenched with the need to hit something. "What happened?" he asked.

"Nothing. Greg closed out his bill and thanked me for being a great waitress. He handed me a tip." She inhaled a shaky breath. "But the smell of whiskey on his breath…" She paused and swallowed. "I had this sudden flash of Todd. He'd been drinking whiskey that night."

All Shane wanted to do more than anything at the moment was wrap his arms around her and comfort her. But he knew she might not want that. She might need the space. Touching her could make everything worse. He took his hands from his pockets. "What can I do?"

She launched herself at him and hugged him tightly. He let his arms circle her gently. If this was his sole purpose for wasting an entire night at O'Leary's Pub, it had been worth it.

"I know it's stupid. Greg was really nice. He wasn't a jerk and didn't hit on me. It was the smell…" She inhaled slowly again, this time a little steadier. "I didn't even see it coming."

He rubbed a hand down her back. "Now you know it's a trigger." He paused and weighed his next words carefully. "Maybe you're trying too much at once, Mags. The apartment, working here, blind dates. Maybe it's too much."

"It can't be, Shane," she mumbled against his chest. "It's how normal people live. And I need to be normal."

After a few more breaths, she eased away from him. "Thanks. You're always here for me, knowing just what to do. I know you don't agree with how I'm handing it, but I *need* this." She swiped a hand over her face and pressed her lips together. "I have to go finish up for the night."

With a stiff nod, she turned and walked away.

~

Maggie forced a smile as she walked back toward the main bar area. The whole way, hiding behind that fake smile, all she could think was how stupid she felt. She'd gotten cocky in her ability to handle being at the bar. She hadn't even thought about how the smell of whiskey on some stranger's breath would make her want to vomit. The guys had been nice and fun and hadn't been rude or disrespectful at all, which made the whole experience frightening. How would she ever be able to handle being at a bar or on a date if she couldn't anticipate triggers?

As she scrubbed the tables before closing, she felt Shane's watchful stare again. For a while, it had been like old times. They joked and had fun teasing each other, but they each had a job to do. While she'd been grateful for his presence when she came out of the bathroom, she didn't want him staring.

She did her best to ignore him and finished cleaning up. There were a couple of people still at the bar, but Jenna waved her off.

"Are you sure?" Maggie asked.

"Yeah. Steve has the door and he'll walk me to my car. You look rung out. Go on home."

"Thanks." She didn't want to admit how messed up she felt—not to Jenna, and certainly not to Shane who stood by the back door waiting for her. "I don't need an escort to go upstairs."

"I'm aware, but since we're headed in the same direction, I thought I'd wait for you." He held the door open and a blast of cold air shot in.

She walked through the door, and Shane was immediately by her side with an arm around her. His heat radiated through her chilled skin. His solid mass offered whatever support she needed.

When they were upstairs, he asked, "How are you?"

"I'm okay. It was rough for a few minutes. Thanks for being there." *Like always* she almost added.

"You had me worried. I saw you change."

"Change?"

"Your color, your expression, your body language. At first, I thought the guy did something, but when you smiled before running off, I knew it had to be something else."

"If I looked that bad, I'm surprised I got such a good tip. I thought my acting had improved over the years."

Shane reached out and tugged at a lock of hair. "You can't act in front of me. I know you too well."

He looked tired, but he smiled in a way that warmed her from the inside. They stood in silence for a minute and the air felt charged, like something was about to happen, but she had no idea what.

She retreated a step and the moment slipped by. "Good night."

"Sleep well, Magpie."

She rolled her eyes. "You know I hate when you call me that."

"That's why I do it."

She turned and went into her apartment, completely aware that Shane stood in the hall until she was locked inside.

Although she was tired—having her fear and anxiety triggered like that always caused a crash—Maggie puttered around her apartment, relishing in having new furniture. She put her new sheets on her bed and ran a hand over them. They were the most expensive length of material she'd probably ever owned, but the luxury in bed was worth it. They were so soft she just wanted to roll around naked in them. Then she smiled. She lived alone. She could sleep naked, walk through her apartment naked, eat her cereal in the morning naked. Without any further consideration, she stripped off her clothes.

With a lingering look at the sheets, she moved to the bathroom for a quick shower. Her night of work after moving furniture left her feeling funky. She wanted to really enjoy the experience of the smooth, cool cotton against her bare skin.

After her hot shower and lathering her favorite lotion on her skin, she strolled naked back to bed. She locked her bedroom door, flicked off the light, and crawled under the covers with a sigh.

She turned and rolled and moved her legs to feel as much of the softness as she could. With both her body and mind soothed, she relaxed.

In that weird space between sleep and wakefulness, Maggie's mind floated. The sensual nature of lying naked in bed aroused her. Every inch of skin exposed and sliding against the cotton.

Her hands slipped across the sheets and back to her body. Gentle fingertips glided over her abdomen and lower. Regardless of who had spooked her earlier, she owned her body.

Her right hand skated over her clit and between her slick folds. In her mind, the big guy made his appearance. Bare-chested, with bulging biceps, he leaned over her. *His* hand pushed into her, pushing her toward orgasm. His thrusts increased, harder and faster.

Her hips bumped up seeking release. A moan rose in her throat, and as she came, her eyes flew open and met the gaze of the man above her. Her heart raced and she sat up in bed.

The face of the man was clear as anything. Shane.

CHAPTER 8

The following morning, Maggie lay in bed feeling weird. When she'd fallen asleep the night before, she'd tried to convince herself that her imagination had gotten away from her. Shane had been the last person she'd seen before bed and he was on her mind. His presence in her fantasy meant nothing. Part of her wanted to call Dr. Janzen and confirm that, but she worried she was wrong. What would she do if the dream meant something? What could that something be?

Sunlight peeked through her bedroom window. It was early, but the bit of sunshine at this time told her spring was on its way. She heard movement out in the hall, and based on the jingle of keys and thump of footsteps, she knew it was Shane. She closed her eyes and imagined him in his work clothes leaving for a day on the job with his dad. She pictured his smile and then remembered her dream.

She'd seen Shane shirtless before. They'd spent too many summers together for her not to notice. Her friend was hot. Objectively, she knew that. She wasn't one of those oblivious women who didn't appreciate men. But had she ever thought about Shane naked and sexy?

Nothing came to mind. Shoving out of bed, she decided it was a silly thing. Shane would probably have a laugh over it. She brushed her teeth and dressed. Moira was coming over that afternoon to help her think through career options, so she figured she should have some ideas.

Mary would be downstairs doing her morning prep, so Maggie decided to snag a cup of coffee there instead of making her own. She grabbed a mug and stepped out her door. As she exited the building, she almost walked into Shane.

"Uh, hi." Her damn cheeks were turning red and she would've given anything to not be picturing him naked right now. "Thought you were gone to work."

"I was. Forgot my tool belt." He shook his head.

That's when Maggie saw how tired he looked. She wanted to reach out, but another flash of his smiling eyes over her as she came rolled through her. "Have a good day," she choked out, and ran down the stairs.

"You too," he called to her back.

She needed to get rid of those images or she would lose her best friend. Walking around embarrassed and unable to interact with him would kill her. She'd never felt awkward with him and she didn't like it.

She ducked in the back door of the bar. This time of day, she needed to use the door that led to the back hall. The kitchen wouldn't be open yet. Only a few lights had been turned on, and the silence was strange. She'd forgotten how quiet the place could be. "Mary?"

"Up here," Mary called.

Maggie followed the sound of the woman's voice. Behind the bar, Mary stood over a newspaper.

"You do know you can read that online, right? Most people don't actually read the paper anymore."

Mary looked up. "I like the paper—the smell, the feel, the way the ink leaves smudges on my fingers. You don't get that with a computer. We still get the delivery for all the old guys who come in to hang out. Ryan likes to continue some of the things your dad always did."

"Sometimes even when he shouldn't." Maggie walked behind the bar and poured her coffee.

"How did last night go?"

"Good. We were busy and I made great tips." No way would she tell Mary about her little freak-out. Mary would immediately tell Ryan, and that couldn't possibly help.

"I'm glad to hear it."

Maggie sipped the coffee and watched Mary. The woman would be objective. She wouldn't jump to conclusions, and while they weren't close, they were friendly. And she was a woman. "Hey, Mary, can I ask you a personal question?"

"Sure." Her gaze left the paper again and met Maggie's face.

"Have you ever had a dream or fantasy about someone you shouldn't?"

Mary's eyebrows furrowed. "What do you mean by shouldn't? Like about my brother?"

"Eww. Gross. No." Maggie tried to wipe away that mental image. "I mean like a good friend. You're just friends."

"Sure. Nate and I were just friends until we slept together. Once we had great sex, it only made sense to get married."

Maggie nodded, unsure of what to say to that.

"Anyone I know?"

Maggie's cheeks warmed again. "Rather not say."

"So that's a yes." Mary sipped her coffee. "It's possible your mind just wandered to someone you know and held that image."

Relief washed over Maggie.

Mary smirked. "Or maybe you're into your friend and you've been lying to yourself. Either way, you need to think about it. If it was a one-time deal, I wouldn't worry too much."

Maggie bit the inside of her cheek. "Thanks."

Not that the conversation had been all that helpful, but at least Mary had tried. Maggie thanked her for the coffee and went back to her apartment to think. Was she lying to herself? Did she have a thing for Shane that was so secret she didn't even recognize it?

SHANE GOT TO WORK TWENTY MINUTES LATE. HE LOOKED AT his dad and readied for the complaint. He hadn't been late to a job since high school when he'd always been too tired to get his ass out of bed in the morning.

Instead of yelling, his dad simply said, "You look like shit."

"Thanks, and good morning to you, too." He'd already downed two cups of coffee, but he still felt sluggish.

"Who kept you up so late that you couldn't be on time?"

"Maggie."

His dad's eyes widened and Shane realized what his dad was really asking. "No. Not like that. I worked closing at the bar last night with Maggie."

"I told you this wasn't a good idea." His dad hefted a sheet of drywall across the room.

The man was getting too old to do this kind of work. Shane took the sheet from him. It looked like he was never going to escape drywall. "Early on in the night, I started to think you were right. She was running around, owning the room. It was like nothing bad had ever happened."

"But?" his dad asked as he followed with another sheet of drywall.

"Right before closing, this guy got too close with whiskey on his breath and she panicked. She covered it well, but when I caught her outside the bathroom, she was shaking." He focused on installing the sheet in front of him and taking over for his dad.

His dad stepped back and let Shane handle it. "You can't stop that kind of stuff from happening."

"I know." He'd give anything if he could. "But being there after made a difference. Helped her." He believed that.

As he worked, he remembered the look on her face this morning. She'd acted weird, like she couldn't get away from him fast enough. He couldn't figure out what would make her act that way. They'd ended the night on a good note, even after her problems with the Marines.

By the time lunch hit, Shane was exhausted. He hadn't thought it possible to be more tired than he was when he got to work. He sat on an overturned bucket and devoured the sandwich he'd hastily made that morning. He looked at the cooler his dad unpacked. One thing he definitely missed about living at home was his mom packing his lunch.

As if he felt Shane staring, his dad looked up. "You want some?"

"Whatcha got?"

"A couple of turkey sandwiches, chips, cookies—"

"Mom made cookies?"

"Of course." He tossed a baggie. "She sent extra like she always does."

Shane munched on the cookies and wished for a glass of milk. As if by divine intervention, his dad passed him a thermos. Milk. He laughed. How many grown men had their moms making lunch for them?

But he wasn't silly enough to say no to her cookies.

"Any word from the police department yet? I read in the paper they're going to be calling up the next class."

Shane lifted a shoulder. He'd about given up on becoming a cop. "Nothing."

He remembered Mrs. O'Leary saying Jimmy O'Malley might have some pull. Maybe it was worth looking into. It couldn't be worse than sitting and waiting.

They cleaned up after lunch and finished the drywall in the basement. It was good work for the winter, but Shane hated working indoors. He missed the sun and fresh air.

"You should go home," his dad said.

"We have a few more hours before quitting time."

"The drywall's done. I don't need your help to start taping. Go home and take a nap."

Christ, the idea of a nap was more appealing than it should have been. "I can finish out the day."

"I know you can, and there will be days I won't be able to let you go early. But you're working too many jobs right now. Go home."

He felt bad knowing his dad was right. His proposal was not well thought out, because he enjoyed sleep. He didn't function well without it, and on a job like this, he'd probably start making stupid mistakes. He'd have to plan better, look at the nights when Maggie would be working, and do his best to rest up instead of working on his apartment.

"You sure?" he asked.

"Yeah. Tell Maggie I said hi."

"Thanks, Dad."

His dad nodded and plopped drywall mud into the pan. Shane gathered his tools and went out to his truck. When he sat down and started the engine, his exhaustion expanded. He could almost lay his head against the steering wheel and sleep. As soon as the truck was warm, he drove on autopilot to his apartment. He took the quickest shower imaginable and crawled under the covers. He glanced at the clock and realized he was worse than an old man. At four in the afternoon, he was in bed.

MAGGIE AND MOIRA SAT ON THE COUCH, DRINKING COFFEE and talking for hours. The career hunt went in circles.

"You need to finish school and get your degree."

"In what? It seems silly to finish and get a degree I won't use."

Moira rolled her eyes. "You said you were almost done when you switched to English as a major and wanted to write. I can help you get some freelance gigs. You need some pieces for a portfolio, though."

"I don't think I'm a good-enough writer to make it a career." She sighed and tried to find the right words to explain it. "I thought that I lacked experience. I believed if I got out and lived life that it would translate into better writing." She scrunched her nose. "It didn't."

"Okay. Let's go back to things you like."

She immediately thought of photography, but dismissed it. She had no chance of getting a degree for that. She hadn't taken any formal classes.

"There!" Moira yelled. "What was that?"

"What?"

"Whatever you were just thinking about. It was something that made you smile. You don't smile when you think about working at the bar."

"I was thinking about photography, but it's just a hobby. I enjoy it. You're supposed to enjoy your hobbies. That doesn't mean it should be a career."

Moira stood and went to the kitchen. She returned with

the coffeepot and refilled both their cups. "But it might be worth looking into. There are all different kinds of photographers."

"I wouldn't know where to start."

"Isn't that what you have me for?"

Moira was probably the best older sister anyone could ask for. Because of that, Maggie decided Moira could be her sounding board for what she'd been considering all day. "So, I had this dream last night. You know, the one I told you about?"

"The mystery man," Moira replied with an exaggerated wag of her eyebrows.

Maggie immediately began to doubt the intelligence of having this conversation, but she soldiered on. "Last night, he had a face." She swallowed hard. "It was Shane."

Moira jumped up, sloshing hot coffee over her hand and on the floor as she squawked. "Oh, my God. Was it good? I bet he's good. Well, of course he was good in your dream. Why would you imagine him as being bad?"

Moira dashed out of the room and grabbed a paper towel to clean up her mess.

"The thing is, I'm not sure what the dream means. I had this freak-out with a customer last night at the bar, and Shane talked me through it. After my shift, he walked me upstairs. So part of me thinks that since he was the last person I talked to and I trust him and he knows about my past, which are all things Dr. Janzen said are vital, my mind plopped him in as mystery man." She reached over and lightly slapped her sister's leg. "And add to that you pointing out the other day how Shane is a big guy…"

Moira shifted on the couch and narrowed her eyes. "What about the other part?"

"What?"

"You said part of you thinks that."

Of course, nothing slipped by Moira. She bit her lip. "The other part thinks Shane would be a perfect experiment."

Moira's eyebrows shot up, but she said nothing.

Maggie twisted her hands together in her lap. "Like I said, he fits everything Dr. Janzen said is necessary for me to be comfortable enough to have a sexual relationship with a guy."

"So you're finally going to make a move on Shane? I've always thought you two would make a great couple."

"No. Not a couple. An experiment. Just sex. You know, to see if I can."

Moira did her beady eye thing again. "But he's your best friend."

"Who better to help me? He cares about me, and he knows everything, so I don't have to worry about that God-awful conversation. He's always taken care of me."

"Before approaching him with anything like this, you really need to think about it. This is big."

Maggie waved a hand. "It's sex. Hookups happen all the time. For most people our age, it's not a big deal at all. I don't want it to be. Can't you see that?"

Moira was making her question her plan. When the thought had struck her hours ago when she was supposed to be thinking about careers, it sounded like the best idea.

Her sister scooted closer and put an arm around her shoulder. "I do get it. I just don't want you to rush."

She snorted. "Funny coming from you. You rush into everything."

"So learn from my mistakes. You're not me. Every decision you make has pros and cons."

"Jeez. Now I'm supposed to make a list? I just had the idea."

Moira leaned back. "Not a list. What's the absolute worst thing that could happen if you do this?"

Maggie closed her eyes and voiced her worst fear. "That I

won't be able to do it. If I try with Shane, someone I love and trust, and I can't have sex, I'll never be able to."

"And what's the absolute best outcome?"

"I have sex, of course. And if I enjoy it, I'll know I'm not completely broken." She drank a gulp of coffee. Admitting those things aloud was harder than she thought.

"What about Shane?"

"What about him?"

"There would be a pro and con for him, too. Did you think about that?"

"Well, he'd get laid. That would be a pro, right? It is for any guy. The con…" She closed her eyes again. She didn't want to think about what the con would be for Shane. If she couldn't have sex with him, he would hold on to that guilt, too. "He'd feel responsible if I couldn't." She opened her eyes. "But it wouldn't be his fault. I'd have to make him understand."

Moira gave her a weak smile and patted her hand. "Don't assume anything when it comes to Shane. It would have to be a serious conversation."

Maggie nodded. She knew that. Talking with Shane had never been an issue.

"I'm going home. Jimmy should be off soon. Get a portfolio together of your photography and I'll ask around. If nothing else, I know I can get you some freelance work. You can try it out to see if you like it." Moira stood and grabbed her coat. Before heading toward the door, she pulled Maggie into a tight hug. "Remember not to rush anything and really listen to Shane."

"Okay." Maggie felt like Moira was trying to tell her something more, which was strange because Moira always said exactly what was on her mind. She walked her sister out. Before locking up, she glanced at Shane's door and wondered if he was home.

Then she thought about him shirtless and sweaty, so she closed herself in her apartment. She couldn't possibly have a serious conversation with those images in her mind.

*M*aggie slept in the following morning. She had another day shift at the bar, but Ryan and Colin had called a staff meeting. Looking at the clock, she realized she was going to be late. Part of the reason she'd overslept was because Shane had taken over her dreams. Again.

As she rushed past his apartment door, she felt like a seventh grader crushing on a guy. In some ways, it was exciting because she couldn't remember the last time her mind and body acted together like this. At the same time, she wished it were someone other than her friend.

She ran through the rear door of the bar and crept to the back of the meeting. Ryan and Colin were discussing Saint Paddy's Day, which was in just a couple of weeks. They were saying that everyone was expected to work. As if she didn't know this. The entire family worked on that day. No matter what their regular jobs were, they all became O'Leary's Pub employees for the day.

Except her. She hadn't since the rape. And no one had expected her to. She halfway listened to the meeting.

Someone asked about green beer and she could sense Ryan tense. He'd always hated the idea of green beer.

Colin stood up and said, "We haven't decided yet. We'll have all promotions set by Monday and we'll let you know."

Everyone moved slowly as the meeting concluded. Most employees chatted with each other, but Ryan and Colin stood and headed toward the back, probably to the office. Ryan's gaze met hers.

"You were late."

"By a couple of minutes. Are you going to give Shane grief for not being here at all?"

At the mention of Shane's name, Ryan's eyes darted away. "He'll be fine."

"Plus, I know it's been a long time, but I know the Saint Paddy's Day routine. I'm sure you haven't changed it."

"We don't need you to work."

"You just got done telling an entire room of people that it's all hands on deck and if they don't show, they'll be out of a job. I'm not looking for special treatment."

Colin stood beside Ryan with his arms crossed, but he said nothing.

Ryan rubbed a hand over his face. "You remember how crazy that day is. It's wall-to-wall people."

"Which means lots of tips. I'll be here."

Ryan shook his head and turned to walk away. Maggie followed.

"I also think we should sell green beer."

Ryan stopped but didn't turn back.

Colin, on the other hand, practically did a jig. "Yes!"

Ryan turned his head to Colin. "What are you getting excited for? She's been working here for a couple of weeks. She has no idea what's good for the bar."

Maggie stomped around until she was in front of both of them. "First of all, this is the *family's* bar, so the family should have input. Second, no, I don't run a bar, but I know people. People who aren't Irish think it's cool to go to a pub and drink green beer after they see the Chicago River dyed green and watch the parade."

"It's stupid. And the beer is crap."

"But they pay for the crap. And because it's a holiday and it's a novelty, you can charge a premium for it." She crossed her arms.

"Dad never sold green beer."

He didn't wait for her retort, not that she had one. He walked around her and went into his office, closing the door behind him loudly enough to let everyone know to leave him alone.

She looked up at Colin. "What was that about?"

"He doesn't like change." He ruffled his hand against her hair. "See you later. I'm going to the bowling alley."

She smoothed hand over her head. "Later."

As she set up for lunch, her irritation with her brother grew. He never wanted to listen to her. It was like she would never know anything because she was the youngest. It was ridiculous. By now Ryan should know better. She was trying to have a life and be part of the family.

She worked her shift with a smile, and in the back of her mind she planned how to create a portfolio of photos. It occupied her brain to keep thoughts of men at bay. She didn't need to think about Ryan or Shane.

As she cleaned up and closed out her remaining tickets, Shane walked through the door and sat at the bar. He looked better than he had the other day, but still tired. She sat on the stool next to him.

"You missed a meeting this morning."

"Meeting?"

"Ryan called a staff meeting. You missed it. He'll probably yell at you." She bumped his shoulder. "You didn't miss much, though. Everyone has to work Saint Patrick's Day. No drinking on the job. Blah blah."

The set of Shane's shoulders stiffened.

"I was just joking. He's not mad. He probably won't remember. He was too busy ignoring me."

Mary put a beer in front of Shane, and he took a long drink.

"Why was Ryan ignoring you?"

"Because I said I would work, and I also said selling green beer on Saint Paddy's Day is a good idea."

Shane's lip curled. "It tastes like shit."

Maggie rolled her eyes again. "But people pay for it. It's special, limited-time-only stuff. Makes them feel Irish."

Shane tilted his head in agreement. He was quieter than normal. "You shouldn't work that day. It'll be crazy in here."

"I can handle it." She laid a hand on his arm. "Are you okay?"

"Yeah. Tired. And hungry."

"What do you want? I'll run to the kitchen and get it." She hopped off her stool.

"I'll wait until Mary's free. You can go back to your tables."

"My tables are clear. Kelly's on her way in. I'm going back to get myself dinner anyway."

"Then I'll have fish and chips." He offered her a weak smile.

She went back into the kitchen to place the order. She wished she could read Shane as well as he read her. She knew something was off, but she couldn't guess what. He always seemed to know with her.

When their food was ready, she brought the plates to the bar and sat beside him. His beer was half gone and he seemed to have relaxed. "So what do you think about this thing with Ryan?"

"What thing?"

"His ignoring me and my input. He never takes me seri-ously. He still wants to treat me like the baby." She bit into a French fry.

"So stop acting like one."

"What?"

"You're sitting here getting all huffy because your brother wouldn't listen to you. How exactly did that conversation go? Knowing you, you yelled at him, maybe stomped your feet a bit."

"I did not." But even as the words left her mouth, she knew that was exactly what she'd done.

"You do it all the time, Maggie. I think you enjoy being treated like the baby of the family. You take advantage of it." He bit into fish, cursed quietly because it was hot, and took another swig of beer.

"What do you mean, I take advantage of it? It's not my fault I was born last." Anger began to build with each sentence coming out of Shane's mouth, but she wanted to hear it all.

"Maggie, I love you. We all love you. But you're used to getting your own way. You say you want to be treated like an adult, but you don't act like one."

"Yes, I do."

"You're working in your family's bar, living in one of their apartments. Knowing you, you probably got your brother to help pay for your furniture and called it an advance on your pay."

Shane did know her too well. But she had every intention of paying Ryan back. Shane took another drink of beer and focused on his meal.

"I lived on my own for more than a year, thousands of miles away."

He looked at her from the corner of his eye and spoke

while chewing his fish. "Who paid your cell phone bill while you were gone? Did you pay your cousins rent while you lived there?"

"I bought groceries and I cooked and helped out around the house. I tried to give them money, but my family's not like that. And as far as the cell phone goes, Ryan insisted on getting me a new one with an international plan so *he* would worry less."

Shane shrugged. "I'm not saying it's all on you, but you enjoy some of it."

"Of course I do. I'd be stupid not to. It doesn't mean I'm not an adult."

"So act like one."

Her temper flared and she wanted to yell at Shane, which was exactly what he was expecting. Well, she could hold her temper. As proof, she grabbed her plate and took it into the kitchen. She dumped her food into a to-go box and returned to the bar to let Mary know she was done for the night.

"Aw, come on, Maggie. Are you really going to run off like this?"

"I'm not running anywhere. I'm going upstairs to my apartment. I'm avoiding an argument with you because I'm angry right now. The immature Maggie would scream at you and call you an asshole. I'm choosing to walk away and calm down in order to think about things. See you later."

He chuckled as she left, and it took every ounce of strength to stop herself from turning back. She knew her anger came from a place of irritation because part of what Shane had accused her of was true. She knew how to play her siblings to get what she wanted. It was one of the perks of being the youngest.

Upstairs, she sank onto her couch. Her food no longer held any appeal. She wanted to stay mad, mostly at Shane, but she couldn't. She'd come back home to build a real life.

Doing that meant growing up and moving on. Wasn't that what she'd told Moira earlier?

She pulled out her laptop and began to work on her portfolio. She didn't know if she could be a photographer, but she wanted to give it a shot. She paused as she clicked on an article about developing a portfolio.

Would using Moira's connections to land a job fall under taking advantage as the baby of the family? She understood the idea of going it alone, but the O'Learys always said that if you have a big family, use it. It wasn't something only she was guilty of. Plus, how else would she get her foot in the door to decide if this was the right career for her?

She pushed doubt aside and focused on accomplishing something.

~

MAGGIE SPENT THE NEXT TWO DAYS WORKING ON HER portfolio and talking with Moira about job prospects and possibly going back to school. She worked her shifts at the bar, made good tips, and didn't have any more episodes. All in all, life was good.

Except for the whole no boyfriend, no dating, no sex thing. And to top it off, she kept seeing Shane in her dreams. She decided it was time to do something about it. She grabbed a six-pack of beer and knocked on Shane's door. Getting things out in the open would be best. Even if he thought she was crazy for thinking they should sleep together once as an experiment, at least then she could put the fantasies to rest.

The radio blared on the other side of the door, and Maggie thought that maybe he hadn't heard her knock. She raised her hand again and the door swung open as her fist came down. She looked like a cat batting a toy. Shane stood in the doorway, shirtless—like that was going to help rid her of crazy dreams. He walked to the radio and turned it down.

"Hey. I brought you some beer."

"Do you mean you swiped some beer from downstairs?" he asked with one eyebrow up.

She wrinkled her nose at him. "No, smart-ass. Want to see the receipt?" She really hoped he didn't ask for one since it didn't exist even though she'd paid for it. She hadn't swiped the beer, but it had come from the bar's stock.

He opened the door wider. "Is it cold?"

"Who the hell would show up with warm beer? That would be like saying, here, have a brownie, and throwing a box at you." She walked past him and took in the sight of the apartment. It was completely bare.

He closed the door behind her and took the beer from her hand. Setting it in the fridge, he took one bottle and drank. "Does this mean we're good?"

"We're always good."

"You seemed a little snippy after dinner the other day and you haven't said two words to me since."

He had her there. She was still mad when they worked a night shift together, but then she hadn't seen him. "I was, but I did some thinking and realized you were right."

"Whoa." He held up a hand and pulled his phone from his pocket. His thumb scrolled through the screen. "I gotta have an app for that."

"For what?"

"I need to record you saying that. Not only will I replay it every time we argue, but I'll play it for my sisters when they tell me I don't know anything."

Maggie rolled her eyes. "Shut up."

She walked through the living room and decided maybe this wasn't a good idea. He had nowhere to sit. "Are you done working?"

"For now."

"Want to come over and watch TV?"

"Do I get to pick?"

"As long as it's not sports."

"Cool. Let me take a shower and I'll be right over."

She nodded and went back to her apartment. Suddenly, her stomach began to flip. Why was this making her nervous? Then she realized she didn't know what the outcome would be. She didn't know what Shane would say, which went against the way she liked things.

If he agreed, how would they proceed? Would they have sex now? Tonight? No, she hadn't even shaved her legs and she was wearing her old college sweats. This was just conversation. She would feel him out—not feel him up.

Grabbing a Coke from the fridge, she checked her cabinets for snacks. What do you serve a guy you're going to ask to sleep with you? Chips? Cookies?

Maggie took a deep breath. She was overthinking. This was Shane, and she'd always been able to talk to him about anything. She settled on the couch and turned on the TV. About fifteen minutes later, there was a thump against her door.

She got up and looked through the peephole. Shane. She unlocked the door.

"You knew I was coming over. Why'd you lock it?"

"I always lock it." It was one of the many things she always did now. She locked her apartment door. She locked the bathroom door even when she was home alone. She locked her bedroom door at night.

"Probably a good idea. I just thought you would've left it open for me." He walked into the kitchen and put two bottles of beer in her refrigerator. "Shoot. I didn't know you still had some."

"I don't drink it. And you're the only person I've had over, so there's beer." She sat back on the couch and waited for him to join her. When he did, she took a moment to drink in the sight of him.

He was all clean, no sign of sawdust or drywall mud on him. The crisp scent of soap tickled her nose. He wore an old T-shirt that had seen better days. The collar had been cut and the hem at the bottom was frayed. Like her, he wore loose sweatpants.

"Before we pick out a show to watch, I want to talk to you about something."

He took a drink of his beer and watched her. "Is this the real reason you got me a six-pack?"

"No." She looked at a spot over his shoulder and tried to get the words right so he could understand. "You know I've been trying to date. And the part I was telling you about, how I'm still not all myself?" She blew out a breath, puffing her cheeks out. "I'm afraid of wasting my time. What if I find another great guy and I still can't have sex? It's not fair to either of us."

"What are you getting at, Mags?"

"I need to know if I'm broken."

"You're not."

She held up a hand, and when she felt it wobble, she tucked it between her knees. "I might be. I just want to know."

He set his beer on the table and leaned closer.

She licked her lips, closed her eyes, and jumped in. "You're the one person I've always been able to count on, other than my family. I feel safe with you."

"I'm glad." His hand landed on her thigh.

She opened her eyes and looked into his. "Would you be willing to have sex with me?"

His entire body froze. "What?"

CHAPTER 10

Shane forced air into his lungs as he listened.

"Dr. Janzen pointed out that in order for me to feel safe enough to have sex, I need to trust the guy and he needs to know my history. I'm already there with you."

Shane heard the words, kind of, if he focused over the sound of his heart thundering in his ears. Maggie wanted to sleep with him?

"I'm not looking to pressure you into any kind of commitment. It would be like an experiment. I trust you, and I know you would never hurt me. If I can have sex with you, I'll know I can find a guy and give it time to get there, you know?"

Christ, she wanted to just fuck. She didn't want to change the parameters of their relationship. She wanted to use his body. How fucked up was that?

"Maggie, I don't know. We've never…"

"I know that's not how we work. And I totally get it if you think it's too weird. But I had to ask."

She was sitting close enough that he could smell the soft, powdery scent of her perfume. Her skin was warm where his hand lay on her thigh. He pulled back and rubbed a hand on his head.

"It's weird, right?"

"Not weird, exactly. Did Dr. Janzen think this was a good idea?"

"I didn't ask her. I don't run every decision past my therapist. She gave me the guidelines. You fit the guidelines. If I can't sleep with you, then no other guy has a shot. I know not to bother. At least not now. I can focus on other things." She gave a careless shrug like it didn't matter.

But she forgot he knew her. She was a crappy actress when it came to him. She was pinning some great hope on him sleeping with her. She wanted him to have sex with her in order to pave the way for some other guy. The thought alone bugged the shit out of him.

He could just blurt it out. Tell her how he felt. Let her know he wanted more from her. But instead, he said, "I need to think about it."

"Fair enough," she said all perky. She tossed the remote onto his lap. "Pick something good to watch. I'll make popcorn."

She stood and left the room. How could he think about a TV show when all his brain could do was focus on sleeping with Maggie?

He flipped mindlessly through the channels, avoiding anything that looked remotely romantic or sexy. He needed action and adventure. From the kitchen, he heard Maggie humming softly while she moved around. She couldn't sing for shit, but her hum was calming.

He'd forgotten how she used to do that all the time. She'd mumble or hum. It had been a surefire way to determine her mood. Humming meant happy, mumbling meant pissed off. He wished he knew what had made her happy. Was it the act of asking him, or was she so sure he'd agree, she thought his taking time was simply a formality?

Her request weighed heavily on him. He didn't want to be the factor deciding whether she'd remain happy.

Part of his brain, the primal part, wanted to jump on her offer immediately. He wanted the chance to know her body, show her how good they could be together, but he didn't want to risk what they had. Not if that wasn't what she wanted.

Ten minutes later, Maggie returned with a bowl of popcorn and another bottle of beer for him. She plopped beside him as if the conversation hadn't happened, and they watched TV like they always had. Except he had no idea what was happening on the screen. He was too busy weighing the possibilities of Maggie's proposition.

By the time the movie ended, he still had no answers, but a headache threatened to ruin the rest of his night. Credits rolled across the screen. Maggie was curled comfortably on his side. He shifted to move away.

"You gotta go?"

"I should. Early day with my dad."

"I'm sorry I was bitchy with you over dinner the other night. I don't like it when people call me on shit. I do"—she waved her hands in swirly motions as if she didn't know the word she was looking for—"finagle what I want from my siblings. I've been doing it my whole life. But you're right. If I want them to treat me like an adult, I need to stop."

He chuckled. "Those are some pretty words, but I know you better than that."

"I'm serious. I'm not saying I'll never ask my family for anything because *hello*, that's what family's for. However, I plan to go into Ryan's office tomorrow and explain to him why I think he should take my opinion into consideration. I won't stomp my foot or scream. I'll be professional, just like any other employee."

Shane stood and stretched. "Let me know how that goes." He knew her brothers. They would never listen to her. It had been part of the reason why she'd been wild as a teenager. She wanted attention and she yelled instead of talked, partied instead of interacted, got arrested instead of playing by the rules.

He'd never understand where she was coming from, because he was the oldest and none of his sisters had sought attention like that. His sisters tended to be a little more straightforward.

"You'll see. I'll win him over with my charming wit and personality."

He grabbed his empty bottles to throw out. "It's your charm that usually lands you in the most trouble."

"You have so little faith in me."

"Never."

She followed him to the door. "You'll really think about what I said, right?"

"Of course."

Narrowing her eyes, she said, "You sound like my brothers when they say they'll think about something."

He reached out and grabbed her hand. "I promise to give it real consideration. I'm not blowing it off. It's just a lot to process all at once."

She nodded.

"See you tomorrow?"

"Probably." She held the door open for him to leave. "Have a good day at work."

He trudged back to his apartment, more tired than he thought. As he crawled into bed he thought about whether he could have sex with Maggie and then walk away, just be her friend again. With other girls, he could, but he'd never had a close relationship with another girl like he had with Maggie. He'd dated some girls, slept with others.

But Maggie had always come first.

He sat up in bed with the harsh realization. Of course he'd always known Maggie was important to him, but these thoughts made him wonder if maybe his relationship with Maggie was holding him back.

"Fuck. Now I'm thinking like a shrink," he said to his shadow.

MAGGIE GULPED DOWN A HORRIBLE CUP OF COFFEE IN HER apartment before heading down to talk to Ryan. She'd have to ask Mary how she made such good coffee. Walking through the back door of the bar had begun to feel second nature, much like it had five years ago. Maggie paused and let the enormity of that sink in.

She was getting her life back.

With an extra spring in her step, she strode to the office door and knocked. When Ryan called out, she walked in.

"Hey, Maggie, what are you doing here?"

"I want to talk to you."

"Shoot."

She sat in front of him and placed her folder on his desk. He continued to stare at his computer screen. "I want you to listen."

She paused, waiting for him to look at her. When he realized she was silent, he turned away from the computer. He leaned back in his chair and folded his hands across his stomach.

"I'd like to talk about Saint Patrick's Day."

"Go ahead."

"I know you despise the idea of selling green beer, but it's a Chicago tradition."

"Not an O'Leary's tradition."

"True. But you don't have to do everything the way Dad did. Sometimes things need to change."

"Maggie, I'm trying to be patient, but you don't know anything about running the bar."

"That's because you've kept me and everyone else out of the loop. You like to handle it all. I'm surprised you let Colin do anything." She took a breath. This was going in the wrong direction. She pushed her folder toward him. "I did some research."

"On what?"

"Bars in the area. The number of customers expected to be out drinking on Saint Paddy's Day."

He flipped the folder open and looked at her chart. "How did you get this information? Why would any bar give you their numbers?"

She winked. "You underestimate my ability to charm anyone. I told the owners I was a reporter doing a story on Saint Paddy's Day in Chicago and how it impacts local businesses. I might've said I was writing for a trade magazine."

Ryan shook his head slowly. "You and Moira would make a deadly combination." He sighed and closed the folder. "Give me the summary."

"Most bars see an uptick in business after the parade. Those bars that appear to be more *Irish* do better because people believe they're getting some authentic experience. Among those making the most money are those selling green beer. It's a gimmick, but it's one customers like."

"It's still bullshit."

"I agree. But even Dad could understand playing the game to increase the bank account. Do I need to point out the O'Leary sign hanging on that cow's neck by the bar? Dad let people think we were related to the woman whose cow started the Great Chicago Fire. Our family wasn't even in the states then. It's all part of the game."

Ryan stared at her. For the first time, she felt like he really saw her.

"I'll think about it. "

"All we need to do is add food coloring to each glass. They can order whatever beer they want, except for the dark ones, obviously. Food coloring won't change the taste. I don't know why everyone keeps telling me how it tastes like crap."

"Because most bars use the cheapest stuff they can and color it by the keg."

"Then we can be extra special. We just need to get food coloring." She stood and left the office. Ryan ultimately might still decide not to go with green beer, but at least he wouldn't be likely to dismiss her again.

She went back up to her apartment to continue working on her portfolio. Chiming in on bar business was fine, but she didn't plan on working there forever. Moira had a point; she needed a plan and it was time to make some choices.

Shane walked into his parents' house and in an instant knew all three of his sisters were there. An argument was escalating in the living room and the pitch would soon hit an octave only animals could hear.

"Quiet!" his dad bellowed.

His dad's yell was like a tremor through the house. Without being in the room, Shane was able to picture all three girls frozen in place, mouths hanging open. There had been a time it would've worked on him as well. Now he didn't have much to fight about when it came to his sisters. Being the oldest, and only boy, had its perks.

"What the hell is going on here?" Dad asked as Shane rounded the corner.

All three girls started in again, pointing fingers at each other, all saying little more than gibberish. Beyond the bellow, Dad never knew how to handle this. Where was their mom?

Shane whistled loudly to get them to quiet. Then he pointed at Alyson. "You first."

"I'm only here for dinner and to do a load of laundry and discovered that bossy pants over here"—she pointed at Cara —"decided my box of books and some clothes I had in storage were free game."

Before the last words were out of Alyson's mouth, Cara jumped in, pointing a finger at Alyson. "I am not being bossy. I was just trying to settle things between you and Riley. Riley opened your box."

"I didn't know it was yours."

"My name in big black letters on the side didn't clue you in?"

"Besides, Riley has a point. If you're not living here, your stuff shouldn't be here."

"Who are you to talk? You don't live here and you still have a bedroom." Alyson's arms waved as she yelled at Cara.

"I do too live here. Just not when I'm at school."

"You live on campus nine months out of the year."

"But it's not a permanent residence. I have to move out over the summer; therefore, I cannot bring all of my possessions with me. You, however, have your own apartment."

Riley, being the little sneak that she was, started drifting farther away from the cluster like no one would notice. Shane knew her well enough to know she probably asked Cara to get involved as a distraction to what the real problem was.

Cara and Alyson continued to argue the finer points of

their living arrangements, so Shane pointed at Riley. "What did you do?"

She shrugged. "I found a sweater I liked and she busted me wearing it."

Clothes. Why was it always clothes that girls fought over? He shook his head and slapped a hand on his dad's shoulder. "This is all yours."

Shane went back to the kitchen just as his mom walked through the back door carrying grocery bags. "Shane, honey, you're here."

His mother always sounded so happy to see him. "Need help with groceries?"

"That would be fabulous. The trunk's open."

She began emptying bags while he went back to the car. He slipped his arms through the plastic bags and hauled them all in one trip. He kicked the door closed behind him and set the bags on the table. His mom was already stirring something in a pan on the stove.

"You're staying for dinner, right?"

"Yeah."

"Excellent. I love having you all here at the same time."

He thought about the O'Learys and their Sunday dinners. Maggie said they ate as an entire family at least once a month. He thought for a minute. The last time all of the Callahans sat down for dinner together had probably been Christmas. Holidays and birthdays were expected family time.

"Maybe we should do this more often."

"What, honey?"

"Dinner together. All of us."

She waved a hand. "As much as I would love that, trying to align everyone's schedules would be insane, don't you think?"

"Just a thought."

"I miss when you all lived here. Even if we didn't eat together, I saw all of you every day. I miss that."

"Everything okay, Mom?"

"Yes. Go tell your sisters to stop fighting."

"Already tried. They don't listen to me now any more than they did when we were kids."

"What is it this time?"

"Clothes. Again."

She tsked but ignored the noise from the other room. Shane briefly wondered what had happened to their dad, but then he figured Dad had given up and went to change out of his work clothes.

His mom handed him a spoon. "Stir this."

He turned to the stove and began stirring the sauce. He sniffed, trying to determine what it was. From the living room, he heard his mother's sharp voice telling both Riley and Cara that Alyson had every right to leave whatever she needed in *her* house. Moments later, he heard stomping on the stairs, which meant Riley was pissed.

As much as he'd loved moving away from home to be on his own, he missed the noise of his family. There was a certain predictability to it.

His mom came back into the kitchen. "What is this?" he asked.

"Something new. As long as you're all here, I decided to experiment. You know how your father is. He hates to try different things."

She lifted the lid on a nearby pot, saw the water boiling, and added pasta.

"Anything else I can help with?"

"No. Have a seat and tell me what's been happening in your life. You hardly come home anymore."

He sat at the table and had no idea where to start.

"Are you dating anyone new?"

"Nope."

She reached across the counter and started slicing a loaf of bread. "Would you tell me if you were?"

"Nope." He walked over and snatched a piece of bread before giving her a kiss on the cheek. "You'd just pressure me for grandkids. I'm not ready for that."

"By the time I was your age, I already had two."

"And you'd also already found the love of your life." He sat back down at the table.

"Are you sure you haven't?"

When he didn't answer, she asked, "How is Maggie doing?"

Shane bit back a sigh. He'd come home to put Maggie out of his head, and here was his mom putting Maggie's name beside the idea of true love. "She's okay."

"Glad to hear. Why don't you call and invite her to dinner? I haven't seen her in ages."

Even with her back to him, Shane knew the scheming look in his mother's eyes. She'd tried to push him and Maggie together often enough as teens for him to know what she was after. He couldn't expose Maggie to that. Not in light of their current situation. "She's probably busy."

"You could call and see."

"I don't think it's a good idea."

"Are the two of you fighting?" She turned and took a seat across from him.

"No. We both have a lot going on right now."

Alyson and Riley came into the kitchen then. As they started a new conversation with their mom, Shane couldn't help but think how much he wanted this for himself. Home and a family. More than he had. Most important, he wanted it with Maggie.

CHAPTER 11

It had been days since Maggie talked with Shane. An awful, unsettled feeling consumed her. This wasn't them. She always talked to Shane. Even when she was thousands of miles away, they talked more than they had this week where they shared a freaking hallway. She began to think that asking him to have sex had been a huge mistake.

He hadn't been dodging her exactly. They worked together twice and they joked and talked during their shift, but something was off. And they didn't see each other the rest of the week. Not for a meal or TV or anything. She felt like she was losing her best friend.

Tonight, she'd make it right. She'd let him off the hook. For real. Of course she told him when she asked that it didn't matter and if he said no, it would be no big deal, but she also knew Shane. He would do almost anything for her. So he was probably trying to figure out how to turn her down without hurting her.

She'd have to reassure him and then find some other guy to have sex with. She shoved that last thought away. Right now, she needed to focus on Shane. She'd heard him come in earlier and bang around his apartment for a while. Since it sounded like he was working, she decided to wait to go over.

And maybe she was a little bit chicken.

She shook her body loose and then straightened her spine. She could do this. As she swung open her door to go to Shane's apartment, she nearly jumped out of her skin. Shane was standing in the doorway.

"Crap. Don't do that to me."

"Do what? I was coming over to see you."

"So was I." She stepped back to let him in.

He stared at her as she closed and locked the door. When she turned back, she couldn't help but smile. He had that effect on her. When he returned a grin of his own, she knew on some instinctual level they would be okay.

"What were you coming over for?" she asked, still procrastinating.

"Come here." He grabbed her hand and tugged her toward the couch. He pushed her to sit down, but he walked in small circles. "About what you asked the other day, about having sex—"

God, she needed to put him out of his misery. Shane didn't get uncomfortable around her. Yet, here he was, stumbling over words. "You can forget it. It's okay."

"What?"

She sighed and stared at her hands in her lap. "I figured you were trying to tell me I'm crazy without hurting my feelings. You're obviously uncomfortable."

"No." He knelt in front of her and held her hands again. "A little, but it's not what you think."

Her eyes met his, and whatever turmoil had been curling in her settled.

"I've been giving it serious thought. I know you try to play it off like it's no big deal, but it is. Deep down, you know it is." He shifted and sat beside her. "I'll do it. We'll do it—or at least try."

Her heart swelled. If anyone could make her feel normal, it would be Shane.

"But we do it my way."

The simple words shot through her and offered a bit of excitement. Would Shane be the man from her dream? The bossy, controlling guy?

"Maggie?"

"Yeah?"

"Do you agree?"

"To what exactly?" She hoped she didn't sound like a complete idiot. Getting turned on when a man expected to have a conversation probably wasn't a good idea.

"Total honesty. That's the only way I'll do this."

"Of course."

He grabbed her chin and held her face. "I mean it, Mags. If something makes you uncomfortable or, worse, repulsed, you have to say something. You need to be open and honest and be able to actually talk to me."

"I talk to you all the time, and I'm always honest with you."

"But you have to tell me everything. Every. Personal. Detail." His voice dropped. "Things we've never discussed. What you like. What turns you on." He swallowed hard.

She watched his throat work and almost jumped in his lap and told him. This. Him. Right now. This turned her on. She nodded because she didn't trust her voice to work.

"You're sure? Because doing this my way means I'm not just pulling my dick out and looking for a hole. It'll be a process."

Now it was her turn to gulp. Although she hadn't imagined a quickie with Shane, she hadn't exactly pictured lots of time.

"You're in?"

"If you are," she whispered.

His thumb caressed her jaw. "Yeah."

Her heart rate picked up. She licked her lips and then took a long, slow inhale.

"Then let's get the worst of it out of the way."

"Like what?"

"Tell me your triggers. When you were with what's-his-name in Ireland, what made you stop? What makes you freak out? Besides the smell of whiskey."

She bit her bottom lip. She'd thought telling Shane what turned her on would be hard? No, coming clean about all of her triggers might make him realize she was crazy. She puffed out her cheeks with a heavy breath.

"My way, Maggie, or we stop completely."

"I know." She slid her hands away from his and rubbed them on her thighs. "I'm trying to think. It's not like I carry a handy list." Start with the obvious. "I don't like being closed in. Like trapped." She closed her eyes. "I sound crazy."

He patted her thigh. "Not crazy."

She stared into Shane's eyes. The intensity she found there grounded her. Even though the next part might've been a little embarrassing, she continued. "It needs to be slow." She swallowed. "Todd was fast, rushed."

Shane snorted.

"Not like that." Well, maybe a little like that. "Sometimes hard and fast was okay, before. But it's one thing I remember from that night. It happened so fast."

She felt Shane tense next to her, but she forged ahead. "Not rough." Her voice cracked on that last one.

"Fuck." The word was barely a whisper, and Shane stood and paced.

This was a bad idea. She pulled her knees up and wrapped her arms around them. This was why she didn't have this conversation with Ian. Shane already knew what happened, and his reaction still caused a storm of emotion in her. Resting her forehead on her knees, she closed her eyes. She didn't know what else to say.

SHANE WANTED TO HIT SOMETHING. NO, HE WANTED TO destroy it. Preferably Todd McCann. If Shane had had these details years ago, he probably would've killed the guy instead of just beating him senseless. He watched Maggie curl into herself while he paced.

As much as it might kill him, he sat back down and put a gentle hand on her back. He forced the words out despite not wanting to go on. "What else?"

Maggie turned her head to the side without lifting it. "I don't know. As much as I'd like to think I know what will freak me out, I don't. Just like the whiskey breath. I didn't see that coming."

"Fair enough. But when you feel something coming, you have to promise not to brush it aside."

"Okay."

"Now tell me what you do want."

A bright pink spot appeared on the cheek he could see. "I thought that was self-explanatory. I know you've had sex before."

"And so have you. But never together." His heart crashed in his chest. If he couldn't get through talking about it, he'd never be able to do it.

"So now you want to know what turns me on?"

His mouth became a desert. He bit his tongue to make things work. "It would help."

She laughed. Maybe it was more of a snicker. "Shane Callahan, looking for a cheat sheet. I never would've expected that. I thought Casanovas like you just *knew* what to do. Maybe explored your way through being a master of women's bodies."

As she joked, she opened up, kicking her legs out and leaning back on the couch.

"I can explore with the best of them. I was trying to take it easy on you."

"I think I can handle you."

This was where they were comfortable—flirting and kidding—but he knew it wouldn't be enough to get them through. "Seriously. I don't want to make you uncomfortable. I assume kissing is okay?"

She shot him a look. "Of course."

"Anywhere?"

Her eyes popped for a second, then she nodded.

"Favorite position?"

"I don't have one."

He raised an eyebrow.

"I'm not the same person I was years ago. I need to discover who I am now. I don't want to give you a checklist to follow. It would be too confining." Her face became stern and she pretended to hold a paper and pen. "Kissed neck. Check. Fondled breasts. Check." She dropped her hands. "I want it to be natural."

Natural. Like it was natural to have sex with his best friend. But she had a point. He'd never needed a list with any other woman he'd been with, and he hadn't received any complaints. He was so worried about damaging Maggie after she'd come so far.

"Okay. You win. Natural it is."

She jumped up from the couch. "Should I get naked here, or are we going to the bedroom?"

His lungs forgot how to operate. Every fantasy he'd ever entertained about being with Maggie flashed through his head.

Suddenly, she was doubled over laughing. "If you could see your face." She slapped her thigh. "Crap, Shane, even *I* know it wouldn't be natural for us to strip down this second."

"Funny," he finally managed.

"I so got you. Master jokester. That's me." She began to dance around.

He slapped her ass playfully. "Better watch it."

She straightened. "Hmmm...I don't know if that should be on the no or go list."

"What?"

She bent over slightly and stuck her ass out. "Spank me again and we'll see if it's okay or not."

He tightened his jaw as he rolled his eyes. This girl would be the death of him.

"Lighten up, Shane. If we can't make jokes, it's going to get really awkward."

Again, she had a point. She seemed totally at ease and more like herself than he'd seen her in a long time. "You're having a lot of fun with this."

"I'm finally gonna get lucky. Why wouldn't I have fun?"

Yeah, but no pressure. "It might not go as you plan."

Her whole face frowned. "True, but I have faith in you."

He couldn't stop the smile. He turned to leave.

"You don't have to go. I promise no more jokes about getting naked."

He spun to face her, and she pulled up short where she had been following. "I have to wake up early for work in the morning, so I'm going to bed. When I'm ready to get you naked, trust me, there will be no jokes, and I plan to make sure I have plenty of time without worrying about work."

Her jaw dropped, the glimmer of mischief in her eyes gone. This was no game to him, and she needed to understand that. He unlocked her door and let himself out. As he reached for his door, Janet's opened.

"Hey, Shane. Hold on a minute." She disappeared back in her apartment.

He leaned against the wall and waited. When she came back, she carried a plate. "This is for you. A welcome-to-the-neighborhood treat. Peanut butter cookies."

He forced a smile. He hated peanut butter but took the plate to avoid being rude. "Uh, thanks."

She stepped closer, again only wearing a tank and a pair of shorts. "Do you want to go downstairs and get a drink or something?"

"Thanks for the offer, but I'm headed to bed. I have to get up early for work in the morning."

"Work? I thought you worked downstairs."

"I do. A little, but I'm a carpenter by trade, remember?" He knew they had a version of this conversation already.

"Do you think you can do me a little favor?"

"What?"

"I tried turning off one of the radiators, but the knob thingy is stuck."

"I'll see what I can do. Lead the way." He followed her inside her apartment, which was crazy hot. She obviously hadn't taken his advice and opened a window. The room was dimly lit and what he could see was overstuffed, comfy furniture and an obscene amount of pillows. Total chick place.

"It's over here. In the bedroom." She shot him a look over her shoulder. "I talked to the new girl...Maggie. She suggested I turn off the bedroom one to control the temperature."

Thank you, Maggie, for putting me in a position to be in this girl's bedroom. As if he needed to be thinking about some other woman when Maggie already filled his head. Shane sidled through the room beside the bed to the radiator. He set the plate of cookies on the dresser.

"Can I get you something to drink while you work?"

"Uh, no. This shouldn't take long." He bent over and it sounded like she sighed. He turned the knob without effort. She could've at least attempted to make it look difficult. "All set," he said as he straightened.

"Thank you so much. I'd like to buy you dinner. It's the least I can do to thank you for your help."

"It's no problem. Just being neighborly." He moved to leave the cramped room.

She stepped in front of him. "I'd like to see you again. For dinner, or drinks, or…" Her eyebrows lifted suggestively.

"Thanks. That's a great offer, but I'm kind of seeing someone."

"Shoot. Figures. I guess I'll see you down at the bar some night. I'll buy you a drink when you get off."

"Thanks." He moved around her to leave.

"Wait," she called. "Your cookies." She handed him the plate he'd left behind.

"Thanks again." He went across the hall to his apartment. He looked at the cookies and debated tossing them directly in the trash, but he couldn't bring himself to do it. Maybe he'd take them to work. Those guys would eat anything.

He crawled into bed and replayed his entire conversation with Maggie. He'd never in his life treated sex like a negotiation, but that's what tonight had felt like. An important conversation because Maggie would push things, and that scared him.

Maybe he should've taken Janet up on her offer for drinks or something. She could've taken the edge off everything he was feeling. But it wouldn't have been right coming from Maggie's apartment where they'd discussed having sex. He reminded himself he wasn't dating Maggie. For her, he was a means to an end.

Unless he could convince her otherwise.

Lying in bed, he used his phone to log on to the rape survivor forums he hadn't visited in years. If anyone could offer advice, it would be those who had walked in his and Maggie's shoes. Plenty of women survived rape and led full lives with sex. Before posting, he scrolled through existing questions and comments, hoping for the answers he needed.

CHAPTER 12

*M*aggie had no shot of sleeping. Her emotions had wrung her out. She'd put on a good show for Shane with flirty jokes, but he knew her well enough to know how deep parts of that conversation hit her. But his parting words continued to echo in her head.

Every time she closed her eyes, the mystery man from her dream popped up. This time, not only did he have Shane's face but also his voice. There was no escaping it. After a long time of tossing and turning, she gave up. She went to her living room, turned on some quiet jazz, and went to work on her photography portfolio.

She'd decided to create a couple of different portfolios that could be used depending on the type of job she was going after. Some photos overlapped the two, but she kept her more artistic ones separate from the portraits. If someone wanted her to shoot their wedding, they would want to see portraits, not a random picture of a strawberry.

As she scrolled through more of her photos—she had no idea she had taken so many—they brought back memories of her trips. Time spent with her cousins, new friends she'd made on a bus tour, gimmicky places she thought were cute. As she continued to organize them into folders, she meticulously backed them up to the cloud.

Of course, she had no idea what the cloud was exactly, but after her cousin lost everything on her computer when her brother spilled a cup of tea on it, Maggie learned to back up everything. She would be crushed if she lost all these pictures.

She found an image of a sunset. Simple, nothing fancy. She hadn't Photoshopped any part of it, but it was spectacular. It had been her first full night away from home in London. She'd taken the picture with her phone and sent it to Shane.

He'd responded with a text: It's beautiful, like you. I miss you already.

She couldn't remember if she'd answered his text, but she remembered how lonely and lost she'd felt in that moment. The sunset was beautiful, but she hadn't felt beautiful in a long time. The ache in her chest had blossomed because of her loneliness, but she also realized that even back at home, surrounded by people who loved her, she'd been lonely.

She'd wanted to believe that trying new things away from Chicago would fix that. It hadn't. She spent more than a year away from her family and friends, and she still wasn't sure if she'd accomplished anything.

But now, she was finally moving forward. Moira was helping her figure out a career. And one way or another, with Shane's help, she would come up with a plan for her love life.

It should've made her feel better, but the mass of confusion still threatened to swallow her.

She shoved it down and focused on the task at hand. She needed a job that would offer her more than tips and compliments from drunks.

~

SHANE GOT OFF WORK, CHECKED THE SCHEDULE AT THE BAR TO see when Maggie had to work, then went upstairs to make a plan. The idea of sleeping with a woman had never stressed him out so much. At least not since he'd lost his virginity. He couldn't just knock on her door with a bottle of wine and expect to get laid.

Technically, he wouldn't even need the wine, but he still wanted to make it perfect. He debated taking her out to dinner versus ordering in. He looked around his apartment, walls unpainted, floors covered in dust. Not exactly a romantic atmosphere, especially since he still had no furniture other than a bed.

As he turned his attention to choosing a restaurant, a frantic knock sounded at his door.

"Shane, it's me."

He opened the door to a slightly freaked out Maggie. "What's up?"

"Please tell me you have your computer hooked up here."

"I have it, but it might not be charged." He hadn't needed it since she came home. He went to his bedroom and pulled it from his dresser drawer along with the charger.

"What are these?" she called from the kitchen. "Peanut butter cookies? You hate peanut butter."

He barely came through his bedroom door, and she snatched the computer from him. "Our neighbor across the hall, Janet, made them for me."

"Funny, she didn't make me cookies." Maggie snickered.

He ignored the comment because the last person he wanted to think about at the moment was Janet.

Setting the laptop on the counter, she said, "Thank you so much. Mine just crashed. I need to make sure all of my backups saved."

While she powered it up, Shane ran the cord to the outlet.

"Please, please, please," she mumbled.

The page opened to his e-mail in-box, which was a little embarrassing since the only e-mails he had were either from her or spam. Thankfully, she was so focused on clicking away on the keys that she didn't take note.

A new page popped up, and the look on her face intensified. She tapped the track pad, opening more things. Some of her pictures appeared.

"How did you do that?" he asked.

"What?"

He pointed at the screen. "Get your pictures on my computer."

"I opened my files from the cloud. It looks like everything is there except for the last project I was working on. At least it's only about an hour or so lost." She exited out of everything and closed the laptop. "Thanks."

"You can use it if you need to."

"I can't take your computer. I'll figure something out."

"Take it. I'm not using it."

"If you don't use it, why do you have it?"

"Honestly?"

She nodded. "Of course."

"I bought it when you left so we could Skype."

Her eyebrows drew together. "You dropped hundreds of dollars on a computer so you could *talk* to me?"

"Yep."

She smacked his arm. "Are you nuts? We could've just talked on the phone. Or texted."

He lifted a shoulder. "Not the same. I like to see your face." He rolled up the power cord, stacked it on the laptop, and handed it to her.

She stared with her mouth hanging open.

"When you left, I didn't have a smartphone, so I bought

this. For the limited stuff I do online, I use my phone now. If I need a computer, I go home and use my parents'." He shoved the computer at her.

She finally took it. "I'll use it for now. Until I buy a new one." Stepping closer, she rose and kissed his cheek. "Thank you."

"How about dinner?"

"Sure. What do you want?"

"Let's order in." He pointed at the door. "In your apartment since you have furniture and all." He followed her out the door and to her apartment, trying to find a balance between hanging out with his friend and making this a date. He figured the sooner they made the attempt to have sex, the better off they'd be and things would be settled between them.

If it played out the way he wanted, they would be a couple. They made sense together.

She unlocked her door and he went in. After locking up behind them, she set the computer on her counter and grabbed the phone. "Where do you want to order from?"

"Whatever you want."

"Want me to call downstairs?"

"It's fine. I'm not picky."

While she called in their order, he settled on the couch and found a romantic comedy for them to watch. Like most guys, he found them sappy and a little silly, but they always made Maggie laugh, and she sounded like she had a rough day.

She plopped next to him. "Food will be ready in about fifteen minutes."

"So what did you do today?"

"I worked on my portfolios some more."

"What portfolios?"

She bit the corner of her mouth. "Promise not to laugh or tease me."

"Never."

She swatted his leg. "I talked with Moira about a career. Although she could help me get some writing gigs, I think I want to take a stab at being a photographer." She paused, and when she opened her mouth again, words flooded out. "I don't have any formal training, but I enjoy it. A lot. So I'm creating a portfolio to see if I can get a job. Maybe at least an internship somewhere so I can learn. I might take a class or two. I don't know. But this is the first thing I've been excited about in I don't know how long. It's just so much, it's a little overwhelming. And…"

He smiled, thinking she'd stopped because she finally needed a breath, but then she didn't continue. "And what?"

"What if I flake on this, too?"

"What if you do? It's one more thing you know isn't right for you."

"But I feel like such a loser. All my friends have settled into careers. Even if they don't love their jobs, they have real careers. I've stagnated. It's like I never moved past being twenty-one."

"None of that matters. There's nothing wrong with wanting to do a job you love, that you're passionate about. Do you think I want to work for my dad forever? We do what we have to do until things fall into place." He took her hand and held it. "You're doing fine, Maggie. Stop doubting yourself."

"Easy for you to say." She leaned back into the couch and he scooted closer.

He continued to hold her hand on her lap and she rested her head on his shoulder as the opening credits rolled on the movie.

"You're too nice to me. You hate these movies."

"Next time, I'll pick and there'll be blood and gore." He watched the first scene of the movie and then stood. "I'll go down and grab the food."

They ate their dinner and watched the movie, with Maggie curled up close to him. They laughed and joked about the characters, and when closing credits came across the screen, he leaned over.

Maggie didn't say anything, but her eyes widened. This was it, the moment he'd wanted for a long time. His fingers wrapped around the back of her neck and her pulse throbbed against his palm. Only her rapid heartbeat let him know she wanted this, because the rest of her was stock-still. Her eyes told him she wasn't afraid.

"Relax," he whispered against her lips.

And she did. She closed her eyes and her lips softened. He brushed against them, her breath quickening. He tried to follow his own advice, but there was no turning back now. This was no friendly kiss meant to comfort. This one conveyed his lust. He'd wanted this for so long, he almost couldn't control himself.

She was everything he imagined. Soft and warm, gentle and open.

His heart crashed against his ribs and his blood thundered through his system, urging for more. But this was Maggie, his friend and soon-to-be-lover. She deserved better, so he kept the kiss soft and slow, as slow as he could bear.

THIS WAS IT. SHANE CALLAHAN WAS KISSING HER AND OH MY freaking God was it good. A giggle bubbled up but was squashed by how good the kiss was. She tried to focus to remember what it was like to be kissed like this, but she couldn't concentrate. His tongue ran along her lip and eased into her mouth. Shane was gentle and slow, but he controlled every move, every shift, every second of pleasure.

She grabbed his shirt and held on, needing to pull him closer, to feel his body touching hers. She felt the tingle of excitement and wanted to hold that feeling. Shane deepened the kiss, his tongue swirling around hers. While his hands stayed near her face, touching her jaw, her neck, her hair, hers roamed down his chest.

Time ceased to exist. The only air was the breath they shared.

By the time he pulled away, she was pliant and beyond relaxed, yet her nerves still thrummed with excitement. Maggie opened her eyes.

Shane's thumb stroked her cheek. "You okay?"

"More than." She leaned forward, wanting more.

Shane took the hint and shifted closer, angling his head and capturing her mouth again. Part of her wanted to feel silly. This was Shane, her buddy. She never knew he could do this. She imagined an awkward fumbling between them. Not this kind of simple magic.

Her heart raced and then her blood weighed heavy in her veins as lust took over. His fingers threaded into her hair and pushed it aside. His lips left hers and he kissed a trail across her jaw to her ear and down her neck. His hands finally— finally!—began to move over her body. He skimmed down her sides, barely brushing the sides of her boobs.

She gripped his head as he continued to lick and suck at her neck, his hands spanning her rib cage before they moved up and pressed against her breasts. Her nipples were hard points, sticking out, begging for attention. Using his whole hand, Shane kneaded one breast and then the other while he returned to her mouth just in time to swallow a moan.

Her entire body hummed and thrummed. If she had

never vibrated with need before, she knew exactly what it meant at this moment. She tugged at his T-shirt and pulled it up to reveal his tight muscles and line of hair leading below his waistband. Desire pooled low in her belly and she welcomed it.

She trusted Shane to make this happen. She shoved at his pants, barely getting past his hipbones before he shot away from her.

"Whoa. Slow down, there."

"What? No!" She reached for him, but he pulled his hips away.

He grabbed her hands and held them. "Maggie." His voice was strangled. Inhaling deeply, he leaned his forehead against hers. "Slow, Mags. I'm not stripping you on the couch."

"We can go to my bed. It's not that far." The bulge in his pants made her mouth water.

He sighed, then kissed her cheek. "Good night, Maggie."

He stood.

Wait. What? He was walking away? She jumped off the couch to follow him. "Shane Callahan." He looked over his shoulder. "Get your butt back over here and finish what you started."

"I will. Just not tonight."

"Why the hell not? What's the point of getting me all hot and bothered and then walking away?"

He walked back to where she stood and held her hand. "You trust me, right?"

She nodded.

"We do this my way." He kissed her again, this time on the mouth. Their lips interlocked and she still wanted more, but he pulled away. Again.

Damn him.

He walked to the door, and as he opened it, facing the hallway, he said, "One more thing. Don't finish without me."

The man was crazy. He got her horny and now he expected her not to get off at all?

When she didn't respond, he turned to face her. "I mean it. You agreed to do this my way."

"You're insane." She crossed the room and poked his chest. His very hard, muscled chest. "You don't get to control my body. I can do whatever the hell I want."

He smirked. "But what you want is me. Whatever you can do alone won't be enough. Trust me. It'll be worth the wait."

He didn't wait for a response. He walked across the hall to his apartment, leaving her gaping at him. He waved with a smile as he opened his door.

She slammed hers shut. Unfortunately, it barely took the edge off her frustration.

CHAPTER 13

*S*hane stood at the doorway to his apartment and withheld the laugh at Maggie slamming her door. As he was about to cross the threshold, Janet stepped out into the hall.

"So, you and Maggie, huh?"

He smiled. "Yeah." At least as far as he was concerned.

"Yet..." She pointed back and forth between the two apartments.

"It's complicated," he said with a lift of his shoulder.

"Nothing should be that complicated." She then pointed at his hard cock and smirked.

He swallowed a groan and waved. "See you around."

He couldn't explain to a stranger what was going on between him and Maggie. He knew it sounded crazy.

Christ, his dick hurt. He hadn't walked around like this since he'd first discovered girls. Why he'd thought a make-out session on Maggie's couch was a good idea now escaped him. He eased his sweats off and cringed as the elastic bumped his hard-on on the way down.

Fuck this. He told Maggie not to take care of herself, but

he'd never made any such promise. Once the shower had hot water flowing, he stepped under the spray. Wrapping his fingers around his cock, he stroked. The only thought in his head was Maggie: the way she smelled, the way lust filled her eyes, the way she moaned when he'd barely touched her.

His whole seduction plan might kill him before he could get her off. His hand pumped his heated flesh. It didn't take long until he spurted across the tiles. He finished washing up and got out. He'd managed to take the edge off, but thinking about Maggie sitting in her apartment all horny wasn't doing him any favors.

Both he and Maggie were working at the bar tomorrow night, so there would be no date and no sex. He wasn't about to rush anything after working until closing. The weekend would have to do.

His biggest concern, besides the obvious—the effect having sex would have on their relationship—was that he worried about making sure she was comfortable with the idea of him touching her long before they had sex. She hadn't been able to go all the way with the last guy because he didn't know her and therefore couldn't understand her. Shane wouldn't make the same mistake.

He lay in bed and listened to the sounds of the building. The music from downstairs still filtered through the floor. He could hear Maggie banging around in her apartment. She always did need a physical outlet when she was frustrated. He rolled over with a smile on his face.

Maggie hadn't seen Shane before or after he worked his construction job, so she went down to the bar without waiting to see if he was on his way. She'd spent a good portion of the previous night scrubbing her bathroom.

Although the space now sparkled, it had done nothing to ease the ache of lust.

She put on her apron and got ready for her shift. Once again, she was relieving Kelly, so she got the lowdown on remaining customers and cleaned off unoccupied tables. As soon as Shane entered the room, she knew it, felt his gaze land on her back. It was like he homed in on her every time he walked into a room.

She ignored the shiver that skated down her back. If he could play it cool, so could she. It wasn't like he was the first guy she'd ever made out with and hadn't gone further. As she walked back to the bar to place an order for one of her tables, she smiled at Shane. "Hi."

"How are you?"

"Good. And you?"

His gaze wandered the length of her body and every one of her nerves perked up at the attention.

"Very good," he answered.

She wanted to ask if he'd spent the night thinking about what they could've done, but the bartender set a martini and a glass of scotch in front of her. After placing the drinks on her tray, she smiled and said, "See ya."

As she walked away, she emphasized the sway of her hips. She was out of practice, but she knew what drew a guy's eye. If Shane wanted to watch her, she'd give him something to see. Luckily for her, the table waiting on drinks faced Shane's location. She set the drinks in front of the customers and bent over more than necessary to set napkins down and collect menus.

If the customers thought anything was odd, they said nothing, but when she straightened, she saw Shane shift in his spot.

For the entire night, they played a game of cat and mouse. For every time she bent or stretched in his direction, he'd pass by and glide a hand along her hip. An innocent gesture one might make as he passed, but with Shane, there was an added flex of his fingers. When she licked her lips suggestively, he groaned. *Point Maggie.*

His heated glare let her know he'd get even. Whether planned or not, Jenna asked him to carry a case of beer from the back. Shane lifted it over his head to bypass customers. Biceps bulged and his shirt rode up from his pants, revealing that delicious strip of stomach. A hint of muscle, a patch of hair. Just enough to make her want to explore.

It was her turn to groan.

Then when he got behind the bar with the case, he bent over to fill the cooler. Damn. The man earned extra points for that.

The night sped buy with their nonverbal game in play. It was a blur of orders and tips interspersed with strategizing. When she'd asked Shane to sleep with her, she'd agreed to doing it his way, but she'd thought they'd actually do it.

By the time they were done with their shift, Maggie was horny all over again. She couldn't remember the last time she'd flirted with one guy for so long. And it was Shane. She'd witnessed his flirtation skills before. Hard to have such a good-looking guy friend and not see that in action. But it felt so different when it was directed at her.

He followed her to the back door and asked, "Good night?"

"Pretty good. Weekends definitely have better tips, but it'll do. Kind of quiet."

He held the door open and she braced herself against the cool air. "Quiet is good. No fights."

He shook his head at her as she crossed her arms outside.

"Quiet also means less money in tips."

"Why not wear a jacket if you're cold?"

"Because it would be one more thing for me to remember.

Plus, it's a quick trip upstairs." She jogged up the stairs as if to prove her point. Inside the hall, she paused at his door and waited for him to catch up. She tilted her head toward her apartment. "Want to come over for a while?"

"Sorry. Not tonight. I have work early in the morning. Are you free tomorrow?"

"I work the lunch shift."

He grabbed the waistband of her jeans and pulled her closer. His lips brushed hers and then he licked at them. When she opened her mouth in invitation, he pressed her against his body. She became slightly light-headed and giddy. Was it the lack of oxygen or was something else about him intoxicating?

He pulled away and whispered, "Dinner tomorrow?"

"How about late-night snack now?" *Please say yes.*

"Sorry. Work, remember?"

"Stupid job."

He chuckled. "Tomorrow will be here soon enough."

"So tomorrow you'll finish what you started yesterday?"

"Maybe. But there's lots of fun to be had between starting and finishing."

Her fingers curled into his T-shirt. "But I *really* want to finish."

He peeled her hand away and kissed her palm. "Soon."

"Jeez. I've never heard of a guy playing hard to get." She stepped away and swept a hand over her body. "Lots of guys would jump at the chance."

"I'm aware." He winked. "I'm also not most guys. Good night, Mags."

She huffed out a sigh. "'Night."

She entered her apartment resigned to play Shane's way.

CHAPTER 14

Maggie filled her day working at the bar, which was busy enough to keep thoughts of Shane and their date at bay. Was it really a date? Sure, the end goal was having sex, but dating was for people who needed to get to know each other. She and Shane knew almost everything about each other.

Was there a point to dating?

She thought about Shane's playfulness the night before at work. Yeah, dating was definitely worth it. The flirting kept her hot and bothered since their make-out session days ago. She debated getting all dressed up for the date, but decided against it. Shane didn't need her to pretend to try to impress him, just like she didn't expect him to put on an act.

They were always just Shane and Maggie.

After her shift, she changed into a pair of comfy sweats and worked on her portfolio while she waited for Shane to call. Once she knew where they were going and what they were doing, she could decide on an appropriate outfit. What she hadn't counted on was for him to show up at her door unannounced.

She opened the door to see him freshly showered and smelling wonderful. He glanced down at her clothes.

Self-consciously running a hand over her hair, as if it could change her appearance, she said, "I figured you'd call and tell me where we're going. I can change fast."

She opened the door and he walked in. "No, you look comfortable. I was just thinking a movie and maybe a pizza from Sorrentino's."

Her stomach grumbled at the talk of pizza. "I'm still a little underdressed even for Sorrentino's."

"If you'd prefer to stay in, we can. It's up to you."

Maggie weighed her options. Staying in with Shane would be like any other night they hung out. It wouldn't feel like a date. That would probably be for the best. "You sure you don't mind?"

"Why would I mind?"

"You're the one who seems to have some master plan I haven't been clued into. I wouldn't want to mess with it."

He grabbed her hand and pulled her into the living room. "Where we eat dinner has no impact on the plan."

So, he did have a plan. Somehow, Maggie found this funny. Shane never struck her as the kind of guy to come up with a schedule for seduction. She wondered what other surprises he might present.

His thumb stroked along her hand. "How was work?"

"Busy, which was good, but I'm glad I have tomorrow off."

"You have Sorrentino's number so we can order?"

She pulled her phone out. "I should probably have them on speed dial."

For the next few hours, they chatted about work and watched a movie while they ate pizza. Shane sat close on the couch, keeping his arm around her shoulder and his thigh brushing hers. The hand on her shoulder toyed with her hair.

She wasn't sure how much was part of his plan, but it sure felt good.

This was a major portion of what she missed most about being with a guy. This kind of casual closeness.

When the movie ended, anticipation curled through Maggie. She didn't have to wait long, however, for Shane to make a move. He leaned close and kissed her cheek. "Tired?"

"Not particularly," she whispered.

"Good." His breath caressed her cheek as he spoke. His lips trailed along her jaw across to her ear and down her neck. As his tongue circled the skin over her thundering pulse, her eyes fluttered closed.

He moved gently and slowly. Her breath came quick as he stroked down the side of her body and then back up to cup her boob. *Woo-hoo! Second base.* She arched into his hand, inviting him to continue, hoping he'd round third any time now. This was where he'd stopped last time. She almost whimpered at the thought.

Her nipples ached, and the slight pinch he offered just increased her need for more. She pushed him back against the couch and climbed onto his lap, straddling him. Stretching her thighs wide, she pressed down on him, his hard-on stiff against her. He groaned in her mouth as she returned to kissing him. She rocked against him, hot and wet.

Suddenly she was flipped on her back and Shane hovered over her. Her heart practically beat out of her chest. This. This was what she craved.

But his eyes widened. He stood and held his hand out for her. She took it without question. They were going to do this. She was finally going to have sex. It might not be her exact fantasy, but it would be sex.

He led her to her bedroom. He walked through the dark room like he knew exactly where everything was and flicked on the bedside lamp. While he fiddled with that, she eased the door closed and twisted the lock.

She turned and waited as he came to her. His arm circled her waist and his hand landed on her hip, drawing her closer to his body. He kissed her again, but kept it short. Brushing her hair off her shoulder, he kissed her neck, sending a shiver through her. When he swirled his tongue below her ear, her knees threatened to buckle.

"I think we need to get naked." The words left her lips a little more raspy with need than she would've liked, but they were out there. She took a half step back and pulled her shirt over her head, hoping he'd take over.

Instead, he followed suit. So she continued. She dropped her pants and stood in front of him in her bra and panties, almost wishing she'd planned something sexy. Shane slid his jeans to the floor, and judging by the bulge in his boxers, her underwear had no negative impact.

He pulled her close again. This time, the hand that wrapped around her edged up her back, and with a flick of his fingers, he released her bra. With his lips on her neck, he reached between them and pulled the bra away.

And then it happened. The unthinkable at this point. Her stomach turned and her heart stammered, and not in a good way.

Crap. Not now. Not again. This is right.

She had no idea what she'd done, but Shane froze. His lips pulled away from her skin. Skin that now felt clammy. His hand that had been making a slow journey down the side of her body halted. She didn't want him to stop. She reached out to touch his bare chest, but her fingers trembled.

Shane stepped away. "What is it?"

Her throat clogged and tears burned her eyes. She couldn't talk, so she shook her head. Trying to swallow, she willed her throat to work. Her diaphragm wobbled inside as if caught in a storm of hiccups.

Shane took another step back. She couldn't look at him. She stared at her feet, flexing and relaxing her fingers repeatedly, waiting for the wave to pass. In her peripheral vision, she caught movement. Shane stood close again, holding her shirt. He slipped it over her head and she forced her arms through.

"It's okay, Maggie. We'll figure this out."

She pressed her cheek to his chest and let the first tear fall. One hand fisted against his skin. Anger crashed through her, causing more tears.

"Do you want me to leave?"

She shook her head as best she could without lifting it.

"Come on." He pulled her toward the bed and he sat down. He welcomed her to sit not quite on his lap, but more between his legs.

She curled against him but beat back the remaining tears. She'd cried enough. Shane's hand stroked down her back, comforting her like he always had.

"Are you ready to talk?"

She hiccupped and snorted. "What's there to talk about? I'm never going to have sex again."

"I said we'll figure this out and I meant it."

"Don't you get it? I'm horny. I want to have sex."

"Then what happened?" His voice was barely above a whisper.

"I don't know. It's not a thought. It's not even a feeling." She inhaled slowly. "It's like a sudden wave crashes over me and I'm stuck."

He shifted beneath her and the realization hit her that she was lying on what would've been his hard-on if she hadn't ruined it.

"Are you sure you really want this?"

"Uh, yeah."

His hand stopped its rhythm on her back and rested in place. "I'm asking if maybe your head has it built up as something you want, but your body doesn't agree."

Her panties were still wet. Her clit throbbed. She swallowed.

"You promised to be honest here, Maggie."

"I know what it feels like to be turned on. Just because I haven't had sex with a guy doesn't mean I haven't...you know."

A quiet laugh rumbled in his chest. "Jilled off? Flicked the bean?"

She slapped his chest. "See, that's why we don't have conversations like this. You sound like a thirteen-year-old."

He kissed the top of her head. "So you can self-service with success."

"Sounds much better." She took a breath. "After last time, I wanted to self-service, but since you commanded me not to, I didn't. But overall, I guess I have some modicum of success."

"That needs explanation. Either you come or you don't. There's no *modicum*."

She sighed and searched for the words. "I'm able to orgasm, but it's not the lights-behind-the-eyes, thighs-trembling, heart-racing, hips jumping-off-the-bed kind of orgasm."

She couldn't believe she was having this conversation with Shane. It wasn't even all that difficult.

"Show me."

She jumped away, and for the first time since he'd stripped away her bra, she looked at him. "What?" She was surprised the word came out, because her throat was so damn tight.

"Shhh." He took her shoulders, turned her, and pulled her

back toward him. "You said you're horny. Show me how you take care of yourself."

"I can't do that. Not with you watching." Could she? She'd never done that with anyone else in the room.

His hands skated down her arms. Nothing overtly sexual in the touch, but his work-roughened palms reignited an itch deep below her skin. The whisper at her ear caused a heat wave to roll through her. "My way, Maggie. You agreed to my way."

He reversed the path of his hands, stopping when they reached the short sleeve of her shirt. "Close your eyes and pretend I'm not here."

As if that was even in the realm of possibilities while the heat from his chest seared into her back. But she closed her eyes and brought back the feelings she'd had when he first kissed her. If nothing else, she wanted to reclaim that. Now it was her turn to let her hands roam. Instead of moving over her own soft skin, she touched his thighs, the crisp hair tickling her palms.

His body was warm at her back. His strong muscles surrounded her, making her feel safe.

With her eyes closed, she didn't bother with a fantasy. She conjured memories of Shane kissing her in the living room, pulling her close in the bedroom, his tongue on her neck. She wanted it there again.

She pulled her hair away from her right shoulder, baring her neck. As she pushed her hand beneath the waistband of her panties, she whispered, "Kiss me," and tilted her head to give him access.

Her middle finger skimmed along her slit. Shane's lips touched the side of her neck, followed by his tongue, wet and warm. She bent her knees and pushed inside herself. Using her own wetness, she circled her clit.

She pretended Shane wasn't watching her every move,

that his body wasn't against her back, that his hard dick wasn't pressing into her spine. The rhythm she created was familiar, almost comforting.

Shane didn't touch her, other than his mouth on her neck and shoulder. But as her fingers went up her shirt and pinched her nipple, she imagined it being his hand. He was no longer Shane, her best friend. He was now Shane, hot guy who made her horny. She picked up the pace and wiggled her hips in jerky movements. Tension coiled low and built.

She was almost there and she wanted that orgasm more than anything at the moment, but it felt like it was just out of reach. Her breath caught and she forged on, determined to come. To get some relief.

Her brain and body begged for more. She whimpered. She wanted him to take over, make this happen for her. Resentment bubbled up because he didn't fix it. She hated that she'd fucked up and scared him off. She was ready to give up.

~

Maggie lay cradled between his thighs, half naked and masturbating. He'd always known she was sexy, but this took amazing to a whole new level.

Shane's dick had never hurt more in his life than it did right now. He was so hard he couldn't imagine why Maggie's back wasn't in pain. She continued to press into him, her hand making jerky movements in her panties, her breaths coming in quick little pants. She was close, but she was rushing it, like she had to hurry to get to the finish line.

The smell of her arousal filled the air, and he tensed to stop himself from flipping her over and satisfying his own needs.

He needed to touch her, remind her he was there, part of

this. He reached out with a trembling hand, fear rushing though him as a reminder that he might push too hard and screw this up. Hurting her would tear him apart.

He brushed his fingers on her arm to gauge her reaction. She kept going, so he stretched his arm along hers until his hand lay on top of hers in her underwear. His intrusion hadn't interrupted her rhythm. With his hand over hers, he slowed the pace. She whimpered and thrust her hips.

Kissing her neck again, he took note that her eyes remained closed. He briefly wondered where her mind was, but ultimately, he didn't care. She was here with him, trusting him with this. His teeth grazed her skin and he nibbled on her earlobe. A slight shudder ran through her.

His free arm circled her waist, keeping her close. Holding her in place, he reached beneath her shirt, following along her other hand, and found her nipple. Her fingers had stopped moving and she allowed him to take over, rolling her hard nipple between his thumb and finger.

Her head lolled against his shoulder in surrender. Her hips rolled up to meet his attention, and she pulled her hand out from under his, leaving him to continue alone. She raised her left arm up behind her and held his head while her right hand braced against his thigh.

She licked her lips, and it was the hottest fucking sight he'd ever laid eyes on. She was slick and hot. Blood pounded through him. With two fingers inside her, he pressed against her clit with his thumb and her back arched up. Moaning, she scrambled both away from him and toward him.

He released her nipple and clamped down on her waist. As soon as he did it, he feared she'd freeze up.

"Please."

He loosened his grip a fraction. "Do you need me to stop?"

Her hips continued their frantic movement, and she swung her head side to side.

"I need to hear it, Maggie."

"No, God, no. Don't stop. Please." The hand on his thigh slapped down hard and her fingers pressed into his flesh, nails biting.

He gave her enough room to buck and writhe, but he held her and moved with her from behind, his cock so hard it was invincible.

Her inner muscles squeezed his fingers and he knew she was there. Maggie, however, seemed to be caught off guard. Her entire body stiffened, and she clutched at his neck behind her. He continued to stroke her and kiss her as she broke. Her body shuddered and her thighs trembled between his.

Although he had no idea what was going on behind her closed eyelids, he got no small amount of male satisfaction of feeling the tremors run through her.

As her body calmed, he removed his fingers but kept his hand in place, covering her. Her arms relaxed and slid away from him. He figured that was his cue to get out of her pants. After a minute more of heavy breathing, she covered her face. "Oh, my God," she mumbled from behind her fingers.

Crap. Now he was going to have to deal with her being embarrassed? "Maggie." He tugged her hands away.

She turned and her face was filled with happiness. "That was so fucking amazing. Thank you." She leaned forward and kissed him hard. "Thank you. Thank you."

He smiled as she moved back. "I take it it was good for you."

She swatted at him again. "You know it was. It was like somewhere deep in my memory, I knew it could be that good, but I haven't, you know, not on my own." Her face scrunched up then. "But you..." She waved in the general area of his still hard dick.

"I'm fine." Which was a total lie.

She reached out. "We can try—"

He pressed his back against the pillows behind him and held up a hand. "Don't touch me." Her face looked more confused. "Trust me. I'll just embarrass myself at this point. Plus, you don't owe me anything. This was about you."

"I know, but...It wasn't sex. It was a truly phenomenal orgasm, but it wasn't sex."

He moved his legs around her and swung them over the side of the bed. "I am completely aware of what that was. I told you we'd do this my way and it would take time."

Time that might kill him given how much his cock hurt. He walked stiffly to the bathroom. As much as he wanted to jerk off right now in front of her, to show her the effect she had on him, he couldn't do that. He didn't want her to feel any pressure.

"Are you okay?"

"Fine." He flipped on the bathroom light and locked the door. He eased his boxers down to free his dick. His hand was still a little wet from Maggie, and he stroked himself. With his eyes closed, he imagined her in his arms, begging for release. Her soft skin gliding along his inner thighs. He braced a hand on the wall and rubbed himself until he spurted, which didn't take long at all.

He groaned with the release and then had to sit on the toilet to regain his composure, his ability to think and move, every fucking thing. After cleaning up, he went back to her bedroom, dick still noticeably hard in his boxers.

He sat on the edge of the bed and asked the question that worried him. "Do you want me to go home?"

"No." She scooted over and moved the blanket out of the way to make room for him.

When he lay down, she stared at his dick.

"Ignore it. It'll go away."

"You sure?" she asked, like she didn't believe him.

"I'm sure." He reached over and clicked off the light. His eyes adjusted to the dark. The moon filtered through the sheer curtains and her eyes glinted. He reached over and smoothed her hair along her ear. "Are you okay?"

"Amazing." She turned her face and kissed his palm. "Do you have to work tomorrow?"

"It's Saturday. I don't usually work weekends. That's why I planned to come over here tonight to seduce you."

She giggled. "Ordering in pizza for dinner and watching a chick flick was your seduction? I always thought you had better game than that."

"It did the job, didn't it?"

"Yeah, it sure did." She tucked her hands between her cheek and the pillow and stared at him.

It wasn't really awkward, but it wasn't them either. This was new territory, a place where he'd longed to be. Now he wasn't quite sure how to handle it. "Go to sleep," he whispered.

She smiled and turned over, giving him the chance to curl up behind her and spoon her body. He hesitated, wanting nothing more than to hold her all night but unsure of how it would affect their relationship.

A few minutes later, she asked, "Did you close the door?"

"Yeah."

She heaved a sigh and got out of bed. She put her palm flat against the door, which he had, in fact, closed. After climbing back into bed and curling up next to him, she said, "Sorry. It bothers me if it swings around at night."

"Okay."

When they'd slept together in the past, they'd both been, fully clothed and stayed on their own side of the bed. Now, he reached out and curled an arm around her waist, tucking her against the curve of his body. She settled in like it was the most natural fit.

She interlocked her fingers with his over her stomach. "I'm glad you came over tonight."

"So am I." He kissed the back of her head and focused on sleep. Her scent lingered in the air, making promises of what was to come. There was no way he could ever look at her again as just a friend.

$\mathcal{M}$aggie woke in the morning, her body still completely relaxed. Before opening her eyes, she reveled in the comfort of orgasm afterglow. Then she reached behind her and realized Shane was gone. He'd said he didn't have to work today, but he was gone.

The idea that what they'd done would make things weird between them hit her again. She didn't want things to get weird, and last night Shane seemed totally fine. Except for the raging hard-on. She swung her legs over the side of the bed and, in doing so, noticed her bedroom door cracked open.

A surge of panic struck, but she took a slow breath to push it down. Of course the door was open. How else would Shane have gotten out? He probably just forgot to close it again.

As she stood, determined to squash the anxiety, she heard a noise, movement somewhere else in the apartment, and the panic returned twofold.

Her heart leaped into her throat and she scrambled to find her pepper spray on the dresser. She turned the nozzle on and edged toward the door, to quietly close it. Silently, she placed her fingertips on the edge of the wood, and met with force.

"Good morning, beautiful. I have coffee," Shane said as he muscled through the doorway.

Maggie jumped back from the door with a scream. All she heard was the thundering in her ears. Her hands shook and she dropped her canister.

"Whoa. Are you okay? I didn't mean to scare you. I thought you were still asleep."

Maggie dragged air in, but her lungs wouldn't fill. She grabbed at her shirt on her chest. In her peripheral vision, she saw Shane set coffee on the dresser. She took a step back and waved him off.

Sitting on the edge of the bed, she bent over and focused on breathing. She closed her eyes and counted. She was safe. She knew where she was and who she was with. She was safe.

She eased her eyes open to see Shane squatting in front of her, his hands out like he wanted to touch her but was afraid. "I'm okay." Her voice was still a little weak, but she was able to talk. "I just got scared. I thought you'd left and then I heard noise."

"Oh, Christ, Maggie. I'm so sorry. I didn't think." He reached tentatively and set his hand on her forearm. His eyes were filled with pain.

"You don't need to apologize. You had no idea." *Because I didn't tell you.* She remembered a similar incident with Ian in Ireland. Not only hadn't he apologized, but he'd had a good laugh over it. Not that she could really blame him either.

Her nerves began to settle and her breathing returned to normal. She was so tired of this shit. What she wouldn't give to be normal again. She stood, almost knocking Shane on his ass in the process. He stumbled to catch his footing, so she held out a hand to help him up.

He grabbed hold, but then they both lost their balance and she tumbled on top of him. A fit of laughter ensued, and she braced a palm on his bare chest to push herself up. "You did that on purpose."

"I did not. Why would I want you to fall on me?"

"To make me laugh."

He smirked but didn't deny her accusation. This time when she held her hand out he allowed her to pull him up off the floor. He handed her one of the cups from the dresser. "You want to tell me about it?"

She raised her eyebrows and thought about dodging it, but she knew it wouldn't work with Shane. "I heard noise and panic hit me."

"Does that happen a lot?"

She took a mouthful of coffee and debated how to answer. "The panic? Not often. And I can usually control it. This was bad because it caught me off guard. I wasn't prepared to hear noise in my apartment."

"I'll keep that in mind. Finish your coffee. We need to get going."

The sudden change in topic startled her. "Going where?"

"I have a plan. Something fun." He drank from his cup.

"What if I already have plans today?"

"Do you?"

She rolled her eyes. "No, but what if I did?"

He stepped closer, his bare stomach brushed against her arm. His skin was warm. He leaned over and kissed her head. "Then I would have to beg you to break them to spend the day with me."

She didn't have a smart-ass remark for a response. In fact, she had no response at all. Something was different between them this morning, and she wasn't sure how she felt about it.

He gulped the remainder of his coffee and scooped up his pants from the night before.

"I'll go to my place to shower and change. I'll be back in a few." He turned to walk away, but looked over his shoulder. "Will you be ready?"

"Are you going to tell me where we're going?"

"Nope. But dress warm."

He walked out of her bedroom, set his cup on the kitchen counter, and paused to tug on his pants. She followed as he walked out of the apartment and locked up behind him. She leaned against the closed door and sipped her coffee.

She felt like she was trapped in her own personal cloud of fog. As much as she feared things being weird between her and Shane, he acted almost as though nothing had changed.

On one hand, he gave her what she wanted: normalcy with her best friend. On the other hand, he'd given her an amazing orgasm. Shouldn't he have had some reaction other than telling her to get ready?

It was all too much to process. How could he not be as rattled as she was?

AS FAR AS DATES WENT, ATTENDING A SAINT PATRICK'S DAY parade was far from the most romantic he'd ever planned. It was a small parade, not the official North Side or South Side parades that would take place next weekend. They wouldn't be able to get away for one of the big ones because of the bar, so this one would have to do.

When he went back to her apartment, he wasn't too surprised that although she wore a sweater, she still didn't have a warm coat. "Don't you have a winter coat?"

"Nope," she said as she pulled her door closed and locked up.

"Hold on." He ran back to his place to grab an extra jacket. "Here."

"I'm fine."

"You won't be."

They headed out the door with her carrying the extra jacket. "Now you're worrying me. Where are we going?"

"Saint Paddy's Day parade."

"That's next weekend."

"This is a small one in the western suburbs. It won't be quite the same, but it's been a long time since we did the parade thing. Senior year?"

She crossed her arms as she walked toward his car. "No, we went to both parades our first year in college. That was one hell of a drinking weekend."

He'd forgotten about that. They had the fantastic idea to do the South Side parade, get drunk at parties all night, and then go to the dyeing of the Chicago River in the morning and stay for the North Side parade. Most of it was a blur. They were nineteen. What had their parents been thinking?

Maggie smiled. "That was the last time I was allowed to go to the parade, because I got so sick. Ryan was pissed. I think he was madder than my parents were. Because of you, I was stuck working at the bar."

"Sure, blame me. Whose idea was that excursion?"

She gave him a little shove. "Don't remind me."

He unlocked his truck and she climbed in without help. On the way to the parade, he stopped at a drive thru to get hot chocolate for Maggie and another coffee for him, along with some doughnuts. He drove near the end of the route since they'd missed the beginning. He found a parking lot for the truck, and they walked to get to the parade.

Maggie had pulled on his jacket before getting out of the truck, and it swallowed her. The sleeves dangled past her hands and the shoulders sat somewhere around the middle of her bicep. But at least she'd be warm. They found a decent spot at the curb. The first few groups had already gone by, but a marching band could be heard down the block.

"Hold this." She handed him her cup and rolled the sleeves of his jacket enough to reveal her hands. "Better." She took the cup back and watched the parade.

A group of kids from a Catholic school walked by, tossing candy to the crowd. They were followed by a politician whom he'd never heard of, and his entourage was passing out shamrock stickers and flyers about the guy's policies. Maggie took both, stuck the shamrock on her cheek, and shoved the flyer in a pocket.

The high school marching band came in full force. They marched, they danced, they even had a baton twirler. Maggie yelled and clapped for each performance. A couple more groups passed and he leaned over to ask, "Having fun?"

"Yeah."

Then it was the group he'd been waiting to see, a troupe of Irish dancers. Maggie had taken dance when she was younger but stopped before she got to high school. He'd often teased her about it.

The girls with their springy hair and stiff limbs stopped right in front of them and executed an awesome dance.

Shane put an arm around Maggie's shoulder and pulled her close. "Were you ever that good?"

"I was better."

He laughed, which earned him an elbow to the gut.

"Take my empty cup and I'll prove it." She shoved the cup at him and stepped off the curb. Locking eyes with him, she bounced to find the beat and then jumped up and started to dance. Arms stiff at her side, she began with a few small skips. Then she launched into hops and high-kicking jumps. Although he knew nothing about the technique, he thought she looked amazing. She was fierce and cocky and he loved it.

The dancers moved on and Maggie took a little bow. They watched a little more of the parade, but his ass was numb from the cold and Maggie's cheeks had turned red, so they decided it was time to move on.

"That was fun. I wish my family could do something like this. I remember when we were little, my dad always took us to the parade. Well, technically, he made us walk in the parade, but it was always fun." A wave of sadness crossed her face. "I miss that."

"You miss him a lot, don't you?" As soon as he asked the question, he realized how stupid it sounded. He couldn't imagine not having his dad around all the time.

"Most of the time, I think I'm okay, but then I come to something like this and I realize how much I miss him."

"I didn't want this to be a sad thing."

She took his hand. Her fingers were frozen. "It wasn't. I had a lot of fun."

"I never knew you had those moves. I think you should do a regular show at the bar."

She laughed. "I actually wasn't sure I'd remember the steps. I guess it had been drilled into me so much as a kid, I'll never forget."

"You looked good, though."

"Yeah, sure. You're just trying to get in my pants again."

The joke halted him in his tracks. He licked his lips and the wind whipped at them painfully. "I'll get where I want to get, babe. I don't have to pretend to compliment you."

"Big talker."

He tugged her close. "I guess I'll have to prove myself again. Last night wasn't enough?"

She winked. "Last night was great, but as I pointed out, it didn't totally fulfill our agreement."

"And as I pointed out, we do this my way."

The banter and jokes kept him at ease. The gray space they were dancing in felt dangerous, but as long as they could keep it light, they'd be okay. He hoped Maggie knew that too. Although she must've since she was the one who kept playing.

He drove to a restaurant so they could eat. The doughnuts had barely taken the edge off his hunger.

After they'd ordered lunch, Maggie asked, "So what are you doing about the police department?"

"What do you mean?"

"I assume they haven't called. If they stop hiring, what's your plan?"

"I don't have one. Keep working with my dad, I guess." He unwrapped his silverware from the napkin and toyed with it.

"That's not much of a plan."

"You're one to talk. A couple of conversations with Moira and all of a sudden you're a master planner?"

"God, no. But I have a plan. It might not even be a good one, but I'm doing something. I'm being proactive. You're sitting on your ass and hoping it comes to you." She stretched her leg out under the booth and set her foot next to his leg.

"What do you expect me to do? March into the police station and demand they hire me?"

She rolled her eyes. She could offer classes in doing that in such a way to make anyone feel stupid.

"Have you talked to Moira and Jimmy like my mom suggested? Have you applied anywhere besides the CPD? There are suburban districts you could go to."

"Talking to Moira and, by extension, Jimmy seems weird. It's not like talking to you. You're my friend, Moira isn't, and I don't even know Jimmy. I haven't looked at other places, because they're small. I want a job that will make a difference."

"Call me stupid, but wanting to work in a place where forty people get shot in a weekend doesn't sound like fun."

"Imagine how much worse the city would be without cops."

"I didn't say we didn't need cops. Just…why do you need to be one here? It's dangerous. And because you'll be new, they'll stick you in a crap neighborhood."

The waitress arrived with their food, and Shane thought the conversation was over. Maggie, however, continued to talk as she squirted ketchup all over her fries.

"I would worry about you a lot if you were a cop."

He hadn't thought about that, at least not with Maggie. His mom hated the idea of him being a cop, but he hadn't thought Maggie would take issue with it. For her, he would consider a suburban job. But she wouldn't ask. "It would give you a taste of your own medicine. I always worry about you."

She dropped her fork and raised her hands. "I don't actively *look* for trouble, so you don't need to worry about me. I live a quiet life."

"So do I."

"By definition, cops look for trouble."

"Moira's okay with marrying a cop." Crap. He hadn't meant it to sound like that.

"She respects that it's his job, but that doesn't stop her from worrying. Plus, Jimmy's not out on the streets looking for gangbangers and drug dealers." She returned to her food and dug in.

Luckily, his words hadn't struck her as odd, but her argument gave him pause. He was determined to sleep with Maggie so she could feel better, whole, but in the back of his mind, he'd been thinking about them as a couple long term. If the department called, would it be a deal breaker?

He couldn't go there. Not now. The department hadn't called, and Maggie hadn't agreed to give them a shot. He couldn't think about possible problems in a nonexistent relationship. He needed to focus on one thing at a time. And right now, his attention was on getting Maggie naked and horny.

CHAPTER 16

Maggie ate until she was stuffed. Then she watched Shane finish off her food after he cleaned his own plate. The guy still had the appetite of a teenager. She wondered what other appetites had remained from adolescence. Judging by how hard his dick was last night, he could probably go awhile, regardless of what he'd said about embarrassing himself. Every time she looked at his hands, all she could think about was how they had been inside her and she came all over them. As a blush crept across her skin, she started to question everything Shane did.

Was their trip to the parade part of his seduction routine? What about lunch? She began to think they couldn't be just friends hanging out, not until they actually had sex. Then she'd put it to bed, so to speak.

Crap. Every thought she had seemed to have a sexual meaning.

"Ready?"

She almost answered, *Not yet*, but she was getting there thinking about last night. She nodded.

Shane stood and went to the register to pay. Over his shoulder he called, "Are you coming?"

Crap. She needed to stop this. He was talking to her like a regular person. "Uh, yeah." She pulled his jacket back on and inhaled slowly, smelling him surrounding her. It must've been a work jacket he'd given her, because she could smell a hint of sawdust. Which made her think of Shane working in his apartment without a shirt, and…

Christ. He better hurry up and finish doing things his way. She'd had her first real, non-self-induced orgasm last night, and she hadn't been able to think about much else since.

He held the restaurant door open for her. The wind was cold and the meager sun they'd seen during the parade now hid behind some ominous-looking clouds. "Is it supposed to rain? Or, God forbid, snow?"

"It's too warm for snow, but maybe some freezing rain." He opened the truck door for her. "I don't think you'll melt."

"Ha-ha." As he ran around the truck, she buckled in. "For your information, I like rainy days. They're perfect for curling up in bed with a hot cup of tea and a good book."

He started the engine with a smile. "Sweetheart, if that's the best you can come up with for a rainy day, you need some help."

"In my defense, I haven't had a boyfriend in a long time. My book boyfriends are great company. In fact, in a lot of ways, they're perfect."

"They're imaginary."

"But real in my head. They're smart and funny."

"That's the author of the book."

She sighed. "They never do annoying things like pee on the toilet seat."

"Hey, now," he said, raising a hand. "My mom raised me

right. I lift the seat and always put it down. Even in my own damn apartment where I live alone."

"Your sisters trained you well." She smiled. "Book boyfriends are also never needy, but they're there for me whenever I want them."

"But they can't bring you a cup of coffee in the morning either."

The reminder of Shane doing just that brought a rush of lust through her. "True."

"And since they're only paper and ink, they don't have hands and fingers and tongues to play with your body."

"But—"

His hand shot up again. "Don't even try to tell me that flying solo is just as good. I think I proved you wrong last night."

She couldn't stop the smile. Of course he was right on that count. But more than remembering how hot last night was, she was having a great time talking with him. Most guys would never put up with such a silly conversation. It was one of the many reasons she loved Shane. He always put up with her silliness.

A few blocks from the bar, it started to rain. Then it started to pour. It was a weird mix of rain and slush splatting against the windshield. He pulled up behind the bar and said, "Get out. I'll park and meet you upstairs."

She waved him off. "I won't melt. Park the truck. I can walk in."

"Get out of the truck."

"I'm fine." She had no idea why she wanted to argue this point. "I don't need special treatment."

And maybe that was the crux of it. Was he treating her differently because of last night? Because they planned to sleep together? The deal was, they would stay the same.

The muscle in his jaw twitched as he threw the truck

back into drive and pulled away from the building. For a Saturday afternoon, there were a lot of cars on the street, so it took a while for him to find a spot.

After he parked, he got out and waited on her side. He looked really pissed. The rain hadn't let up and the cold mush slashed against her skin. Maybe this was not the time to take a stand with Shane.

He locked up as she took off at a slow jog. She wanted to run, but the pavement was slippery. More than once, she skidded and almost lost her balance. By the time they climbed the stairs to their apartments, her hair was plastered to her head and Shane still looked pissed off.

He let them in the hallway and she tugged his sleeve. "Come on, I'll make you a cup of tea."

"Make it coffee."

"Fine."

As she unlocked her apartment door, he asked, "What was that about?"

"What?"

"Don't play stupid."

"When you pulled up and told me to get out, it was such a gentlemanly thing to do."

"And?"

"And I had this awful feeling you were doing it only because of last night."

"What? Now you're sounding stupid." He took off his jacket and hung it over the back of a chair.

She did the same. "Don't call me stupid."

"Then don't talk like it. Dropping you off so you could stay dry is something I would do for anyone. Even before last night, I definitely would've done it for you. It's courtesy."

She knew he was right, but she was so afraid of things changing. Instead of saying anything else, she went to the bathroom and grabbed a towel to dry her hair. Although her shirt had been dry beneath his jacket, her hair now dripped and left wet spots all over.

Toweling her hair, she tried to explain. "I'm sorry. As much as I really want to follow through on our agreement to have sex, I can't afford to have things change between us. You're my best friend."

"I'm not going anywhere, Mags. Except to the kitchen for the coffee you promised."

"I said I'd make it."

"Yeah, but we both know your coffee sucks."

~

AFTER HER SHOWER, SHANE MET HER AT THE BATHROOM DOOR with a cup of tea. She turned toward the living room, but he laid a hand on her shoulder.

"I thought you wanted to read in bed."

"Are you leaving?"

"No. Unless you want me to."

"Let's go watch some TV then." On the way to the couch, she picked up her book. She sat in the corner, setting her cup on the table, and tossed the remote to Shane.

It was all very homey. She sat and read while he watched some sports crap that held zero interest for her. At some point, she must've dozed off, because Shane was tapping her leg.

"Must be a boring book," he said with a smile.

"Nope. Just a cozy day."

Shane's hand rubbed her calf. "Are you well rested now?"

She stretched as far as she could, her muscles pulling tight. An uneasy feeling crept through her. When was the last time she'd slept anywhere other than in her bed behind a locked door? "Yep. Did you nap?"

"Nuh-uh. You're cute when you sleep."

"You sat here watching me?" She chuckled. "Creeper."

"I thought about waking you up." He leaned over and kissed her. "Like this," he said against her lips.

She placed her hands on his face and stared into his eyes. "You make me feel safe."

"That's good."

"No, I mean, really." She still couldn't tell him about her need to be behind a locked door for sleeping. Her lips brushed his. "Thank you."

"Let's go to the bedroom." He waited for her response.

She nodded. This felt right. She'd made a good choice in asking Shane. He always made her feel safe and secure. This afternoon was proof.

He pulled back and stood, holding out a hand. When her palm met his, she was reminded of how he'd touched her last night. Her heart swelled with comfort and her blood began to race. If last night was any indication of how good it could be, she was in for one hell of a ride.

Shane led her to the bedroom, and she quietly closed and locked the door. Meager light came through the window, so he turned on the bedside lamp. "I need to see you. To know you're okay."

She almost smiled. "I said I wouldn't lie."

"But you would try to push through even if it wasn't working for you. You'd try to pretend you weren't freaking out even if it meant tearing yourself apart."

She nodded. He was right. She wanted this so much she would let it happen no matter what. But Shane wouldn't let it be bad for her. He'd stop and make her feel better.

He pulled her close with his arm around her waist. His other hand guided her at the base of her skull as he leaned in to kiss her. The warm, cozy feeling fled her body and was replaced by the rush of desire. She wanted more of what she'd experienced last night, and she wasn't ashamed to admit it to herself.

She tugged at Shane's shirt, and her fingers brushed across his skin. His hard-on pressed against her middle. She rubbed her body along his, causing a hiss to escape his lips.

"I want to get you naked," he whispered.

"So do it." Images of Shane tearing at her clothes doubled her desire.

He eased away from her. "After what happened yesterday, maybe it would be better if you did it yourself."

As if she needed the reminder of her meltdown. But she wouldn't let a memory ruin this. He was right; she'd been able to get down to her underwear without issue yesterday. She pulled her sweatshirt over her head and he groaned when he saw her bare chest. No bra to worry about tonight.

"You could've warned me."

"But I like surprises." She shoved her pants off and stood before him naked.

He whipped off his shirt and dropped his pants, leaving everything in a pile at his feet. He smirked and kissed her collarbone. Before going any further, he looked up in question. She nodded. She didn't want anything to be off limits with him. Not tonight. Or ever.

Crap. There was only tonight. Succeed or fail, this was it. She closed her eyes against the sensation of his mouth on her nipple. Her hand gripped his shoulder, feeling the strong muscle bunch underneath his smooth skin as he moved. After giving both of her breasts ample attention, which left her nipples hard points, he kissed lower.

Warm, wet kisses trailed down her ribs, across her belly button, then down her hip to her thigh. Anticipation sent shivers through her. She didn't know what to expect, and in some ways the not knowing was worse. But still good.

He stood and guided her backward until her knees hit the bed. She flopped back thinking he was going to follow. Instead, he grabbed her hips and pulled her to the edge of the mattress. He knelt in front of her and used his hands to spread her legs. Propping up on her elbows, she stared at him.

He looked up, met her gaze, and when she didn't protest, he lowered his head. Running his tongue along her slit, he moved slowly, methodically. She stayed on her elbows and watched. There was something completely erotic about watching him go down on her. She was nervous but excited. She had vague memories of how good this could be.

Shane moaned, and with his gaze still on her, one of his eyebrows arched. The simple act loosened her nerves. She mimicked the move in challenge. If he wanted a moan, he'd have to work for it. Using his fingers, he spread her lips and swirled his tongue around her clit. Her breath caught, but she didn't lose eye contact.

He flicked her with the tip of his tongue and her hips jumped, but her eyes remained steady. She had no idea what game they were playing, but it was exciting. His hands massaged their way up her thighs. He pulled his mouth away for a brief moment and shot her a cocky grin.

He pressed a finger into her and began thrusting. She bit her lip. He winked and put his mouth back on her. Her clit became the center of his attention and she lost focus. A second finger joined the first, and as he moved them inside her, his tongue was relentless.

First, her head lolled back. Then her arms weakened. She didn't care if Shane won their battle. If this was losing, it was one hell of a way to go. Her mind blanked out with the pleasure. She felt the tension coiling and building. She raised her foot and sought the edge of the bed for balance, but it kept slipping.

She finally braced her heel against Shane's shoulder and

held his head in place with her hand. Her hips bucked, but he didn't let up. Her nerves tingled throughout her entire body and her mind saw nothing but white. Her muscles trembled and she thought she was done. This was the most she could normally hope for in an orgasm.

But then Shane did something with his hands and his tongue, and damn, she had no idea what it was, but her whole body was gone, floating, and all she could say was, "Oh, God, Shane" over and over.

She had no idea how long she lay there with Shane touching her everywhere. She came down from the high of her orgasm, but she wasn't done. Her body craved more. She opened her eyes and found him staring at her. "That was amazing."

"I'm glad."

She tugged his arm. "But I want you. Inside me."

He didn't move, but continued to gently caress her with his fingertips.

"Preferably now, Shane."

He shifted away from her toward the head of the bed. "I think you should be on top."

Not that she minded being on top, but she wasn't all that sure of herself, and part of her really liked him taking control.

"If you're on top, you can stop the second something doesn't feel right. There's no way for you to feel trapped."

She nodded but didn't say anything. Her body craved his touch and longed for him to be inside her. But she wished she could tell him he didn't make her feel trapped. She turned and saw his hard-on curving up on his belly. She crawled toward him and he groaned.

On her path up the bed, she ran her tongue over his balls and up the length of his dick. His hands fisted in the blanket. She took him in her mouth and swirled her tongue over the head. His hips jerked. Part of her wanted to make him come like this, but she was selfish. She wanted all of him for her.

She reached over and grabbed a condom from the nightstand where he'd tossed one earlier. She opened the package, but he took it from her and rolled it on. On her knees, she moved forward and grabbed his dick. Moving it along her wet slit, she bumped her clit and realized how turned on she was. She could've just done that a couple more times and come again.

Shane hissed and she smiled before doing it again. As much as she wanted to prolong that sweet torture, she wanted him inside her more. She placed the head at her entrance and eased down.

It hurt. She hadn't expected that. It didn't hurt a lot, so she pressed down a little farther. Shane held her hip with one hand, his fingers making indentations in her flesh. He licked the thumb of his other hand, reached between them, and began massaging her clit again.

She dropped her chin to her chest as he created small circles that rippled pleasure through her. Her hands braced on his chest and she felt his hips raise. He entered her slowly, taking his time. She stretched from within until she was gloriously full.

She sat still for a minute and enjoyed the sensation. Then she opened her eyes and looked at Shane.

"You okay?" he whispered.

Not sure if she could form words, she nodded. His thumb pressed against her clit, and she needed to move. She rose a little and dropped back down, her muscles slightly burning with the movement, but it felt so damn good. Shane moved both hands to her hips, and she expected him to drive into her, but he just held on. Every movement was hers. Every thrust. Every grind. Every wiggle.

She picked up the pace, unsure if she could come again

but needing to know he would. She stayed close to his body and slid back and forth, riding the length of him. She grabbed his hands and moved them to her chest. He took direction well. He kneaded her breasts and lightly pinched her nipples.

She was getting close again, but she couldn't read Shane. She had no idea how close he was. Leaning down, which knocked his arms away from her, she kissed him hard.

"God, I'm close, Shane."

"So let go."

She shook her head. "Come with me. I don't know…." Her thoughts blurred. After a slow inhale. "I don't know if I can again."

"You want to?"

She slapped his chest. "God, yes."

With a hand on her cheek, he kissed her. "Touch yourself. I'll take care of the rest."

Their eyes locked again, like they had earlier. He continued to kiss her and while his tongue was in her mouth, she snaked a hand between them and rubbed her clit. Stars spiked behind her eyes. Shane thrust into her hard and fast. She felt his hips lifting off the bed, but he held on to her. This time when she came, she had no words. Air froze in her lungs.

But a moment later, Shane stiffened beneath her and he stopped kissing her. His dick pulsed inside her and she laid her head on his chest, listening to his heart beat. The racing thump comforted her as she caught her breath.

They were wet and sticky and panting, but she had no desire to move. She'd discovered perfection.

Shane's hand smoothed over her back, his rough palm slightly scratchy. "Still okay?" His voice was quiet, and he sounded like he was still out of breath.

"Yeah." She followed with a nod and slid away from his body.

He kept his hand on his dick, holding the condom in place as he stood to get rid of it. She watched him walk out her bedroom door and close it behind him. A sudden spike of panic struck her again.

No. I will not let this happen. This was good. Nothing is going to take this from me. She squeezed her eyes shut and thought of Shane. He would be back in a minute. The fear subsided.

When she reopened her eyes, she briefly wondered what Dr. Janzen would say about her using Shane as a calming device.

But she didn't have time to ponder the thought, because Shane was back through the door with a glass of water.

CHAPTER 17

While he'd been in the bathroom and then the kitchen, Shane had convinced himself when he came back to the bedroom, he would know what to say or do. His body moved on autopilot, closing the door behind him, which was good because his brain fuzzed out looking at Maggie lying naked on the bed waiting for him.

He shook his head. No, she wasn't waiting for him. She was just lying in bed after having sex. He had to remind himself she wasn't yet his. But if that round of sex didn't convince her how good they would be together, he had no idea what would. He strode to the bed and handed her the glass of water.

"Congratulations," he said, and immediately regretted it, but he couldn't undo the stupid word.

"You weren't so bad yourself." She propped on an elbow, took the water, and gulped down half the glass. Then she held it out to him before flopping back down on her stomach.

"I didn't mean it like that." He sat beside where she lay. He spoke and struggled to keep his eyes on her face instead of on the naked curve of her ass. "No matter what you use to measure the definition of sex, I think you accomplished that tonight."

She reached across and wrapped her fingers around his. "*We* accomplished it." She pressed her lips together, then said, "Thank you."

Her thank-you wasn't quite as stupid as his congratulations, but it irked him. Did she think he was looking for gratitude? He'd just had some of the most amazing sex of his life and she was tossing off a thank-you.

"Mmm…I forgot how sleepy great sex makes me." Her eyes fluttered closed.

Shane watched for a minute, trying to decide if he should stay or go. He wanted more than anything to stay, but he didn't want to push things. Well, yeah, he did, but he didn't want to freak Maggie out. And he'd stayed last night, so tonight shouldn't matter.

"Come to bed," she mumbled. "And turn out the light."

He stretched out next to her and reached for the light switch. Before plunging the room into darkness, his gaze coasted over her bare body. He'd agreed to a single attempt at sex, but now he had no idea how he could continue on without this, being with her in every way.

He flipped the switch and settled against the pillows, which smelled of Maggie's shampoo. She rolled over and snuggled against him while pulling at the blanket to cover herself. Shane sat up and snapped the blanket over both of them, even though he wasn't cold. He just wanted to be as close to her for as long as possible.

Shane did his best to control his thoughts and relax enough to sleep. Instead, he began to plan his conversation with Maggie explaining why they should be a couple. So many things flashed into his head that he knew he would sound insane if he said them at once. It would be so much easier if she had given him some hint of what she was thinking.

Was it possible she could have sex with him and not feel the connection they had?

Shit. He thought thinking like a shrink was bad, but now he sounded like a chick. What the hell had Maggie done to him?

He turned to his side and breathed in her scent. His brain finally turned off, and as he began to doze, Maggie shifted and got off the bed. He assumed she needed to go to the bathroom, but she went to the door, fumbled around, and then returned to bed. Was she sleepwalking? Then he realized she was checking the door again.

She said nothing, but climbed back in beside him and hugged her pillow.

He could definitely get used to this.

Maggie woke in the morning, feeling sleepy and a little sore. She rolled over and looked at Shane, who was snoring beside her. Something felt right waking up beside him and she didn't know what to do with that feeling. This was Shane and she'd woken up with him before. Over the years, they'd spent the night together after watching movies or after a party.

This was different. Last night changed something, even more than the previous night. She'd known the possibility existed that having sex might change things between them, but she had faith that they could make sure it didn't impact their relationship. In truth, she didn't believe she'd be able to follow through and have sex.

Holy crap! I had sex. And it had been good—more than

good. She hadn't felt frozen or trapped or freakish at all last night. She did it.

Dr. Janzen had been right. If Maggie took the time to get to know a guy and really trust him, she could have a positive sexual relationship. She could ultimately find what her siblings had. She could eventually have a husband and kids—not that she was in any hurry. It was the knowledge that it was a possibility that made her a little giddy.

Armed with her new knowledge about herself, Maggie eased out of bed without waking Shane. She looked over at him. He'd been perfect. He'd given her what she needed. Only for one night, she reminded herself. A slight pain poked her heart. Nothing should hurt. It all went according to plan. She wanted to face her day and figure out what to do next. She was back on the market for a boyfriend. Thinking it didn't make her feel any better, but she had to keep the momentum going so she didn't lose ground.

She gathered clothes and went to the bathroom to shower and dress for the day. It was family dinner day today. Maybe she'd talk to Moira for ideas about where to find a good date. But if she did that, Moira would guess that Maggie had had sex and she'd want details. Maggie wasn't sure if she wanted to share those details.

Something great happened last night and she wanted to keep it just for her.

By the time she got out of the shower, Shane was standing in his boxers in the kitchen, drinking a cup of coffee.

"You could've slept in. I would've brought you coffee."

He made a face as he drank.

"My coffee's not that bad."

"Yeah, it is."

She reached around him and filled her own cup. She was at a loss for what else to say and she didn't like feeling that way. Talking with Shane had never been a problem and neither was being in silence with him. This shouldn't be awkward.

"How are you feeling?" he asked.

"Great." She couldn't hide her smirk. "Last night was … Wow. I never thought I'd be okay." She sighed and set her cup on the counter. Just get it over with so they can go back to being Maggie and Shane. "I can't thank you enough. Dr. Janzen was right. I just need to open myself up to a guy and trust him enough to take care of me. I have to have the tough conversations, but if I do, everything will fall into place."

Shane's face hardened while she talked, but then he smiled. It wasn't a real smile, though.

"Something wrong?"

"No."

But he didn't expand. An uneasy feeling crawled over her. "What is it?"

"I'm fine, Mags. I'm going home to shower."

"I have family dinner today. You're welcome to come if you want."

"No, thanks. I think I'm going to hang out with my dad."

"Want to get together later for a movie or something?"

"Maybe. Give me a call."

He dumped the rest of his coffee down the drain. She picked up her cup and drank as he walked toward the bedroom. The uneasy feeling deepened and pressed on her. Something went wrong, but she had no idea what.

She recalled their brief conversation. Could it be Shane was mad that she talked about finding a boyfriend? Would that make him mad? She was putting them back to normal. It was what they'd agreed on.

Her heart rate kicked up. She followed him down the hall. Leaning against her doorway, she watched him jump into his jeans and gather his other stuff in his arms.

"What's wrong?"

"I'm fine."

"No, you're not. You're mad. I want to know why."

He sighed and his chest made it look like the air weighed a ton. "I'm not mad."

She straightened away from the frame. She didn't like these games. "Are you mad because I talked about finding a boyfriend?"

Rather than step into his shoes, he carried them. "I'm not mad. I'm worried, Maggie. You're so impatient. I'm afraid you'll think one sexual encounter makes you…"

She knew where this was going, and it pissed her off. "Makes me what?"

"Just don't rush it."

"Makes me what, Shane? Normal, right? That's what you were going to say?"

"Yes, Maggie, normal. I love you, but you're not normal. You were raped. That is never going away."

Her throat tightened and her eyes burned. Not Shane. Everyone in her life had tiptoed around her for a long time, treating her like she was fragile. But not Shane. He'd always treated her the same. "Don't you fucking think I know that? I live with it every damn day. I don't need you to tell me I'm not normal. I know that, too. But that doesn't mean I don't get to live a normal life."

"That's not what I meant." His voice was quiet. He sounded hurt.

But she couldn't care. She was pissed. And hurt. "You did, or you wouldn't have said it." Her cup shook in her hand.

"Fuck." The curse came out as a sharp whisper. "Maggie." He stepped toward her.

She backed up. "I'm pissed off now, Shane. Go home. We'll talk later. Maybe. You know, if I'm not too fucked up in my own head to be normal."

She turned and went back to the kitchen. She heard his heavy footsteps behind her. His hand landed on her shoulder and he spun her around. "Don't twist my words. I wasn't trying to say that there's something wrong with you—"

"But there is."

"Christ, Maggie. I don't want you to take this one victory and rush into some asshole's arms."

He stopped. Maggie had the impression he planned to say more, but he stopped himself. She stood and stared into his eyes. She saw pain, which was like a stab to the heart. "I won't. I need to move on with my life. I have to learn to trust myself to choose a good guy and then trust him enough to take care of me."

He backed off, dropping his hand from her shoulder. She missed the reassuring weight.

He disappeared back to the bedroom and walked past her again with his things. A rock sat in her stomach. She had no idea how things had gone so wrong. She and Shane had fought before, many times over the years, but this felt different. This was real pain, not just anger.

She swallowed past the lump in her throat and pushed down the urge to go after him. She needed to understand why she was so angry first. It shouldn't have surprised her that Shane would tell her what to do. In that way, he was very much like her brothers.

Maybe that's why she was so upset. He was the one person who was supposed to be in her corner. She'd calm down and talk to him later, when she could be rational and not accuse him of being like Ryan.

In the meantime, she had to go see her real brothers.

CHAPTER 18

Shane walked into his apartment and slammed the door. It didn't make him feel any better. What. The. Fuck. How could Maggie make love to him and then talk about moving on with some other guy who would take care of her? The damn bed wasn't even cold yet.

He'd expected a conversation in the morning, but not that one. He scrubbed his hand over his head in frustration. Breaking something would feel awesome right now. But since everything in his apartment was new, he wasn't about to undo all of his hard work.

He threw his shoes against the cabinets and went to his bedroom. Pulling fresh clothes from his dresser, he realized he still smelled like sex and Maggie. He couldn't work like that, so he opted for a shower.

Once he was clean, his head was also a little clearer. He'd made a deal with Maggie. He knew that going in, and his own silly romantic ideas wouldn't change that. They'd talk later and they'd be okay. He'd told himself from the beginning that if all he got was one shot to be with Maggie, it would be enough.

But it's not, a sneering voice in his head pointed out. It would have to be enough because he couldn't imagine his life without her. He turned on the radio to drown out the sounds of the nasty voice in his head that reminded him that as long as Maggie was in his life, he'd have to see her with other men. He turned to the classic rock station, blaring the Stones singing "Satisfaction." He started a pot of coffee and surveyed the work he needed to finish.

The drywall was done and ready to paint. He hated painting. It wasn't physical enough and it didn't require mental power. He'd buy and install the trim today. Trim would keep his mind occupied and off Maggie. While his coffee brewed, he measured the walls again as if he didn't already know the dimensions. He made halfhearted notes for his shopping list.

He filled his to-go cup, grabbed his list, and turned off the radio. Before leaving, he opened his door and peered out. He wasn't sure if he was hoping to see Maggie or avoid her, which was really sad. Shaking his head at himself and his stupid ideas, he went to his truck.

AFTER SPENDING MOST OF THE DAY CUTTING AND INSTALLING trim, Shane didn't feel any better. He'd managed to keep his mind off Maggie mostly out of sheer determination. If he got distracted, he'd screw up the trim, and his dad had taught him a long time ago he needed to measure twice, cut once. The simple mantra kept him on task and focused. When he decided to call it quits for the day, he was coated in fine sawdust.

He brushed himself off, and then took off his shirt and pants and shook them out. He checked the time. Maggie would still be at dinner with her family.

He needed to stop thinking about where she was and

when she might be back. He needed to step back from her if he wanted to keep their friendship.

The thought irritated him almost as much as his conversation with Maggie this morning. He took a shower and went to see his family. Hopefully, only his parents would be at home. He didn't need any more time with crazy females today.

When he got to his parents' house, he didn't see his mom's car. Dad's truck was in the driveway, but that didn't mean much. Shane let himself into the house. "Hello?"

No one answered. Didn't that just figure. After spending the entire day by himself, he needed the noise and distraction of his family, and they weren't home. He tossed his keys on the counter and pulled out his phone to contact his dad. He texted and waited for a reply.

Just as he settled at a kitchen chair, the back door opened and Cara walked in.

"Hey, what are you doing here?"

"I could ask you the same. I thought you stayed on campus."

"I live on campus, but this is still home. I get tired of roommates and parties." She narrowed her eyes at him. "What's going on?"

"Nothing. I came home hoping to get a real meal. My apartment is still under construction." The half truth should've been enough, but not for Cara.

"And?"

"And what? I should've called first, obviously, because no one's here. So that means no dinner."

"I'm here. And I cook. I'll even cook for you if you tell me what's bothering you."

"Nothing's bothering me."

She smiled. "That means it's girl trouble." She bit the

inside of her cheek as she thought. "This is tough because I don't remember Mom talking about a new girlfriend."

"There is no girlfriend."

"So it's someone you slept with."

"Shut up, Cara."

"I love it when I'm right. What's the problem? You screwed some girl and she thought it was going to be a lifetime commitment?"

Just the opposite. "You have no idea what you're talking about." He felt uncomfortable under her steady gaze. She had their mom's eyes, and she could stare down anyone.

She rolled her eyes then. "Men," she huffed. But she went to the refrigerator and scoped out the options. "Mom has leftover pasta in here. That good for you?"

"Yeah. Whatever."

Cara pulled out the plastic containers and then dishes from the cabinet. The sounds in the kitchen brought him back to being a kid. It didn't matter that it was his sister and not his mom making the noise and the food; it felt the same.

She set a plate in front of him. He went to the fridge, grabbed the milk, and poured a glass for each of them.

He picked up his fork. "For the record, this doesn't count as cooking. All you did was reheat. I could've done that."

"But you didn't. So I get credit for feeding you. Make sure you tell Mom."

They ate in silence for a few minutes. "So how's Maggie doing since she came back? I overheard Dad saying she's working at the bar."

"She's fine. Good."

"Isn't it weird for her to work at the bar?"

He lifted a shoulder. "She has some bad days, but overall she missed being part of the family business."

He shoveled more pasta in his mouth. He definitely didn't

want to talk about Maggie. It was his whole reason for coming here. "How's school?"

"Fine. Same shit, different day. I'm ready to be done."

He remembered those days. The last few months of senior year had been horrible. "That doesn't make much sense since you just signed on for three more years of school."

"That's different. That's law school. The stuff I learn there will be useful. It's what I need for my career. These classes, not so much."

He couldn't argue. He still wasn't using a damn thing he'd learned in college. Of course, he hadn't gone to school to be a carpenter. Watching his younger sisters grow up and move into their careers unsettled him. Was this all he had to look forward to? Being his dad?

Maggie had a point. He had been sitting back and waiting for the job to come to him. With Chicago, he didn't have much of a choice. Maybe it was time to look elsewhere.

"You're quieter than usual. Something's wrong. You can tell me. I'll even promise not to tell Mom and Dad."

Could he talk to Cara? She could keep a secret. Surprisingly, all of his sisters were good at that.

"You're a girl, right?"

She grunted. "Last I checked."

"That didn't come out right. I mean, you know girls and how they think. Is it possible a girl could sleep with a guy and have it be just sex?"

She laughed at him. Then laughed some more. "Lord, Shane. Welcome to the twenty-first century. Guess what? Women like sex. Guys don't have the corner on the market. Yes, girls have sex just to have a good time. We're not all weepy women, mooning for some soul mate."

"I know that." He inhaled to get it right this time. "Before I go on, it would help if you didn't include yourself in this conversation. I really don't want that information. But if a girl cares about a guy, they have a relationship, and they sleep together, what's the likelihood it was just biology?" He knew in his gut it wasn't just biology with Maggie, but he had no idea how else to explain it.

"Look, I can—I mean, a girl can like a guy and not want a relationship. Relationships take work. School is time-consuming: reading, homework, papers, friends. Many of us —many women—just want a good time, a physical release. It doesn't mean they don't like the guy. In fact, lots of people I know hook up routinely for a 'friends with benefits' thing." She finished her dinner and stood to take her plate to the sink.

"No, it's not that. She definitely wants a relationship."

"Then maybe you're not good enough. A girl doesn't want a relationship with a guy who can't get it right."

"I got it right. I'm *not* having that conversation with you. I knew this would be a mistake." He stood and put his dish in the sink.

"No, wait." She laid a hand on his arm. "You're really worked up about this. It's not like you. Isn't this normally the kind of thing you'd talk to Maggie about?"

As soon as she finished the question, he saw the idea flash in her mind.

"Oh, my God. You and Maggie slept together." Although she whispered the words like they were a huge secret, she followed it with a squeal-giggle and a jump that only sisters knew how to do. "This is so exciting!"

He shook his head and loaded their dirty plates into the dishwasher.

"Now that I know what this is really about, I need the full story."

He sat back at the table and explained the situation, leaving out the specific details. He knew the physical part was not an issue. He needed help navigating the emotional situation with Maggie.

"I always knew you guys would be great together."

"I thought so, too."

"Thought?"

"She's…I don't know. Determined to find some other guy. It's like I don't exist as a guy for her."

"Trust me, if she slept with you, and it was her idea, she's well aware you're a guy. Did you bother to tell her how you feel?"

Shane stared at his sister.

She rolled her eyes. "Men. You're so stupid."

"I'm not stupid."

"Yeah, you are. Is Maggie supposed to be psychic? Guys always accuse women of not saying things straight, using some kind of code when we talk, but at least we talk. You have to tell her how you feel."

"What if she doesn't feel the same? Then I lose my best friend."

"What did you expect to happen?"

"I thought she'd feel it. I did. It wasn't just fucking, Cara. It's different when it's someone you love. I always thought that was some bullshit Mom and Dad spewed to get me to keep it in my pants as a teen. But they were right."

"I know."

He shot her a look, but her eyes darted away. When had Cara ever been in love? "Who?" he asked.

"We're not talking about me."

"I kind of wish we were."

"You need to talk to her. Take that risk. Otherwise, you keep things as they are. You need to decide what's more important."

Maggie. She was all that was important. But that wasn't

much of an answer. Could he just tell Maggie he wanted that relationship with her?

He still wasn't sure. Talking with Cara didn't make him feel any better. He had no idea why women advocated all this talking shit. It hadn't done him any good.

Maggie walked into her mom's house, late as usual. All of her siblings were already there. In the past year, they'd added so many family members, the house was filled to bursting. Maggie's first thought was that their dad would've loved it.

She walked past her brothers sitting in the living room and into the kitchen to find her mom and Moira at the sink. Quinn was putting something in the refrigerator.

"Hey," Maggie called.

Moira turned. "I'm glad you're here. I need to talk to you after dinner."

"Talk now."

"No. It's too much with all these people."

"Moira, go set the table," their mom said.

"Grab the silverware," Moira said to Maggie.

Together they went back into the dining room. If the family grew any more, they'd need to invest in a bigger table. Not that one could fit in this room. Extra folding chairs had been added to the corners of the table.

"What's going on?" Moira asked.

"You're the one who said she needed to talk to me."

"That's a work thing. We'll talk about that later. I mean, you look different."

Shit. Could Moira look at her and know she'd had sex? She'd been dying to talk to someone. But not here. Not now, with her entire family within eavesdropping distance.

"We'll talk about that later, too."

"What's going on?" Ryan asked. "You two look thick as thieves, just like when you were scheming as kids."

"What?" Moira's eyes widened, trying to look innocent.

Maggie didn't have the heart to tell her she couldn't pull that off anymore.

"Moira, Maggie, come get the food," their mother called.

Both girls rolled their eyes.

"Ryan and Colin have arms too, Mom," Moira yelled back.

"Why do you bother?" Maggie asked. "She'll never expect them to do anything."

"Not true," Ryan said. "We fix things around here. When was the last time either of you mowed the lawn?"

"Uh, never," Moira answered.

"As soon as you mow the lawn or shovel the snow, we'll help with dinner."

"It's a bunch of B.S.," Moira mumbled, but she and Maggie both went to the kitchen.

Over dinner, most of the talk revolved around Saint Patrick's Day and the bar. Ryan had finally agreed to do green beer, but he wasn't happy about it.

"With Saint Paddy's landing on a Sunday, we have to be ready for a full weekend of business. People will start drinking Friday night and not stop until Monday morning when they have to go back to work. I've got the full staff on hand. How many of you will be there?" Ryan asked.

Moira, Liam, and Michael all chimed in with yeses.

"I can do door duty, if you need me," Jimmy offered.

He'd never worked at the bar, but Maggie figured that being engaged to Moira made him family now, so he was willing.

"I'll be there for all the shifts," Maggie said. "Drunk Irishmen tip well."

The entire table quieted. Everyone stared at her.

"What?" she asked. She hated being under the microscope, but it was always the worst when it came from her family.

Her mother's lips thinned and almost disappeared.

"We don't expect you to work," Ryan said.

"But I'm going to." She looked around the room for support. Surely they all didn't think her incapable of working the holiday. She stared at Moira with wide eyes.

Moira looked away.

Maggie stood. "It has been nearly five years since I was raped."

Her mother sucked in a sharp breath.

"Yeah, Mom. I can say it. I was raped. It was horrible and I still have bad days, but I'm better. I want to work with the rest of the family on Saint Patrick's Day."

Looking at all their faces, she knew she couldn't back down now. "I can't believe my own family has so little faith in me. I traveled to Europe by myself. Nothing bad happened. I'm working at the bar, and I'm living in an apartment above it. Across the damn hall from where Todd raped me."

She knew her mother was in shock when she didn't scold Maggie for cursing. She grabbed her plate. "What more do I have to do to prove to you that I'm okay?"

In the kitchen, she scraped the rest of her dinner into the trash and put her plate in the sink. She had the sudden urge to pull a beer out of the fridge. It was something her brothers would do in a situation like this. She hadn't felt the desire to drink any alcohol in years. Not once. But today with her family looking at her like she might break, she wanted to drink.

Man, I'm fucked up.

She heard the sharp whispers from the dining room. They were probably arguing about who had to come and talk to her. Talk some sense into her. She'd place her money on Moira. They'd think she could play the sister card with Maggie to get her to acquiesce.

Sure enough, Moira entered the room a moment later. Maggie shook her head.

"They're all stupid," Moira said.

Maggie's eyes shot up to her sister's face.

"They won't listen to me anymore than they listen to you. Ignore them. Do what's right for you."

Maggie threw her arms around her big sister. "Thank you."

"No problem. Let's get out of here."

"Where?"

"We're going to my house to talk. Jimmy's going to hang out with Liam for a while."

Maggie smiled. Moira was probably the best sister someone could ask for. "You have any beer at your house?"

Moira's forehead wrinkled. "Yeah. Why?"

"I think I'm ready for that, too." Where else could she sample and feel safe? She immediately thought of Shane and how safe she'd always felt with him. But Shane wasn't an option. "I have a sudden thirst for a beer. Part of me wants to pop one open just to scandalize Mom more. And really, if she hadn't had a heart attack, I would."

Moira laughed and put an arm around her. "I don't know why they worry about you. You're fine."

Maggie drove to Moira's new house, which wasn't far from their childhood home. Both she and Jimmy wanted to stay in the neighborhood because of their respective parents. Maggie had been to Moira's house only once, last month when she'd helped them move in.

It was a bungalow designed almost like the house they'd grown up in. Moira opened the door, and Maggie was surprised there were no boxes sitting around. "You have everything unpacked?"

After laughing lightly, Moira said, "Jimmy would have a fit if I left stuff in boxes. It wasn't too hard given that I got rid of a lot of my stuff. We wanted to start building the *us*." She flicked on lights as she walked through the house.

Moira went to the kitchen and Maggie detoured to check the bedrooms on the first floor. They were using one as the master. The other was Moira's office without a doubt. Piles of paper and notebooks were all over. This was the chaos she was used to seeing with Moira.

Moira came up behind her. "We keep this door closed so Jimmy doesn't have a seizure."

"Good to know that falling in love hasn't totally changed you." Maggie turned off the light and closed the door.

"Being in love is supposed to change you some. It's like becoming a better version of yourself."

Maggie sighed. Yeah, she wouldn't mind having that.

"I put coffee on and stole a couple of pastries from Mom's."

"You're good." Maggie followed her back to the kitchen. She bit into the éclair Moira has swiped for her as Moira set a brownie on a plate. "So what work stuff did you want to talk about?"

"I think I might have a job for you."

"What?"

"It's not a done deal, but the paper I used to work for out in the burbs is looking for a photographer. It doesn't pay great, but it's a foot in the door."

"How did you find out about it?" Custard dripped from the pastry and Maggie licked to catch it.

"I had coffee with a reporter I used to work with. She wanted to pick my brain about a new project she's starting. One thing led to another and we were talking jobs. I have the information so you can apply. Put me down as a reference." She took a long drink of her coffee. "The startup Tara is doing might pan out for you, too."

"What?"

"She's starting a new online Chicago magazine. She's just getting it off the ground, so there's no money, but if you help her it'll build your professional portfolio, and when she starts making money, you'll be first in line for a paycheck. And if I know Tara, it won't take long."

"Thank you. It means a lot that you'd put yourself out there for me."

"You're my sister. Why wouldn't I?"

"I don't know. Thank you."

"You ready to talk yet?"

"We are talking."

"Not about what happened at the house. Not about you wanting a beer. And definitely not about the look on your face when you got to Mom's."

Maggie polished off her éclair and her coffee. "For that story, I might need the beer."

Moira went to the fridge, pulled out a bottle, and handed it to her without opening it.

Maggie rolled it between her palms. Would she still like the taste? Did she need the crutch to talk about Shane? Yep. She twisted the cap off but didn't yet drink.

She wanted to make the attempt without it. "I had sex."

Moira choked on her coffee. "What? When? With who?"

Before Maggie could answer any of the questions, Moira asked, "Most important, was it good?"

"Oh, God, yeah." The words slipped from her tongue easily.

"Yay!" Moira clapped her hands rapidly. "Now give me the details."

Maggie exhaled a heavy breath. "It was Shane. I asked him to have sex with me to see if I could."

"Wow. He agreed? I never would've thought."

"Why not? He's my best friend. Wouldn't you do anything for your best friend?"

"Yeah, but…"

"But what?"

"Nothing. So it went well?"

"Not at first. We talked and he was adamant about me being honest, as if I've ever been anything other with him. But he was so worried about me, you know? The first time we tried—"

"Wait. There was more than one time?" Moira leaned forward on her kitchen table, eager for information.

"Kind of. We tried and I wanted it, but then when we got to the bedroom and he took off my bra, I froze. So we stopped."

Moira's face wrinkled with worry.

"But then I started again, solo, and he finished me. And it was so…wow." Maggie threw her hands up like an explosion. "I'd forgotten how good it could be."

She stared at the beer in front of her and then took a gulp. The sting of alcohol hit her tongue and slid down her throat. Not bad. "Then he spent the night, and we hung out the next day and then he fucked me."

Moira's eyes widened with her word choice. She had to phrase it that way in order to keep her distance. It had to be just sex with Shane. She couldn't pretend it was anything else.

Then Moira's face got hard. "What do you mean?"

"He fucked me. Thoroughly. Like I saw freaking stars and my body was wasted." She took another gulp of beer. "It was amazing."

She hoped her voice didn't sound dreamy, but that's what it had felt like remembering.

"So it was a resounding success."

Maggie nodded.

"Now what?"

Another drink of beer. "Now I know that if I invest the time to get to know a guy, trust him, let him in, I can have a full relationship." She finished the last gulp of beer, and the alcohol started to hit her system. "Basically, I'm back on the market for a boyfriend."

She stood and grabbed another beer from the fridge. She held one out to Moira, who declined.

"What did Shane say?"

"About what?"

"About any of it."

"He thinks I'm stupid, and I'm going to rush into a relationship with an asshole because I managed to have sex one time and having sex once doesn't make me normal." Her thoughts began to blur, and she was pretty sure she was rambling. She twisted the cap off her beer and chugged a bit, as if the liquid would stifle her anger at Shane's attitude.

"Are you sure that's a good idea?" Moira asked, pointing at Maggie's bottle.

"I haven't had any alcohol in almost five years. I think I should be celebrating."

"I'll get you a pillow and blanket for the couch. You're not driving."

"Okay." She smiled at her sister. "You don't think I'm stupid, do you?"

"For wanting a complete relationship? No. But you aren't thinking everything through." She stood to leave.

"Like what?"

"Like Shane, honey. Did you think about him in all of this?"

"What's there to think about? He's bossy. And controlling." Her eyes fluttered closed. "And in some situations, that could be a total turn-on."

"That." Moira pointed at her. "That right there. You can't toy with him. Do you think it was easy for him to sleep with you?"

"What are you trying to say? Am I some kind of hardship? I'm not ugly. I know I can sometimes be difficult, but it's not like he didn't get an orgasm out of the deal." The room started to spin, and she slapped her hand against the table to stop it.

"Oh, honey, we need to talk when you're sober. You really have no idea. Shane loves you."

Maggie stood, holding on to the table for balance. "I know. I love him, too. I think I'm ready for bed now. I never used to be such a lightweight. Who'da thought five years without beer would make it hit me so hard?" She giggled and then couldn't stop.

Moira grabbed her arm and led her back to the living room. She pushed Maggie onto the couch. Maggie watched as Moira got a blanket from a hall closet.

"You know anyone who'd wanna date me?"

Moira shook her head. "You don't want me to play matchmaker."

"Why not? You know me. You know what I like."

She put a pillow against the arm of the couch and spread a blanket out. "Not that I agree with everything Shane said, but I don't think you should rush into anything. Take your time. Don't worry about sex until you find a guy you really like."

"I know. But I miss sex, Moira."

"I know." She gently guided Maggie until she was stretched out.

Maggie sighed and closed her eyes. This week was full of renewed firsts. Hopefully she'd have more in store soon. She was ready to take on life.

CHAPTER 20

Shane stopped by Maggie's apartment before work the following morning, but she didn't answer. Her car wasn't parked outside either. She hadn't come home. The thought sank in his gut. In their last conversation she'd mentioned dating. She couldn't have found a date already, could she?

He brushed the thought aside. She wasn't the kind of person to just not come home, so she was probably with one of her siblings or her friend Olivia. It wasn't like she had to check in with him.

While driving to work, he thought about his life. Tonight, he'd get his computer back from Maggie so he could look for other departments that might be hiring. He hadn't considered going anywhere else, which was narrow-minded on his part. If Maggie could be brave enough to explore her options, so could he.

Once in the basement with his dad, he looked around. The job was almost done, then they would be on to something else. As much as he liked working with his dad, he didn't want this to be the rest of his life.

"You okay?" his dad asked.

"Yeah," he answered, not liking the lie but not knowing how to tell the truth.

"Cara said you stopped by last night. What did you need?"

"Dinner." The quip was enough to make his dad laugh and move on to work.

They worked side by side, and Shane knew they wouldn't have too much more time together like this. While he would miss it, it was time to move on.

By the time he drove back to his apartment, he was beat, but he had a plan. He dragged his feet up the stairs and was shocked to see Ryan O'Leary standing at his door. "Hey."

Ryan turned. "Just the guy I was looking for."

"What'd you need?" He walked past Ryan and unlocked his door.

Ryan followed him in. "I know you've been pretty much working every night Maggie is and I said I couldn't hire you when you wanted your old job back, but I was hoping you'd work, for pay, this weekend. With it being Saint Patrick's Day, we're going to be slammed. Maggie is insisting on working."

"I know. Yeah, I can be there."

"Thanks. I appreciate it." Ryan held out a hand and Shane shook it. "She's doing better, right? I'm not imagining it?"

"She is doing better. Better than we all give her credit for, I think." Shane turned toward the kitchen. "Want a beer?"

"No, thanks. I have to head to my other bar." Ryan took a quick stroll through the place. "It looks good in here. You'll be done soon, huh?"

"Yeah. I probably would've been done this weekend, but not with the holiday."

"No rush. Don't kill yourself to get it done. It was just wasted space anyway." He turned away again. With his hand on the door, Ryan asked, "Thanks again for everything."

"No problem."

Ryan left and Shane grabbed a bottle of water from the fridge. While he guzzled the water, he checked his e-mail on his phone. His heart stuttered to see one from the police department. He clicked it open and read. His eyes skimmed over it too quickly, so he started again at the top, wishing he had his laptop to read this on. It was a letter letting him know a detective would be doing a home visit. Shit. He hadn't changed his address.

The CPD would still have his address with Joe on file. He'd need to get that corrected. It was a good sign that he was moving on to the next step in the hiring process.

Then he looked around his apartment. Ryan had been impressed because he knew what the place had started out like. A detective probably wouldn't be too impressed with unpainted walls and exposed electric in the ceiling. As tired as he was, he put his job-hunting plan on hold and opened a can of paint.

Time to make sure his apartment looked like it was livable. He worked for a few hours until his already tired body screamed at him to stop. His stomach grumbled and he figured it was as good a time as any to get some dinner. He washed up, and before heading to the bar for dinner he knocked on Maggie's door again. Still no answer.

He walked downstairs and went through the back door, waving at the kitchen staff as he went. No one ever questioned his presence.

He took a spot at the bar and ordered a beer and a burger. While he waited, he glanced around. This place was almost always busy. Maybe not insanely so, but the O'Learys had a good thing. He took a sip of his beer, and movement off to the side caught his attention. He turned to see Maggie flip open her order pad.

What the hell was she doing? She hadn't been on the

schedule to work. She smiled at the guys as they ordered. When she came toward the bar, she pulled up short.

"Shane. What are you doing here?"

"Having dinner. I didn't know you were working tonight."

"I took an extra shift for Karen. She wasn't feeling well."

He wanted to weep. He was too fucking tired to think about pretending to work tonight. But the bar was full and Maggie was working.

"You look beat. Tough day?"

Looked like it was about to get tougher. It didn't help that she was pretending their argument hadn't happened. "Yeah. I finally got a coat of paint on the walls in the apartment, though."

"That's good." She walked around the bar and tapped away at the computer screen, putting in the order she'd just taken.

"I tried to catch up with you this morning, but you weren't home."

"Checking up on me now?" she asked without turning.

"No." Not really anyway. "I wanted to talk to you. About our fight."

She turned slowly away from the register. "I can't talk about that right now. I'm working."

"We need to talk."

"Later," she whispered.

He sighed, but let her go back to work. He nursed his one beer and then switched to water when his food arrived. He ate as slowly as possible since he wasn't dressed for work and he couldn't run upstairs and change without Maggie noticing. If she found out he'd only been pretending to work here, she'd be even more pissed.

So he spent a few hours sipping on glass after glass of water and chatting with people who were half drunk. He felt

Maggie's stare on him throughout the night, but she said nothing.

His muscles ached and longed for a hot shower. His eyelids scraped like sandpaper against his eyes. There was no way he'd make it to closing tonight. He felt like shit, both because his body was giving out and because he was failing Maggie.

He watched what was left of the crowd. It was near midnight, so the bar would be open for a couple more hours. No one had paid extra attention to Maggie, and no one seemed obnoxiously drunk. The bouncers could handle this.

Maggie will be fine.

Shane slid from his stool, deliberately putting one foot in front of the other. He probably looked drunk. Leaning against the bar, he waited for Maggie to swing by.

When she did, he said, "I'm going up to bed."

"Good. You look exhausted."

"Call me when you get home so I know you're safe."

She rolled her eyes. "I think I can manage to walk up a flight of stairs alone."

"Do I need to ask one of the guys to walk you up?"

"Shut up."

"Then promise you'll call me."

"Why would you want me to wake you up?"

He reached out and gently touched her jaw. "I need to know you're safe."

"Fine."

She tried to look irritated, but he saw her eyes soften. He nodded and trudged out the back and up the stairs.

He went to sleep with his phone in his hand so he wouldn't miss her call.

∼

MAGGIE'S LIFE WAS FINALLY COMING TOGETHER. SHE practically skipped down the street toward her car. In her pocket, she had a list of community events she would photograph for the newspaper. The pay was crap, but she would have her name attached to pictures that were published.

Now all she had to do was sell herself one more time to Moira's friend who was doing the magazine startup. It would take a bit of juggling, but she could handle it in order to build a new career. Moira had done it. She'd worked small, going-nowhere jobs and then started freelancing.

Maggie had already learned quite a bit from her big sister. She drove from the suburbs into downtown to meet Moira's friend Tara at a coffee shop.

Because she worried about being late, Maggie sped across town and ended up arriving early. She ordered a hot chocolate with extra whipped cream as a reward. She staked out a table near the front so she could see people arrive, but not too close to the door where the wind swept in.

After draping her coat on the back of her chair, she settled in with her drink and her phone to play a little Candy Crush. After a few minutes, she felt someone looking at her. She glanced up to see if Tara had arrived and then scanned the room. Her nerves pricked. At the table to her right, a guy looked up.

Their eyes met and he smiled. Maggie couldn't help but return the smile. He was cute. His light brown hair was a little shaggy, and he had the scruff of a beard. He reminded her of a younger version of Ryan's friend Griffin. She'd spent most of her childhood crushing on that man.

She returned her attention to her phone, feeling a little silly now for playing a game. That same prickling sensation of being watched tickled her. She had to squash the negativity the feeling brought. Not every guy who looked at her was bad. From the corner of her eye, she saw him move. Then he was beside her.

"Hi," he said.

Maggie immediately looked over her shoulder as if he spoke to someone behind her before realizing he was talking to her. "Hi."

"I'm Eli."

She smiled again. "Maggie."

"Can I join you?"

"Um…I'm actually waiting for someone. It's an interview, so I'm sorry." She shook her head a little. If she wasn't meeting Tara, would she have invited him to sit with her? For all her talk about wanting to date, she was woefully unprepared for it to actually happen.

"I understand. I was hoping to buy you another drink. Since you're busy tonight, can I have your number?"

"Uh…" Damn. She was too out of practice. She couldn't remember the last time she had a guy hit on her. At least a guy she didn't mind. "Okay."

He held his phone in his hand and typed as she rattled off her number. Then he snapped a photo of her.

Nerves tumbled through her. What if this guy was a predator? She covered the anxiety with a quip. "Afraid you won't be able to remember what I look like?"

"I'd remember." He looked confident. "I like to have a picture with my contacts."

A moment later her phone buzzed.

"That's me," he said. "You can save it so when I call you later to ask you out, you'll know it's me."

"But I'll also know it's you if I want to ignore you."

"I hope you won't, but yeah, you could." He extended a hand. "It was nice to meet you, Maggie."

She shook his hand and liked that he didn't grasp too hard or too soft. He walked away, and when he got to the door, he winked at her as he held it open for someone. Tara strode in, blocking Maggie's view of Eli as he left. Her cheeks were warm after the brief flirtation.

Tara waved before going to the counter to place her order. While Tara's back was to her, Maggie swiveled to see out the window, but Eli was gone. This had to be the strangest day of her life.

To her surprise, Moira came through the door a minute later. Maggie's heart sank. Her sister was afraid she'd screw this up, so she came to run interference. So much for turning her life around. She bit back the sigh when Moira waved like a crazy woman.

Moira and Tara hugged briefly. Tara waited for Moira to order and they approached Maggie's table together.

Maggie stood with her hand extended. "Hi, Tara. It's nice to meet you."

"You too," she said. They shook hands, and Tara took off her coat.

Moira did the same, and Maggie widened her eyes in question. Moira answered with a smile.

Once they were settled, Tara said, "I hope you don't mind, Maggie, but I asked Moira to meet with us. I think between the three of us, we can come up with a game plan."

So this was Tara's idea, not Moira's. Moira hadn't expected her to flop. She relaxed, and her lungs filled easily.

"A game plan for what?"

"My magazine. I want something along the lines of *Chicago Magazine,* but for a younger crowd. People in their late twenties and thirties aren't subscribing to a paper magazine. We live in an online world. My vision is to create a destination they'll come to daily." She took a drink from her cup.

Moira practically danced in her seat.

"That's where you guys come in. I know Moira can write. I've looked at your portfolio, and I think you'll be a good fit."

Maggie's heart started to race. Blood filled her ears, and she slowed her breathing so she wouldn't miss anything. This sounded like the opportunity of a lifetime.

"I want to take what Moira's already doing with the social scene and expand it to include more youthful events. Not that the charity stuff doesn't have a place, it does. But we can capitalize on a different market."

Tara spoke about investors and budgets. Although she spoke like a total businesswoman, her eyes lit the same way Moira's did when she was on a story. They talked for over an hour. Well, Tara and Moira talked, and Maggie mostly nodded.

More crap pay and lots of running around, but she felt like they were on the edge of something interesting and fun and exciting. Moira and Tara looked at Moira's schedule and created a plan. Maggie would tag along and take photos until she got used to the expectations of the job. Then she'd start to branch out and work with other writers as they came on board.

Maggie was almost floating as she left the shop. Even the cold air outside didn't ruin anything. In fact, if she took a deep-enough breath, she was sure she could smell spring. Just a hint, but it was enough to keep any Chicagoan motivated after a long and miserable winter.

She had been so excited about the work that she'd forgotten to tell Moira about Eli. She probably shouldn't jinx herself by talking about a cute guy she'd just met, since they didn't have plans for a date, but the whole day had set her buzzing. Sitting in her car, she wanted to tell someone about all her awesome news. She stared at her phone. Instinct had her thumbing Shane's number, but she paused.

Things were unsettled between them. This was definitely

the type of news she'd normally share with him, but she couldn't talk to him about a cute guy who might ask her out. Especially now. He'd accuse her of rushing into things again.

Instead, she called Olivia and made plans to meet at O'Leary's. As soon as she walked through the door, Maggie decided she needed to find some new places to hang out.

When Olivia arrived a short time later, all of Maggie's news bubbled out of her. Excited didn't begin to describe how she felt. After telling Olivia about the job stuff, she took a deep breath then said, "And while I was waiting for Tara, a cute guy asked me out."

"That's cool. Tell me everything."

"There's not much to tell. We were both sitting there and then our eyes locked and he smiled. And I smiled. Saying it like that makes me feel like I'm twelve years old. But then he came over and asked if he could sit with me, which I declined because of Tara. So he asked for my number instead."

Olivia's eyebrows wrinkled. "You didn't make plans for getting together?"

"No. I was just impressed that he not only came to talk to me but asked for my number. You know there are a lot of guys who won't even get that far. Plus, I was nervous."

"Has he called?"

"No. It's only been a few hours, though. You think I should call him?"

Olivia's hand shot up. "God, no. You want a guy who makes the first move and takes initiative."

"I thought this was the twenty-first century. You know, where women could do everything a man does?" She drank her water while Olivia sipped a martini.

"Of course, some guys like a forward woman, but you have to decide what kind of guy you like. Me, I like a man who takes charge."

Olivia's words caused a ripple of sensation through her.

Yeah, a man in charge was a definite turn-on. "It's not like a phone call turns me into a dominatrix."

"No, but it sets the tone for the relationship. Make him come to you."

"And if he doesn't?"

"Then move on."

"Sounds like a depressing race."

Olivia sighed. "Sometimes it is."

Maggie's phone vibrated on the table. She glanced at the screen. "Oh, my God. It's him. Eli."

"So answer, you goof."

Maggie waved her hand at her friend, and she accepted the call. "Hello."

"Hi, Maggie, it's Eli. Is this a good time?"

"Uh, sure."

"How did your interview go?" His voice was cool and warm all at once.

"Good. Great, actually."

"Excellent. I was calling to see if you're free for dinner tomorrow."

"Tomorrow?" She looked at Olivia, who nodded wildly. She was working the afternoon shift at the bar, so her evening was free. "Sure."

"Can I pick you up?"

She was so out of the dating loop that she wasn't sure how to answer.

"Or we can meet. Whatever you prefer."

Maggie's mind moved a mile a minute. If he picked her up, he would know where she lived. If they met there, it could be awkward having two vehicles. Although it would prevent her from sleeping with him on the first date. She laughed at herself. As if that were a possibility.

Olivia snapped her fingers in front of Maggie's face.

Maggie held up a finger. "You know. I'm working tomorrow. Why don't you pick me up there?"

She gave him the name and address of the bar and disconnected. Placing her phone back on the table, it hit her. She just made a date. Although Ian had been her boyfriend in Ireland, this somehow felt different. Ian had started out as a blind date her cousin had set up, so Maggie didn't have the whole first-meeting-will-it-end-in-a-date thing going on. She did now. A date with a total stranger. And she wasn't nervous.

"Hello," Olivia said. "What happened?"

"We're going out for dinner tomorrow. He's picking me up here."

"Is that a good idea?"

"Even if it's not, it's too late now. Besides, where else am I safer?" There was a time that sentence would never have left her mouth, but now she knew it to be true. "There are big, burly guys working here. My family is always around. Then there's Shane. I can't imagine a guy would want to bug me if it didn't work out."

But Todd had. He kept coming to the bar after she'd broken up with him. It had given him a chance to watch her. A sinking feeling settled in her. Maybe this was a bad idea.

Olivia reached across the table and grabbed her hand. "It's okay, Mags. Most guys are *not* Todd."

"I know." She'd been telling herself that for a long time.

$\mathcal{M}$aggie skated through the bar, trying to go unnoticed. She'd worked the lunch shift and then left earlier to meet with Tara again. She didn't want anyone to ask her to work extra hours tonight because she had her date with Eli. She headed for the kitchen to grab something to eat so she wouldn't look like a pig on her date.

As she snuck behind the bar, Mary called her.

Damn. She looked over her shoulder. "Sorry. I can't work tonight."

"No. We're good." She held up an envelope. "This came addressed to the bar with your name on it."

"Weird." Maggie grabbed the letter. Bile rose in her throat when she saw the return address. Todd's parents' house. Her hand shook.

"Are you okay?"

No. No, she was not fucking okay. "Is—Is Ryan here?"

"In the office."

Maggie stumbled away from the kitchen. Her body felt thick and fuzzy, no longer like hers. She opened the office door without knocking.

Ryan looked up. Her throat closed. She wasn't even sure she was breathing. But she must've been, because she was still thinking. Ryan said something into the phone and hung up.

Then he was in front of her, holding her shoulders, calling her name.

She pressed the envelope to his chest. Then tears started to fall. Tremors rattled through her whole body. Ryan gently pushed her onto the couch.

She leaned over and focused on breathing. Clearing her mind, deep inhale, but the air meagerly inched its way into her lungs.

The couch dipped beside her with Ryan's weight. She closed her eyes against the tears. Ryan rubbed her back. An image of Shane appeared. She would've given almost anything for him to have been there to comfort her.

"How?" The single syllable squeaked past her restricted airway.

"I told you he was getting out."

She rocked a little and pressed her forehead to her knees. Todd didn't matter. He no longer had a hold on her life. She was better. With a burst of energy, she stood. She swiped at her cheeks and looked down at Ryan.

"It's a letter of apology. He's been in therapy and wants to take responsibility for his actions."

"Fuck him."

"Do you want to read it?"

"Burn it." She stopped, remembering how important a trail of evidence could be. "No. Keep it so I can get a restraining order."

Oxygen flooded her system. This was her life and she wouldn't let Todd take any more from her. Again, she thought of Shane. Although he would've offered her comfort, he'd also seek revenge, like he had before. "Don't tell anyone about this. Especially Shane."

"I'm going to talk to Jimmy to see what we can do. This is the only one, right?"

She nodded.

"You okay?"

She swallowed hard. Her body was still shaky, but she was all right. "Yeah, I am."

He stood. "Maybe you should go home to Mom's."

"No. I live here. I'm going to my apartment. I won't let him drive me from it again. He doesn't get to do that."

"Want me to walk you up?"

"No. I'm good. Really." She wrapped her arms around her big brother.

She left through the back door and stomped up the steps. As she put her key in her lock, Shane called to her.

Maggie turned, widening her eyes with hope that he couldn't tell she'd been crying.

He took a step, suddenly looking nothing like the confident man she knew him to be. Just as he opened his mouth, the exterior doorbell rang and he turned to look through the door to see who it was.

Maggie took his momentary distraction as a sign for her escape. She slipped into her apartment and prayed Shane wouldn't follow. She couldn't face him right now. If he asked what was wrong, she'd tell him.

Once behind her locked door, she dropped her keys and bag on her counter. Why did it feel that for every step she made forward, something had to knock her back?

She crawled into bed to reboot her system. The pillow she held against her chest still smelled like Shane. She clutched it and breathed in his scent. She didn't know how long she lay there, but after a while, she remembered her dinner date with Eli.

Mostly, she wanted to cancel. She wouldn't be great company. But then she pushed out of bed. Not going on her date would be giving Todd space in her life.

Not happening.

She rushed through a shower and dressed quickly. Just as she applied makeup, Eli texted that he was parking. She raced out the door but slowed in front of Shane's so he wouldn't come looking for her again. He always knew the sound of her feet.

When she got back to the bar, she scanned the area for Eli. He stood near the front door watching the crowd. She strode over. "Hey."

He smiled. "Good to see you again. Are you ready?"

"Yep."

"Where do you want to go?"

"We can stay here if you don't mind."

"Really?"

"Sure." Being on her home turf might make things easier. "Your call."

She pointed over her shoulder. "We can get a table near the back."

He followed her through at a distance. Far enough that at one point she turned to make sure she hadn't lost him. They settled at a table and Maggie waved Kelly over to take their orders. Eli asked for a beer, but Maggie stuck with water. They decided to share an appetizer platter as their meal.

Eli told her about his job, manager of a sporting goods store. He shared funny stories about customers. While she smiled, nothing made her laugh, and she needed a good laugh.

He was the kind of guy who got into telling a story: voices, gestures, everything. It was almost like he was performing. And he was good at it.

When he talked, though, she didn't feel like he was

speaking to her. More like at her. He barely made eye contact.

Unlike Shane, who gave her his total attention whenever they were together.

She mentally slapped herself. Eli was not Shane. It was an unfair comparison. Shane had known her for a decade. First date nerves never came into play.

When dinner was finished, their conversation faded.

"I've had a good time tonight, Maggie."

"Thanks. So have I." She wasn't lying, but something kept her enthusiasm in check.

He stood and tossed money on the table, enough for the bill and a tip. "I'd like to see you again."

"I'd like that, too." At least she told herself that. "But I'm going to be busy working here all weekend because of Saint Patrick's Day." She stood.

"Okay. I'll give you a call." He leaned in and Maggie expected him to try to kiss her, but he offered an awkward hug with a pat on the back like she was a dude.

"Can I walk you to your car?" he asked.

"No, thank you. I'm going to talk with my friend for a few minutes before heading out." She wasn't ready for him to know she lived there.

She waited until he cleared the front door and she went out the back. As a first date, it might not have been perfect, but at least it wasn't a disaster.

SHANE HAD BUSTED HIS ASS FOR THE LAST FEW DAYS TO MAKE his apartment presentable. He had no idea what to expect from a home visit from a detective, but he did know that if he passed this phase, he would probably get hired. This was it. His dream of becoming a cop was finally happening. He hoped.

He hadn't seen Maggie since Monday. He wasn't sure what to think of that. They'd talked a couple of times and she told him briefly about this new job thing she had going on, but they never got around to discussing their relationship. It wasn't a conversation they could have over the phone.

She hadn't mentioned anything, so it was like she'd simply forgotten they'd fought. And slept together. Yet he couldn't get her out of his head. He'd gone to her apartment twice. More futile attempts to reach her.

Cara's words had haunted him all week. He'd finally decided to talk to Maggie, convince her they should give it a shot, and he couldn't track her down. He knew she was working the lunch shift today, but she'd made it clear that she wouldn't have this conversation at work. He sent her a text telling her to let him know when she got home. She hadn't responded.

With his apartment clean, Shane paced, feeling restless because he had nothing to occupy him. He felt itchy in his own skin. Nervousness over this visit made him miserable. If Maggie were here, she'd talk him down. She'd tell him he was being ridiculous. The visit was a formality. He would make a good cop.

When he heard footsteps in the hall, he raced for the door, sure it was Maggie. No way was he letting her escape again. He swung his door open as she turned her key in the lock.

"Maggie."

She turned, full-on deer in headlights. Fuck. This was *not* how they were. She looked upset, like maybe she'd been crying.

Just then, his doorbell sounded and he turned to see who was standing outside. In that brief moment, Maggie slipped into her apartment. From where he stood, Shane saw a guy in a suit waiting.

Shane was torn. He needed this interview, but he needed to talk to Maggie.

Damn. He strode to the door and opened it. The cold breeze wafted in.

"Mr. Callahan?"

"Yes."

"I'm Detective Carroll. Here for your home visit."

The man didn't look happy. Shane opened the door wider and led the way to his apartment.

In his living room, Shane tried not to fidget. Detective Carroll scanned the apartment and said, "I'm going to look around."

"Okay."

Shane leaned by the kitchen counter then moved back to his living room, wishing he'd bought furniture. Without the building materials he'd had here for weeks, the apartment was too empty. Every sound echoed.

He could hear drawers opening and closing. The door to his closet clicking. The inspection shouldn't take long, since he owned so little.

Detective Carroll came back to the living room. "Why no furniture?"

"I moved in not long ago. I haven't gotten around to getting some."

"Look, Callahan, I'm not going to lie to you. We have a problem here."

Shane's heart sank to his feet. He'd done everything right. What could be the problem?

"You live above a bar. I have to wonder why. Are you a drunk?"

"No."

"Why then?"

Shane thought of answers, wanted to be honest, but even in his own head, knowing his history with Maggie, they all sounded creepy.

"My friend's family owns the bar. This apartment was gutted and needed work done. They offered free rent to do the work. I was helping them out."

Carroll shook his head. "It doesn't look good. It's against department regulations."

Shane deflated. No imaginary pep talk would fix this.

"You did well on the tests. You're in the final stages. I don't see anything here that would cause a red flag, except for the location. If what you say holds true after I talk to your neighbors, I'll recommend you move to the next step."

"Thank you."

"But"—Carroll pointed at him—"before you can be hired, you have to move, which means it needs to happen fast." He moved toward the door. "We'll be in touch."

Shane stared at the door after Carroll left. His sole purpose for living here was Maggie. He'd have to leave her. *Maggie.* He dashed out the door and knocked on hers. No answer. He tried the knob. Locked, of course. She was definitely dodging him.

CHAPTER 22

*M*aggie ran around like a crazed woman. She had no idea how her life had become so full. She was juggling her new jobs because she wanted them so badly, but she still needed her job at the bar because it paid the bills. Then there was Eli.

In the days since their date, they'd talked and texted and she'd enjoyed their conversations. He was a fun guy with a great personality. She attributed the awkwardness at dinner to first date jitters. Plus, it wasn't like she was totally herself that night.

However, even she knew she couldn't assess her compatibility with a guy without kissing him. With the holiday hitting this weekend, she probably wouldn't see him for a couple days. How long did she want to wait to see him again?

She weighed whether it was a good idea to invite him to stop by the bar. Although she hadn't worked Saint Paddy's Day in years, she remembered how busy the bar was. She wouldn't have much time for socializing, but maybe she could take her dinner break with him. After bounding up the stairs to change for work, she almost skidded to a halt as she saw a guy standing in the hall talking to her neighbor. What did Shane say her name was? Janet?

Maggie knew she should be better at the neighbor thing, but their paths hadn't crossed. Just the one time the woman had asked Maggie about adjusting the radiators. She didn't know what the guy said, but Janet answered, "Oh, no. He's a great guy. He came over and fiddled with my heat for me."

Maggie let herself into her apartment, and before she locked the door, someone knocked. Assuming it was Shane, who she'd been avoiding, she swung the door open. It was the guy who had been talking to Janet. "Hi," she said cautiously.

"Hi. I'm Detective Carroll with the Chicago Police Department."

"Okay."

"I was wondering if I could ask you a few questions about your neighbor, Shane Callahan."

Shoot. This was about Shane. Did he do something wrong? Oh, God. What if Ryan told him about the letter from Todd?

Her questions must've shown on her face, because the detective followed with, "He's an applicant for the department, and it's standard procedure to do a home visit."

"Oh." She calmed her racing heart. "What do you want to know?"

"How well do you know Mr. Callahan?"

"Very. We've been friends since high school." She leaned against the doorframe and wondered if she was supposed to invite him in. Would it be better for Shane if she did?

"So you're Maggie O'Leary whose family owns the bar."

"I am."

"Mr. Callahan said he moved in to help your family out by doing work on the apartment."

"I guess so. I didn't ask. My brother handles all of that."

The man nodded and made a note in a notebook. "Does he spend a lot of time at the bar?"

"Define a lot."

One eyebrow rose.

"If you're asking me if he's a permanent fixture, no. Does he go there more often than someone who doesn't live upstairs? Yes. The food's good and Shane isn't much of a cook." She felt like she was stepping in a puddle of goo and not helping Shane, which was the last thing she wanted.

He nodded again. "Anything else you'd like to add?"

She straightened from her spot. "Shane is a good man. He'd make a great cop."

"Thank you for your time." He turned and pointed across the hall. "Do you know when your neighbor might be home?"

"Alex? I've only seen him once in the weeks I've been living here. He works nights and goes to school during the day, so he's hard to catch."

"Thank you again for your time."

Maggie locked up behind her and scrambled to change quickly. When she was ready for her shift at the bar, she peeked outside her door to make sure the coast was clear and then knocked on Shane's door. He didn't answer, so she knocked again.

When he opened the door, he was standing in a towel and nothing else, but drops of water cascading over his skin. She swallowed hard. She'd seen Shane like this probably hundreds of times. But holy crap he looked good. She imagined his broad, bare shoulders between her thighs as he went down on her. Her throat went dry. She shouldn't be thinking about him like that. Eli. Think of Eli.

Shane busted through her thoughts. "What's up? I'm trying to get ready."

"You're working tonight?"

"Yeah."

"There was a cop here a little while ago asking questions about you."

"I figured."

"You knew?"

"Yeah. I had my home visit. He said he'd be back to talk to my neighbors."

Her arms flew up. "Why didn't you tell me? Prepare me so I would know what to say? What if I screwed things up for you?"

"Did you answer his questions honestly?"

"Yeah."

He walked away from her but kept talking. "Then you couldn't screw it up."

She followed until she realized he was going into his bedroom. Where he would drop the towel and be totally naked until he pulled on clothes. This was way harder than she'd thought it would be. "But if I knew, I could've prepared something."

"He's a trained detective, Mags. I'm pretty sure he'd know if you were feeding him a line of bullshit."

His voice carried easily from the bedroom, where he hadn't closed the door. If she angled her body a little, she could probably see everything. She sighed. She'd already seen it all. Felt it all. She closed her eyes and rubbed. *Don't go there.*

He came from the bedroom dressed in jeans and an O'Leary's shirt. "Ready?"

"Yeah." She walked out the door and down to the bar.

As they went in, he said, "We still need to have a conversation."

Before she could respond, Jenna came up and grabbed Shane's arm. "Hey, there was a cop here—"

"I know. I'm on the applicant's list. They have to do a home visit."

"He wanted to know if you're always in here drinking. I told him no, but he didn't seem too thrilled. Then I explained you can't drink on the job." Jenna cringed.

Shane pulled from her grasp. "Shit."

Maggie asked, "What?"

"Cops can't work in bars. Not at all. Not ever. I didn't tell him I was working here."

"I'm sorry. I didn't know." Jenna's face was full of remorse.

"It's okay."

Maggie bumped his arm. "See? If you had warned us, we'd know. We would've been able to help."

"It's fine. It'll either work out or it won't."

HE SURE AS FUCK HOPED IT WORKED OUT. HE'D THOUGHT HE was okay. He wasn't technically working here, but the only one who knew that was Ryan. And because of the holiday this weekend, he was supposed to work.

Now he didn't know what to do. "Is Ryan here?"

"In back."

"I need to go talk to him. I'll be right back." He had no idea if Ryan could help or if he had any ideas, but if Carroll talked to him, Shane wanted to make sure Ryan told him that he absolutely did not work here. He knocked on the office door and waited for Ryan to call out.

He stuck his head in the office and asked, "Got a minute?"

"Sure. Come on in."

Shane walked to the center of the room and paused. He had no idea how to do this. Since he didn't have any older siblings, the idea of asking for help was foreign. But he'd seen Maggie in action plenty over the years. "I have a small problem. At least I hope it's small."

"What?"

"I don't know if Maggie mentioned it, but I applied to the police department, and although I've gone through a bunch of the steps, I've been on a waiting list." Ryan didn't comment, so he went on. "A detective came and did a home visit and wasn't thrilled that I live above a bar. If that wasn't bad enough, he came down here and talked to Jenna, who told him I work here."

"That's a problem?"

"Yeah. First, a cop can't work at a bar. Which isn't huge because I would just quit before starting the academy, but the bigger problem is that I didn't tell him. I didn't mention it because technically I don't work here."

"And now you look like a liar."

Shane nodded. "I assume he hasn't spoken to you?"

"No. What do you want me to say if he does?"

Shane shrugged. "I don't know what the right answer is now."

Ryan stood behind his desk. "Call Jimmy, Moira's fiancé. He's a cop. He'll know the best recourse." He wrote on a scrap of paper and handed it to him. "Jimmy's number."

"Thanks."

"You can still work this weekend, though, right?"

Tension knotted his muscles. He wanted to be here for Maggie. What was the likelihood one more weekend would ruin his chances of being a cop? Shane forced a smile. "Yeah. I'm heading out there now."

"I don't need you tonight. Tomorrow and Saturday should be plenty. Maybe Sunday too."

Shane hitched a thumb over his shoulder. "Maggie's working tonight."

"Okay."

Shane left the office and his muscles were still tense. Maggie was better and he probably didn't need to work tonight. She'd been fine earlier in the week. She even texted him when she got into her apartment.

But if he went back upstairs, he'd drive himself crazy thinking about Carroll and what he needed to say or do to get into the academy. Carroll had said Shane had to move. That meant leaving Maggie here.

He pushed all the thoughts out of his head. There was nothing else he could do tonight. He walked through the crowd of the bar, watching for troublemakers and drunks, but it was too early for any of that. So for a while, he just watched Maggie work.

She smiled as she served customers. Joked while she took orders. Laughed when another waitress leaned over to gossip in her ear.

Although he didn't necessarily enjoy the extra hours at the bar, he would miss seeing her every day.

MAGGIE WORKED HER SHIFT WITH ONE EYE ON THE CLOCK THE whole night. She'd planned for a late dinner break so she could spend time with Eli, since she wouldn't be able to see him all weekend. As much as she'd been watching the clock, Shane had been watching her. He hadn't accused her of dodging him, but that was only because she hadn't given him the chance to say much of anything.

She should probably tell him she had a guy coming to meet her. But she was a chicken. Something about what had transpired days ago picked at her. She didn't want to hear Shane tell her she was stupid for wanting to date Eli. She wasn't rushing into anything. They'd had dinner and talked. A lot. And now they'd have dinner again. It was normal, which was all she'd been looking for.

The bar was busier than she had expected. A constant

stream of customers filled her tables. By the time Eli walked in, her feet were crying for a break. She had no idea how she'd make it through the weekend.

She saw Eli before he saw her. She waved him over. He greeted her with a kiss on her cheek.

"This place is a madhouse."

"I know," she said, pulling him toward a free table. "I had no idea we'd be this busy. I wasn't expecting it to be like this until the weekend."

"If tonight's not good for you—"

"No. I'm due for a break. I can't sit for long, but I'm glad you came." Once he sat, she asked, "What do you want to drink?"

"A beer."

"I'll be right back."

She went to the bar, where Shane stood, still watching her. "Aren't you supposed to be watching the crowd?"

"I am. Who's the guy?"

Her skin warmed. "Eli. We met earlier this week. I asked him to stop by for dinner since I can't see him this weekend."

Shane crossed his arms and the muscle in his jaw twitched. "We still need to talk."

"About?"

"Us. This past weekend."

He was so serious. She didn't like this side of Shane. "I don't think there's anything to talk about."

"Maggie." His voice was soft, but she was able to hear him over the noise.

The bartender slid Eli's beer in front of Maggie. "I have to deliver this."

He laid a hand on her arm. "After we get off tonight, come to my apartment so we can talk."

The warmth of his firm grip reminded her of all the places his hands had been. She pulled away without answering. She didn't want to have whatever conversation Shane seemed to think was necessary. She just wanted to go back to being what they always were.

She delivered the beer to Eli. "Want something to eat? I think I can take my break now and hang out for a bit."

"I ate earlier. I came just to see you."

She didn't hide her smile. "I'm going to grab something. I'll be right back."

As she put in her order for a basket of fries, she asked Kelly to cover her tables for a bit. Most of her customers were fine, but she didn't want to take chances. Sharing a few tips when they were this busy wouldn't break her.

She grabbed her fries and a glass of water and went back to Eli's table. While they snacked on fries, they talked and laughed. Even though she enjoyed herself, Maggie couldn't stop thinking about Shane and what he wanted to talk about. What was there to say?

When Maggie stood to get back to work, Eli asked, "What time do you get off?"

"The bar closes at two. Then I have to help with cleanup."

"Can I call you later?"

"Won't you be in bed? You have to work in the morning, right?"

"Yeah, but I like to talk to you."

"Okay," she answered with a silly grin on her face.

Eli left, and Maggie returned to work. The night dragged on forever and it seemed like people had no intention of ever leaving. Her feet were killing her and all she wanted to do was crawl into bed. She almost raised her arms in praise when the bartenders yelled for last call.

Tables started to clear and Maggie cleaned and refilled napkins and salt as she made her way around the bar. If she stopped for too long, she might fall asleep. As she wiped a table clean, a conversation at the door caught her attention. She looked up.

Eli was back. Jake, the doorman, was stopping him from coming in. From the corner of her eye, she saw Shane stiffen and take a step. She hurried to the door. "Jake, it's okay. He's a friend."

Jake glanced down at her. "We're done serving."

Eli raised his arms. "I'm not looking to drink."

Maggie grabbed Eli's hand and pulled him past Jake. "What are you doing here?"

"I thought about calling you, but then I realized I'd rather see you. Do you have a few minutes?" He interlocked his fingers with hers. His hand wasn't much bigger than hers.

"Yeah."

"Can we go somewhere a little more private to talk?"

"Sure." She led the way toward the back. As she crossed into the back room, she almost crashed into Shane. When had he come back here? His eyebrows slammed together when he took in the scene, but he was on the phone, so he said nothing.

Maggie continued to walk until she got to the back hallway. The space was dimly lit, and except for anyone going to or coming from the bathrooms, they would be alone.

"Private enough?"

"Yeah."

She leaned against the wall and tilted her face up to look at him. "Why'd you come back?"

"Like I said, I wanted to see you. And give you a good night kiss." He leaned one arm against the wall by her head.

Her heart thumped, but she couldn't decipher whether it was a stab of panic at feeling trapped or good old-fashioned excitement. She took a deep breath. "You drove all the way back here for a kiss?"

He dipped his head and smiled. "I thought it might be worth it."

He lowered his mouth to hers and their lips met. Although he started slow, Eli moved from easy to hard and fast in an instant. It wasn't a bad kiss, but all her mind and mouth, for that matter, could focus on was how different this was compared to Shane's kiss last weekend. Someone called Maggie's name from the other side of the room.

Eli pulled away. Maggie straightened. With her arm she pointed vaguely toward the bar. "I have to …"

"Yeah. Good night, Maggie."

"'Night." She moved back to the bar to finish closing. Eli walked past her and out the front door. She looked around to find Shane, but he wasn't around. She tapped Kelly on the shoulder. "Have you seen Shane?"

"Uh, yeah. He said he had to take a phone call, and since he was done for the night he went upstairs to talk."

"Oh." Well, at least if he was already upstairs, he couldn't corner her into having a conversation. Her kiss with Eli just muddled things even more. She liked Eli. She wanted to give him a shot, which meant she needed to get Shane out of her mind.

CHAPTER 23

Shane paced in his empty living room talking with Jimmy O'Malley. He'd already laid out what had happened during his home visit with Carroll and the interviews Carroll had done with Maggie and Jenna.

Jimmy sighed. It was late and the man was probably exhausted, but Moira had made him return Shane's call tonight. Those O'Learys were a pushy bunch.

"I don't know Carroll, but I do know a lie is more than just a red flag during the hiring process."

"But I didn't lie."

"Doesn't matter. It comes across that way. Your best bet is to call Carroll first thing tomorrow and explain."

"Do I tell him about Maggie?"

"Crap. That's a catch-22. From the outside, it sounds like you're a stalker. But I don't know if that's better than being a liar when it comes to being at the bar."

"Is this going to bump me off the list?"

"I have no idea. I've heard of guys doing a lot of stupid shit during the last couple of steps and it ruins their chances.

If you're honest, especially before the final interview, I think you'll score some points."

"Okay. Thanks."

"He was serious about moving, though. You can't play around with that and you can't lie. They're going to want proof that you've moved."

What he wouldn't give for a couch to sit on right now. Or a table to kick. "Yeah, Carroll made that point. Thanks for all your help. You didn't need to call me this late. It would've kept."

"No problem. Moira's persistent."

Shane still wasn't sure how Moira had gotten involved, but he was glad she had. Shane disconnected and took a shower. No matter how hot he made the water, his muscles wouldn't loosen. Between the mess with the CPD and seeing Maggie drag some guy she barely knew through the bar, he was a mess.

He needed to talk to Maggie. No matter what, he had to move. Maybe he could talk her into moving as well. If they gave their relationship a shot, they could live together. That would solve at least half his problems.

As he dried off, he reminded himself he was moving too fast. He hadn't even talked to Maggie about them. And she'd insisted on dating this other guy. What did that say about her feelings for Shane? He pulled on a pair of sweatpants and checked the time. Maggie should be done cleaning up by now.

He walked to her apartment and knocked. She didn't answer. He supposed it was possible that she came up and fell asleep already; she'd looked exhausted tonight.

Or maybe she went home with the other guy, a small voice poked at him.

No. He shoved that thought away. Maggie wouldn't. She had more sense. He went back to his apartment and lay down on his bed. Maybe they were running late downstairs and she'd come knocking in a few minutes.

~

MAGGIE FINISHED WORKING, SAID GOOD-BYE TO HER coworkers, and then crept up the stairs as quietly as humanly possible. She didn't have it in her to talk to Shane tonight. Childish? Yes. But she didn't care. Tomorrow night would start the holiday revelry, and she needed to have her shit together. Unfortunately, by the time she got to bed, sleep eluded her.

She kept thinking about Eli. They'd had a lot of fun over the last few days. They shared a spark. Then she thought about the kiss. Did she really feel a spark, or was she convincing herself she had?

Her phone buzzed on her nightstand. She cringed, afraid it was Shane, but the screen lit with Eli's name. A short text: Still awake?

Unfortunately. Hard to get settled after a long night.

You just need to relax.

She laughed. As if she had any shot of that happening.

I could help both of us fall asleep. What are you wearing?

The simple conversation had taken a turn. An orgasm would definitely help her sleep. If Eli could bring her there? Even better. Her hand glided along the flannel sleep shirt she wore. Not very sexy.

Nothing.

Good. That makes things easier. Imagine me lying next to you. I kiss your lips and work my way down. I lick your neck and feel your pulse pick up. I pinch your nipple, just enough to get you to moan.

Maggie moved her hand to her nipple and tugged.

You with me?

Yeah.

I kiss my way down your body, running my tongue over ever inch. Then I'd stroke your pussy. Is it wet?

Yeah.

I bet it tastes good.

Maggie rubbed her clit in slow circles, but slow didn't last long. She dropped her phone and closed her eyes. As soon as her lids shut, all she saw was Shane's head between her legs. She remembered the look in his eyes as he went down on her.

Her eyes flew open. No. This was supposed to be her and Eli. Her phone buzzed.

You're not into this, are you?

The guilt sat on her chest. She didn't want to hurt his feelings, or worse ding his ego. It wasn't his fault. I'm trying, but it's not working. Maybe I'm more tired than I thought.

Then I guess we'll have to try in person.

Maybe. We'll see.

I'll call tomorrow.

I'm working late again—all weekend.

Okay. Good night.

Good night.

She lay staring at her ceiling trying to sort things out. For a while, she'd been imagining some big guy in her fantasies. It only made sense that now that she was back home and seeing Shane almost daily, he would take over the mental image. Especially after last weekend.

God, that had been *so* good. Phenomenal. A huge part of her was afraid she would never find that with anyone again. No, she would. She just had to give it time. And give Eli a real chance. She picked up her phone.

How about we meet for dinner before my shift? There's a restaurant down the street we can meet at.

I'll be there.

~

SHANE DID WHAT JIMMY O'MALLEY SUGGESTED AND HE called Detective Carroll. The man didn't answer, so Shane left a message. All afternoon, Shane sat with his phone in his hand, willing it to ring.

He had never been so nervous as when it finally did ring.

"Hello."

"Mr. Callahan, this is Detective Carroll returning your call."

"Hi. Thank you for calling back. I think there's been some confusion, and I don't want it to negatively impact my chances for getting on the force."

"What's that?"

"I know you were asking about me downstairs at O'Leary's Pub. I didn't mention on my application that I work there because I don't. Like I told you, I'm friends with the owner, so I fill in when they need some extra help."

Carroll didn't respond and Shane couldn't interpret silence.

"My job, the one that pays the bills, is as a carpenter. I don't rely on the bar for anything."

"If that's the case, Mr. Callahan, I suggest you not only find a new place to live but also stop working there, even to help out."

Shane blew out a heavy breath. "Does that mean I still have a shot?"

"Probably. We'll be in touch. If you get the call for the interview, make sure you can provide documentation of the changes I told you to make."

"I will. Thank you." Shane disconnected and struggled with the combination of emotions gripping him. He was relieved and anxious that his application appeared to be safe, but the nagging thought of leaving here, and Maggie, stabbed at him.

It wasn't the bar or the apartment, even though he had put in a ton of work. He knew it was Maggie that tore at him.

She already appeared to be moving on, just like she said she would. Granted, they'd only had the weekend together, but he knew they had feelings for each other. He couldn't understand why she didn't see it. Surely if she did, she wouldn't be searching for some other guy.

He looked at his apartment. At least he didn't have much to pack. He wondered how he'd be able to find an apartment to move into immediately. He supposed he could always move home, but he really wanted to avoid that. The idea of living with any of his sisters again was enough to knot his muscles.

He loved his sisters, but Riley still lived at home and both Cara and Alyson showed up at least as often as he did. He needed his own space. Looked like he'd have to get his laptop back from Maggie for sure so he could apartment hunt. He changed into his O'Leary's shirt and headed down to the bar for his first paid shift. The crowds would be crazy and would only get worse through the weekend. Keeping an eye on Maggie might prove to be impossible.

After knocking on Maggie's door and not getting an answer, he jogged down the steps and pulled up short at the bar's back door.

～

FRIDAY AFTERNOON, MAGGIE WAS DETERMINED TO HAVE A good time with Eli. They ate pizza and laughed about their failed attempt at sexting the previous night. She was at ease with him, which she considered a sure sign they had possibilities. He held her hand and walked her back to the bar before her shift.

She checked the time. "I'm a little early. Let's take a walk."

He continued to hold her hand and she led him around the corner and down the alley toward the back door of the bar. She stopped there.

"I had a great time tonight. I wish we could hang out more, but the bar will be slammed the whole weekend because of Saint Patrick's Day. I usually don't work this many hours."

"I understand." He leaned back against the brick building, tugging her with him.

This was what she'd been hoping for by bringing him around back. He wrapped an arm around her waist and pulled her tight to his body. He was only about six inches taller than her, so they lined up pretty well. She closed her eyes and leaned in.

It was like he was waiting for her mouth. He didn't make a move other than his first to pull her close. She connected her lips to his, brushed them, and stroked her tongue along them. His hands stayed planted at her hips.

She wanted more: more movement, more action, more passion.

The hairs on her neck bristled to attention, and she knew Shane was there. Felt his gaze on her skin. One look from him, one that she couldn't even see, made her blood race more than having Eli's tongue in her mouth.

Man, was she fucked up.

The back door to the bar slammed with Shane's entrance, and Maggie pulled away. "I have to get in. My shift's about to start."

"Have a good night."

She backed away. "You, too."

As she walked through the back of the kitchen, she wiped

her hand over her mouth. She got to the wall where employees stowed their things in cubbies, and Shane was waiting for her.

"A little old to be making out in an alley, aren't you?"

"We were not making out. It was a kiss." *And not a very good one.* She bit her tongue before those last words could escape. She *really* didn't need Shane's "I told you so."

They walked out to the bar together, and she couldn't believe her eyes. As crowded as they'd been last night, tonight was a wall of people from one end of the bar to the other. "Holy crap."

Shane muscled his way through the bodies and found a spot near the archway that divided the back of the bar and the front. Maggie wrapped her apron at her waist and checked in with Mary and Ryan. This wasn't going to be like a regular shift where she had a station to focus on. In addition to her station, people would flag her down from where they stood in the middle of the floor.

A band was doing a sound check on stage. It was about to get even louder. Maggie pushed all thoughts of guys out of her head and focused on the job. With her pad in her pocket, she walked through the crowd and began taking orders. By the time she delivered the first round, the band had started playing Irish folk music.

The sounds brought her back to her childhood, and she wished she could just stand and enjoy. Someone came up and bumped her shoulder. Maggie turned and saw Moira standing beside her.

"Is it like this every year?"

Moira wobbled her head side to side. "Kind of. It's worse this year because the actual holiday lands on the weekend."

"I'm kind of glad I've missed out on this. It's crazy."

"Yeah, but it's the good kind of crazy."

Maggie lost track of how many employees Ryan had

working. At least two fights were broken up, and twice Shane had to help muscle her through a crowd to deliver orders. Unlike the other bouncers, who simply created a path for her to follow, Shane held her close, one time carrying the tray over his head for her. When he'd put his hand on her hip to guide her through, she'd had a hard time focusing on where she needed to go.

So much for putting men out of her mind. Some of them, she'd like to do more than put out of her mind. As the night wore on, the guys got friendlier and handsier. But Shane acted as her personal bodyguard. She never had to do more than slightly admonish a guy. If another attempt was made, Shane was at her back.

He hadn't thrown anyone out, but Maggie was convinced it had been unnecessary because of the look on Shane's face.

The music was loud and fun. At one point, Moira grabbed her hand and yelled, "Let's dance."

Maggie pulled back, but Moira insisted. She had the band play a song and the two of them did an Irish step dance together like they had as kids. Tomorrow night they would have a real dance troupe performing, but the drunks at the bar were impressed with the O'Leary sisters and their hacked-up, half-remembered steps.

They left the stage completely out of breath from laughing. Customers shoved singles at them for tips as they walked by. Shane met her by the arch and handed her a glass of water. She grabbed it and gulped. "Thanks."

"You looked cute up there."

She rolled her eyes. "You saw the same dance last week."

"But it's better when there are two of you having fun."

"Yeah. It was better." She finished the water. "Well, back to work."

Before she walked back to the bar with her glass, Shane

grabbed her arm. "Don't think I've forgotten about our conversation."

"I know." But she didn't say more. She dropped her glass off at the bar and walked the room clearing empty bottles and taking orders.

By the time the night was done and the last customer left, Maggie was dead on her feet. She looked around the room. All of the O'Learys were there, plus the regular staff filled the space.

Ryan stood at the bar. "Can I have everyone's attention?"

Movement across the room stopped. Everyone faced Ryan.

"First, I want to thank you all for your hard work tonight. We had very few problems and most people seemed to enjoy themselves. I've got a skeleton crew on during the day tomorrow because I'm hoping it won't be too busy. At least until the parade is over. We still have a lot of cleanup to do, but I think you all deserve a drink."

No one moved.

Colin yelled, "Come on. Belly up to the bar."

Everyone moved like a wave. Maggie followed and Ryan and Colin poured shots and beer for everyone. Maggie reached for a glass of beer.

Shane looked at her. "A beer?"

She nodded. "I had a couple at Moira's last weekend. They were good."

When everyone had a drink in hand, Colin raised his. "To Patrick O'Leary for founding one hell of a bar. And to all my O'Leary siblings for showing up today. Sláinte."

Maggie took a drink of her beer. It wasn't as good as the bottled beer she'd had last weekend, but it wasn't bad. She took another sip.

Shane's mug was already half empty. "You're really going to drink a beer. I can't believe it."

"Why?"

"Because you stopped drinking five years ago."

She quirked an eyebrow. "I'm restarting a lot of things I stopped doing five years ago."

Although she'd had only a few swallows of beer, she might as well have been drunk to say something like that.

But Shane smiled. "So you are. That's one of the things we need to talk about."

"What do you mean?"

"This guy you were with—"

"Eli."

"Yeah." His *yeah* was every bit a *whatever*. "Is it serious?"

"How can it be serious? We just met and went out a couple of times. The important thing is that I want to give him a chance. For the first time in forever, I want to see what happens."

She studied his face and tried to figure out where he was going with this. She wrapped her arm around his. "I know you worry, but I'm okay. I'm not rushing anything." She smiled up at him. "Well, maybe I rushed the kiss with him, but you know how important a kiss is. If that's not right, nothing else matters."

"Is it?"

"Is what?"

"The kiss right?"

She took another gulp of beer to avoid answering, but Shane was relentless anytime he asked a question. He was going to make one hell of a cop. A long, slow inhale and then she said, "I'm not sure yet."

Shane snorted and disengaged his arm. He grabbed a broom and started sweeping. She ran around to get in front of him. "Hey, what is that supposed to mean?"

"Nothing."

"Come on. Say it."

He leaned the broom against a table and took two steps toward her. His eyes were hard but not angry. She backed up and bumped into the corner of a booth. Shane kept coming.

"A kiss isn't something to have to think about or decide on. It's right or it's not. In the moment you can't think. You don't analyze. You just feel. And if you're telling me you're not sure, this guy doesn't know what he's doing."

He stood so close that she felt his breath on her face, a warm caress to go with what felt like a warning.

"What do you know?"

He took a full step back. "I know what I'm doing. You know it, too."

Then he turned and went back to sweeping the floor. Maggie stared at him, not sure what to say or do. This was a different side to Shane. This was the Shane that burned a hole in her back while she kissed Eli. This was the Shane who was bossy and controlling.

Unfortunately, she had no idea what any of it meant or what she was supposed to do with it. So she did what she did best: She walked away.

CHAPTER 24

Shane and Maggie worked the weekend with a barely perceptible rift between them. Frustration consumed him. He'd almost kissed her the other night at the end of their shift. He'd been too wound up hearing her talk about giving Eli a chance. He'd wanted to shout that *he* deserved a chance, but that would make him sound insane.

So he dialed it back. His life was out of kilter and he couldn't afford to take it out on Maggie. They needed to have a conversation, a real one without the O'Leary's staff standing by.

He knew the chemistry exploded between him and Maggie. He'd be able to convince her they could be more. But first he had to tell her about moving out and on. He didn't want to start a new relationship with lies between them.

She had the night off at the bar, and he'd already told Ryan that he was done. He ordered a pizza to be delivered to her apartment and now he was just waiting for her to get home. That morning in passing she mentioned a new job, something to do with Moira, and then left.

A thump on his door let him know she was home. "I have pizza."

He swung his door open and Maggie stood there with a bright smile, holding their dinner.

"I have excellent timing. I pulled up right behind the delivery guy. I'm starving." She spun on her heel and walked across the hall.

Sometimes he forgot how much of a whirlwind Maggie could be. He followed into her apartment and watched her carefully lock up. "You look happy."

"It's amazing. I thought when I met with Moira and her friend Tara that I was heading into something good. I told you about that, right? Anyway, part of me was hesitant because, let's face it, I'm not a photographer, but it's fun. And like Moira always says, why work a job you hate? I'm so glad I tried."

Another thing he forgot about Maggie was when she spent a lot of time with Moira, she started to talk like her. He remembered that being at the O'Leary house and listening to the two of them talk was like being caught between dueling tornadoes.

"Are you listening?" She grabbed some water from the fridge as he opened the pizza box.

"Yes, I'm listening."

She inhaled, and he took note of the tight sweater she wore. Bright blue to match her eyes. "So this weekend, even though I knew it would mean going on almost no sleep, I went to the parade and took some pictures and then I snapped some shots on my phone at the bar." She grabbed a slice of pizza and bit into it.

Shane ate without responding because he figured she had more to say.

"I had to play with the ones from the bar, but the parade turned out great. Tara loved them. She definitely wants me to do more, cover more events for her. She plans to launch her online magazine at the beginning of the summer."

"Online?"

"Digital only. In the meantime, Moira and I are going to help her build content for a soft launch."

Shane ate his pizza and tried to figure out what language Maggie spoke. He had no idea what she was talking about. "What does all this mean?"

"It means I'm getting in on the ground floor of a new magazine. If it succeeds, so do we. Although Tara is the main backer, Moira and I are here at the beginning. It's exciting to start something new. To build something."

"Yeah, it is. You don't have plans tonight, do you?"

"I actually have to go take some pictures at a community fun fest for the newspaper Moira got me in with."

"So you're really doing this. Becoming a photographer."

"I think so. I thought about going back to school, but nothing is grabbing me. I'm having fun."

They ate in silence for a few minutes.

"What about you? What happened with the police?"

"Well, I still have a shot, but I need to move out of here and not work at the bar anymore."

"Oh."

"But Detective Carroll led me to believe that if I do that, I'm in. I'll be in the next round of recruits."

"Congratulations." Her voice held no enthusiasm.

"You don't sound very happy for me."

"I am. I mean, I know you want this, but being a cop is a dangerous job. It's scary."

"I'll be fine. I take a greater risk working in the bar." He finished off his pizza and water. "But I wanted to talk to you about the rest. I'm going to be moving out pretty fast."

"Like how fast?"

"Hopefully within a week." He huffed out a breath, not

knowing how to soften the next part. "I think you should move out, too."

"Why? I just got settled."

He knew that no matter how he answered this, she would get mad, but he had to say it. "I won't be here."

"So? We'll see each other often, I hope."

"But I won't be here, Mags. You're already moving on from working at the bar. Move out."

"Wait. I didn't say I was quitting at the bar. Yeah, I have new jobs lined up, but they won't pay the bills yet. I have to keep waitressing. Although I'll miss having you around, you not being here won't have an impact on me keeping my job."

He blew out a heavy breath. "I don't want you to stay here. Not working. Not living."

"So sorry to disappoint you."

Grabbing her hand, he tried again. "I know you're feeling better, Maggie. Things are going well. But I moved in here and worked at the bar so I could keep an eye on you. I didn't trust anyone else to do it."

She slid away from him and crossed her arms. "You told me you were working at the bar to get money for Cara. That it was Ryan's idea for you to move in."

"I stretched the truth a little."

"You lied."

"But I did it for the right reasons. If I told you the truth, you would've been pissed."

"I *am* pissed."

He tamped down his own anger. And hurt. The pain always accompanied the guilt. "Don't you get it? I couldn't live through that again. If I had paid closer attention five years ago…If I had watched you then—"

Her voice was quiet but strong. "There wasn't a damn thing you could've done. Nothing that happened was your fault."

Her words didn't erase the guilt. "Maybe not my fault, but I could've prevented it."

"Don't turn this around. I don't want to feel sorry for you right now, Shane. You *lied* to me. You acted like you were in my corner. Like you believed in me. But you're no better than my brothers."

He reached out again, but she backed away. "Being like your brothers isn't a bad way to live. They care about you and love you and want you to be safe."

"By treating me like a child."

"Have I ever treated you like anything other than the woman you are? Maybe I didn't go about it the best way—"

She snorted hard enough that the neighbors probably heard.

"But my intentions were good. And I'm being honest now because I don't want there to be lies between us."

"So it's okay to lie when we're neighbors and have to work together, but as soon as that convenience is over, it's time to come clean?"

"No. I don't want lies between us as a couple. I want us to be a goddamn couple, and you're not making this easy."

She stopped whatever she was going to say and stood with her mouth hanging open. That wasn't exactly the way he'd planned to approach the topic, but it was out there now.

"Oh, my God. I can't believe you."

Not the reaction he was going for. She sounded even more pissed, if that was possible.

"How could you? You figure that playing the guilt card didn't work so now you play on my insecurities when it comes to relationships? Get out."

What? He didn't even understand what she was saying. "I'm not playing anything, Maggie."

She didn't answer, but turned her back on him. "Go home, Shane. I have to get ready for work."

Shane left her and went back to his apartment totally bewildered. He'd known she'd be mad, but he hadn't expected it to be that bad. He felt like he just fucked up the best thing in his life by being honest. The most he could hope for now was to give her time and space to cool off. To process what he'd said.

Then he'd try to explain again. He had to make her understand.

~

SHE COULDN'T BELIEVE SHANE'S AUDACITY. HOW COULD HE use her emotions against her? She just got to the point where she could have a relationship, and he toyed with her to get her to do what he wanted. She was half surprised he didn't try to blame that on Ryan as well.

She stomped through her apartment cleaning up their dinner mess, and then she changed her clothes to look professional for the fun fest for a school district she was covering for the paper. After work, she had another date with Eli. Tonight, she'd planned to tell him about being raped. Although they'd known each other only a couple of weeks, she knew most guys were looking to get laid a few dates into a relationship.

The fun fest was lively but exhausting. She took lots of photos, and then she headed back into the city to meet Eli. She wondered how he would take it. He would be the first guy she ever talked to about it. Her stomach revolted, and she regretted the pizza she'd had with Shane earlier.

Eli wanted to meet at a bar, and she figured since it was the middle of the week, they could find a quiet corner to talk. She could do this. She'd talked to Shane about all of it, even some of her freakishness, and he hadn't walked away.

But he's Shane. He never leaves.

Parking in the lot of the neighborhood bar Eli had chosen, she told that little voice to shut the hell up. She was still pissed at Shane. No warm fuzzy feelings for him today.

She flipped her visor down, checked her makeup, and smiled. No, she didn't look nervous, not at all. As she walked into the bar, she pulled out her phone and texted Eli.

He responded, Parking now. Be right in.

While she waited, she scoped out the place, looking for a quiet booth. She found one that faced the door, so she could see Eli come in. She hung her jacket on the hook on the edge of the booth and sat.

Eli walked through the door, phone in hand, and scanned the bar. It took him a couple of sweeps and her waving for him to see her. He strode over, kissed her cheek, and took the spot across from her.

"Hi. How are you?"

"Good."

"Looks like you survived Saint Patrick's Day."

"Barely. It was crazy all weekend."

A waitress interrupted. Maggie ordered water and Eli ordered a brandy. Maggie tried not to cringe. This would definitely test her.

When the waitress left, Eli said, "So, what did you want to talk about?"

Maggie wished she'd ordered her drink when she came in. It would give her hands something to do besides fidget. "I like you."

"That's good because I like you, too."

"But I need to tell you something before we try to take our relationship further."

The waitress dropped off their drinks, and Maggie took a gulp of water. Setting the glass back on the table, she used it as an anchor. "I haven't been with many guys. In fact, I've dated very little compared to most women my age."

Another deep breath. "That's because five years ago I was raped."

Once the words came out, she wanted to hide. She had nothing to be embarrassed about. She knew that in her head, but something else washed over her and crawling under the table sounded like a good idea. Her eyes left the cool ice in her glass and met Eli's.

"Wow. I don't know what to say."

"You don't have to say anything. It's just important that you know."

"Did they get the guy?"

The air left her lungs. Her heart squeezed. Her throat thickened. Of all the questions she thought he might ask, this hadn't been one. How should she answer?

Slowly, carefully, she pushed words from her mouth. "I knew who it was. He was my ex-boyfriend."

Confusion came into Eli's eyes. "Oh. So it wasn't like he dragged you into an alley and tore off your clothes or something."

A burst of anger hit her. It seemed as though she had an abundance of that to go around today. "That doesn't make it any less of a rape."

"I didn't mean…I just…" He drank his brandy in one gulp. The glass hit the table with a loud thunk. "I get that it was rape, but it's not the same, you know. The level of violence."

Her anger turned to rage. This was part of why she never wanted to talk to people about this. Her hands shook, and she clasped them in her lap. After clenching and unclenching her jaw a couple of times, she leaned forward. "My ex-boyfriend drugged me and raped me. I was incapacitated and couldn't give consent. He put his dick inside me. Without my permission. What greater violation is there?"

She stood. She had to get out of here. While she yanked her jacket off the hook, Eli stood.

"Maggie, wait."

She turned to face him, but the disgust she felt right now wouldn't allow her to hear anything.

"I wasn't trying to upset you."

"But you weren't very thoughtful either. I'm leaving."

"Are you okay to drive?"

"I'm fine." She walked away from him, repeating that all the way to her car. Eli was not the first person to take that attitude with her, and she knew better than to let it get to her like this, but she couldn't help it. It was easier to not have this conversation with people.

Her hands were still shaking when she got to her car. She started the engine, but just sat while her body calmed and she got her emotions in check.

She should've known. At the kiss, she should've known. Shane had been right. If the kiss was wrong, it wouldn't work. She needed to follow her gut. Her brain engaged with too much noise. Her gut would tell her what felt right.

CHAPTER 25

Shane packed his meager belongings into the boxes he never got around to throwing out when he'd moved in. Something to be said for laziness. It seemed silly to pack when he had nowhere to go yet, but he needed something to do. Dwelling on his conversation with Maggie wasn't doing him a lick of good.

He did some apartment hunting but was too restless to even focus. What he wouldn't give to have a TV right now. Shit, he'd settle for a couch to sit on. The apartment looked good, though, so Ryan shouldn't have a problem finding a renter.

The cookie plate Janet gave him sat on his counter, and an idea struck. He could return the plate and maybe get invited in. She probably had a TV he could watch. So it was a little disingenuous, but he was desperate. His only other choice was the bar downstairs or his parents' house. Or maybe Alyson might be home. He shot Alyson a quick text.

She answered: Sure come on over.

That was a relief. Going to see Janet would probably give her the wrong idea, and he'd done enough of that for one night. He drove over to his sister's apartment and, after circling the block, found a spot that would allow him to park without a permit. As he walked down the street to her building, he filled his lungs with fresh air. It was still cold, but the barest hint of spring was there.

He couldn't wait. The winter had lasted much too long, and he loved summer. He rang Alyson's bell, and she buzzed him up. She met him at the door with a worried expression.

"What's wrong?"

"Nothing."

"Then why are you here? You never visit me."

He took off his coat and hung it on a hook near the door. "I'm bored and I live in an apartment with no furniture and no TV."

She crossed her arms and narrowed her eyes. "There's more."

He walked past her and patted her shoulder. "Maybe. But it's nothing I want to talk about. Got any beer?"

She sighed. "In the fridge."

When he came back to the living room, he took a spot on the recliner she had facing the TV.

"Did you have something special you wanted to watch, or can I pick?"

He slugged back some beer. He could've stayed at the bar and gotten drunk without worrying about driving home. All he wanted to do was forget the fiasco with Maggie. "Whatever you want."

"Excellent. I have *The Bachelor After the Final Rose* saved on my DVR. I've been waiting for this."

He groaned. Getting drunk at O'Leary's was looking better by the moment. Alyson curled up on the couch with a huge bowl of popcorn on her lap and glass of pop on the table. Shane moved to sit next to her to steal her popcorn.

She absently handed him the bowl as the show opened with scenes of some sap handing out roses.

"You can't possibly believe any of this is real, right?"

"Shhh." She waved a hand at him.

He grunted and shoved more popcorn into his mouth. The show wasn't as boring as he'd thought it would be. Some snippy remarks by one woman nearly led to a cat fight. That would've been worth watching. Instead they played a montage meant to show how in love the couple was. As if.

When the forty-three minutes rolled to an end, Shane reached for the remote. "I cannot sit through something like that again."

Alyson shot him a look. "No sports."

She sounded like Maggie. Damn. He was here trying to forget Maggie. He flipped through channels, but felt Alyson's eyes on him. "Stop staring at me."

"I'm trying to figure out what the deal is. You're in my apartment when you could've gone to Mom and Dad's. Or Maggie's. Didn't Dad tell me you lived next door to each other?"

"She's not home."

"Why here?"

"Because you're my favorite sister."

"Now I know you're full of shit."

He tossed the remote on her lap. "You choose something if it'll keep you quiet."

"Oh, now you've done it. No Callahan man has ever given up the remote without cause. Do I need to call Cara and Riley? You know you don't stand a chance when we're together."

"Alyson. Shut. Up."

"Okay, must be girl trouble. If it was work or something equally as boring, you'd never want to keep it from me. I didn't know you were dating anyone."

"I'm not."

She pulled out her phone. "I'm texting Cara. She'll have ideas."

Shane snatched her phone and shoved it between the couch cushions.

"So Cara knows but you won't tell me?"

"This isn't a joke, Alyson. I came here to forget shit tonight."

"Well, someone taught you wrong. You don't forget with a bottle of beer and *The Bachelor*. You need shots for that." She stood and went to her kitchen. She returned with a bottle of cheap whiskey and shot glasses.

She set the glasses and poured. "To forgetting." She raised a glass and tossed the whiskey back.

Shane followed suit. After Alyson poured him two more shots, he felt better.

"Now are you gonna tell me?"

"I fucked up."

She laughed. "You're a guy. Guys always fuck up. Who with?"

"Maggie."

"Ah, damn. What'd you do? Try to get in her pants?"

He chuckled. "Didn't try. Succeeded, and it was her idea."

"Yay!" She smiled and was about to clap, but then frowned. "That's not what you want to forget, is it?"

"No. I want to forget shit I said tonight. It's complicated. I lied to her, but it was for a good reason. I came clean tonight because I wanted to tell her we should give us a shot. Somewhere in the conversation, she twisted everything up and thought I was manipulating her." He filled his glass again and downed the whiskey.

"Were you?"

"Hell, no. She didn't believe anything I said."

"Well, in her defense, you did just admit to being a liar. Why should she believe you?"

He knew he'd had too much to drink when his sister's logic made sense.

"So where did it go wrong, other than the lying part?"

"I think I blurted out that I wanted us to be a goddamn couple and she was being difficult."

Alyson reached for the bottle and poured him another shot. "You're an idiot."

"I know." He drank. "Why'd you say that?"

"Because that was no declaration of love. You made a demand and called her names. More or less. Was that supposed to win her over?"

"No. That's not how it was supposed to go. But she got so mad and she was yelling and accusing me of things and said she wouldn't feel sorry for me." He sagged against the couch.

"Why the hell would she feel sorry for you?"

"She shouldn't, but she thought I wanted her to. 'Cause I feel guilty about her getting raped. And I should feel guilty. It was my job to keep her safe, and I fucked up then, too." His head lolled to the left, and his sister looked a little blurry. "Am I ever gonna get it right?"

"You're drunk."

He narrowed his eyes. "You're not. How'd that happen?"

"A sister never shares her secrets."

"Not cool."

"You'll get it right, Shane. She loves you."

"But I want it all with her. Not just part of her. And she's looking to give it all to some other guy." He pointed at Alyson. "Eli. What kind of lame name is that?"

"Is he cute?"

"Hey! You're supposed to be on my side." He grabbed a handful of popcorn. "And I'm better looking anyway."

"Modesty's not a problem here."

"Did I eat dinner?" He thought back through his night. His stomach sloshed the alcohol around. Pizza. He'd eaten pizza with Maggie. It felt like forever ago.

"Are you hungry? I can make you a sandwich. I think I have peanut butter and jelly."

"I hate peanut butter."

"You do?"

"You're my sister. How come you don't know that? Maggie knows it."

"Maybe Maggie likes you more than I do. You crashed my party here, remember?"

"Lamest party I've ever been to."

"You're calling me lame? You're the one who's drunk at ten o'clock."

"Good point." He smiled at Alyson. He liked his sisters. Not when they were kids. They were just annoying then. But now that they were all grown. They were actual people he could relate to. "Hey, Aly?"

"What?"

"I don't think I'm driving home tonight."

"You're definitely not going anywhere." She stood and disappeared.

He tried to focus on the bottle to pour another glass, but his perception was off and he couldn't grab it.

"You've had enough," Alyson said when she came back. She tossed a pillow and blanket at him. "Sleep it off. I'll wake you up before I go to work in the morning."

"Thanks, Aly."

When Shane woke the following morning, he had a horrible case of cottonmouth and a thumping headache. No, that wasn't a headache, it was awful music. He pushed off the couch and looked across the room. Alyson was dancing in her kitchen to some crap that sounded like someone banging trash can lids.

She smiled sweetly at him and handed him a cup of coffee. "I tried to wake you up nicely, but you were dead. Looks like the music worked."

He waved a hand at her. "Can you turn it off now?"

She tapped her phone and smirked as she sipped her coffee. She was already dressed for work in a skirt and blouse. Her hair was pulled back tightly. She looked a little like a librarian.

"Drink fast. I have to leave."

"Sure. Get me drunk and then rush me out the door in the morning. I hope you don't treat all your overnight guests like this."

"You're my brother, not a guest. If a guy offers me a screaming orgasm, I'd see no need to push him out the door. You just snore loud and take up my whole couch."

"Thanks for that totally unnecessary imagery." He gulped the last of his coffee, which was still too hot and burned his throat on the way down.

"Hey, before you leave…"

He rinsed his cup and faced Alyson.

"Give Maggie some time to think and calm down. Then go back and tell her how you really feel. Forget about the guilt and the lies and stick with the simple stuff."

The problem with that was nothing was simple when it came to how he felt about Maggie.

MAGGIE COULDN'T SLEEP FOR SHIT AFTER HER EMOTIONALLY charged night. Men were stupid. She was beginning to think she'd be better off as a lesbian. Unfortunately, she really liked men. She had to work the lunch shift, but since her energy level was at antsy, she decided to spend her morning taking pictures before work.

Being behind the camera soothed her and took her mind to other places. The temperature was finally warming up, and it was already forty degrees at six in the morning. By the afternoon, it might even hit sixty. Spring was on its way. She pulled on a light jacket and wrapped a scarf around her neck before grabbing her camera bag. By the time she was ready to walk out the door, it was six ten. Being a creature of habit, Shane left every day at six-thirty.

If she moved fast, she wouldn't have to worry about running into him. She opened her door, and as she locked up, the exterior door behind her opened. She turned to see Shane, wearing yesterday's clothes.

Well, that hadn't taken long. He propositioned her to *be a couple* and promptly went out to find someone else. Men.

Don't engage. Do not engage.

"Morning, Mags."

"Whatever."

"Still pissed."

"Beyond pissed."

"Couldn't be me. I haven't seen you since the first time I made you mad."

She pointed up and down his body. "Walk of shame really doesn't look good on you."

He glanced down at himself, paused, then looked up at her. "It's not like that—"

She held up a hand. "Your business, Shane. I don't want to hear the details."

"Maggie."

"See you later. I have things to do." She opened the door and flew down the steps before he'd have the chance to hand her any more lies. The biggest problem was that she always wanted to believe Shane. Their relationship had been strong because of honesty.

With the weather finally breaking, there was only one

place to go: the lake. Not too many people were out because of the cold, but a few hard-core runners slapped the pavement. Maggie sat on a stone wall and aimed her camera out to the water. She'd always loved Lake Michigan. Actually, she loved any water. While she was away, she missed her family, of course, but the city itself didn't do much for her.

Lake Michigan, however, was something she'd longed for. From atop her cousin's stone fence in Ireland, she could see the Shannon River far in the distance. A little sliver of water.

But it could never compare to this. The lake changed with the seasons. Hell, it was different daily, sometimes even hourly. Today it fit how she felt.

Dark blue, violent waves crashed against rocks. Sounds of early morning rush hour whooshed by behind her, but with a camera lens to her face, she tuned out everything in the moment.

For over an hour she sat, then stood, and snapped shot after shot. It was colder by the lake and she hadn't dressed for it. Her cheeks were numb. Both sets. She jogged back to her car and sat with the engine running. Still a beautiful sight.

Her insides were knotted, and she couldn't figure out how to loosen them. First Shane, then Eli, then Shane again. Men were idiots. Why the hell did she want one?

She closed her eyes and remembered the feeling of being held, skin on skin, and the memory brought back the reason. Maybe she was rushing it. Having sex with Shane taught her she could, but if she'd waited, she could've figured it out with another guy.

But the not knowing would've eaten away at her. She'd take a step back and reevaluate. She had a lot going on with starting new jobs and trying to build a career. Not seeing Shane every day would be a blessing and a disappointment. She loved living next door to him and hanging out all the time, but as long as she continued to spend all her time with him, no one else had a chance.

She drove back to O'Leary's and changed for work. Just as she put on her apron, her phone buzzed with a text. Against her better judgment, she looked at the screen. It was from Eli.

I was a total ass last night. I'm sorry. You took me off guard and I didn't know how to respond to what you said. Please forgive me. Can I see you again?

Maggie snorted and rolled her eyes. No one knows how to respond to that conversation. Hell, she barely knew how to have that conversation. Then she sighed. The whole thing was difficult. And he was apologizing. Maybe he deserved another chance.

If for no other reason, she could get a good reading on their chemistry now that he knew her whole story. I get off at 7. Meet me at work and we'll have a drink.

As soon as she hit send, she began to think she would need a drink.

Maggie kept busy working her shift to forget all men. When she met with Eli tonight, she would put the brakes on whatever they had going. Maybe. She feared walking away from something that had potential simply because the timing was off. At seven o'clock, she began clearing her tables and closing out her orders.

No sign of Eli. Although he hadn't responded to her text, she'd assumed he'd come. By seven fifteen she was ready to give up on him, and he strode through the door. Like he had the previous time they met, he scanned the entire bar, completely overlooking her. Why did it always take him so long to notice her? She waved to draw his attention.

As he walked over, she called to the bartender, "Hey, Jenna, can you get me a couple of beers? Put them on my tab."

Jenna nodded.

Eli stood beside her. "Hi."

"Hi."

"I'm glad you got my message and can forgive my attitude."

"Well, I didn't say that I forgive you. I simply invited you out for a beer."

He touched her hand. "The invitation felt like forgiveness."

Jenna handed Maggie the beers. Maggie took them and led the way to the back of the bar to find a table. They sat and Maggie took a drink. She had no idea what to say. She wasn't even sure why she'd invited him here.

Liar. You're still looking for some magic.

"So. About what you told me. I didn't mean anything by what I said. I get it. I wasn't trying to imply that what that guy did was okay. It was a lot to take in at once."

"I know. And that's part of why I offered to have a drink with you. I dumped a lot on you that you weren't expecting." She drank more beer. This was almost more uncomfortable than their last conversation.

"Where does this leave us?"

"I'm not sure. I have a lot going on in my life right now. I'm starting a new career. Working my way up from the bottom in a few ways. And I still have a lot of issues."

"Are you breaking it off with me?"

She shrugged. "I don't know. I think I'm ready for a relationship, but it has to go slow, and even then, I'm not sure. The truth is, I'm not sure of much in my life right now." Another drink for courage and she lowered her voice. "The other part of why I wanted to meet you was to check our chemistry. I mean, if it's not there, it would be silly to continue, right?"

He sat back in his chair and blew out a whistling breath. "You didn't feel it? Even out in the alley the other day?"

She cringed. Was she being a bitch right now? She was just trying to be honest. "I thought so, but I've been distracted." Mostly by Shane, if she was being totally honest, which was completely unfair to Eli. Eli hadn't lied to her or tried to manipulate her.

Eli leaned forward again, this time scooting his chair closer to her. "Are you done being distracted?"

She smiled. "Yeah, I think so." She sure damn hoped so.

He touched her hair, smoothing it back behind her ear, and then cupped the back of her neck. He drew her in and his lips closed over hers.

The kiss was gentle, nice even, but stirred nothing in her. Much to her dismay, her mind conjured yet more images of Shane. Damn it.

Eli's tongue swept into her mouth and she almost gagged. Not a good response. He pulled away with a frown. "It's not working."

She shook her head, afraid any more words would just come out sounding mean.

"Damn. That's too bad. I really like you."

"I like you, too." She sighed and reached for her beer. "Maybe our timing is off. Another place, another time."

He slid from his chair. "Maybe I'll see you around."

She nodded and watched him walk away. After chugging the rest of her beer, she cleared the table and climbed the stairs to her apartment. Once inside, she took a bottle of beer from her fridge and started drinking.

CHAPTER 26

As much as Shane wanted to follow Alyson's advice and leave Maggie alone, he needed his computer. Trying to hunt for an apartment on his phone was unbearable. He needed to find a place fast or he'd have to move into his parents' house. He expected an e-mail from the department any day, which meant he had to be ready for his final interview.

Maggie had to work the day shift and she hadn't been home when he checked earlier, so he'd packed the last of the things he wouldn't need to access. At eight-thirty, he went to check again. Even if she got caught late or stayed to eat dinner before coming upstairs, she should be home by now.

He knocked on the door and heard some fumbling in the apartment.

"Who is it?"

"It's me."

"Me who?"

He sighed. He wasn't in the mood for games. "Maggie, you can stay pissed for as long as you want. Just give me my computer, and I'll leave you alone."

The door swung open and Maggie stared at him with a goofy look on her face. "Shane. Why didn't you just say it was you?"

"Who else would knock and assume you'd recognize his voice?"

She stepped back from the door.

"I need my computer."

"Shit. I haven't gotten a new one yet."

"I don't need to keep it. I need to use it to look for an apartment. You can use it until you're ready for a new one." He walked past her and noticed the empty beer bottles on the table. Did she have a guest? "Am I interrupting something?"

She laughed and stumbled back to the couch. "Just a pity party."

"Are you drunk?"

"Almost. The upside to not drinking for five years is that you lose your tolerance. Only a few beers in and I'll be good and drunk." She picked up a bottle and drained it.

He hated seeing her like this. "What happened?"

She blew a raspberry. "Life. My sucky life."

He sat beside her and waited.

"I met with Eli. Oh, wait. You don't know the first part. Yesterday, I told him I'd been raped, and he pretty much discounted what I said. Like because Todd was my ex, it wasn't really rape."

Shane's blood began to boil. "Fuck him."

Maggie held up a wobbly hand. "That's what I said. But then he texted me and apologized."

Shane clamped his jaw shut. Maggie was too nice. How could she not see that a guy like Eli didn't deserve her?

"So I had him come to the bar tonight for a drink. We talked. He said he felt bad." She picked up an empty bottle and held it up to the light, then pushed off the couch. "Want one?"

He shook his head. Drinking when he felt like this wouldn't be a smart move.

She staggered to the kitchen and brought back two bottles. He waited patiently for her to continue.

"So me and Eli, we talked. He wanted to keep going out, but I told him I wasn't sure about our chemistry."

Shane couldn't hold back the snort. Maggie shoved his shoulder. No matter how fucked up things had gotten, this was how it was supposed to be between them.

"That was pretty much Eli's reaction, but I was distracted when I was with him."

"Distracted?"

She mumbled something, and Shane leaned closer. "I didn't catch that."

"I was distracted by you, okay? You gave me my first real orgasm in years and it was amazing. Every time Eli made a move, I thought about you."

As it should be. His chest puffed. Although he didn't say the words, he let his smile speak for him.

"This isn't funny. We had sex as an experiment just to see if I could. That's it. It's not supposed to mean anything else." Her arms flailed as she spoke, and he took the bottle of beer from her.

"So what if it does?"

"It can't. It was sex. Great sex." She scooted closer to him. "In fact, I wouldn't mind having more of that. But that's all it'll be."

He held her hand. "Why?"

"So many reasons." She waved her hand in front of his face, attempting to tick off her points. "We're friends and I don't want to complicate that. You tried to manipulate me. And you used good sex to do it."

"No, I didn't. Was I supposed to offer bad sex?"

"I mean yesterday. You started talking about being a couple."

"That's what I want."

"No, you don't. You just want to control me."

"No one can control you. I know that."

She closed her eyes. "I forgot how horny I get when I drink. I think we should have sex again. See if it's still as good now that I know I can do it."

"No."

"No, what?"

"I'm not sleeping with you, Maggie."

"I'm not talking about sleeping. I'm talking about fucking."

"Using crass terms isn't going to change what we have, what we did." He stood. "You need to go to sleep. Where's my laptop?"

"Whatever. You wouldn't be able to get it right anyway."

"Excuse me?"

She stood and pointed at him. "Yeah, the sex was good. But you know what I really want, Shane? I want a guy who's going to take charge, make demands, not treat me like I'm fragile."

But she was fragile. She didn't want to be. More than anything else, he understood that.

She disappeared into the bedroom and returned a minute later with his laptop in hand, wearing nothing but her bra and panties.

"Want to give it another try?"

"Nope."

Her face fell. "Why not? You've slept with tons of girls just for sex."

"Because you're not some girl."

"I could be."

"No." He felt like he was dangling from a thread and no

matter which way he twisted or turned, he couldn't find solid ground.

She waved her hands down in front of her body. "Well, I bet I could find someone downstairs who could accommodate me."

"Don't go there. You're not leaving this apartment tonight. If I need to park my ass in front of your door, you're staying put."

She giggled. "I'm just joking. I'm not that drunk. I want you to treat me like a nobody for tonight."

He lost the slight control he had on his temper. "You could never fucking be a nobody to me. I love you, Maggie."

"I love you, too."

"I'm *in love* with you. I have been for longer than I can remember. I thought I could sleep with you once, give you what you needed, and then go back. But you won't let it. It's all or nothing, Maggie. We're either a couple or we're friends. There's no in between."

The look on her face was total confusion. She stared at him, mouth hanging open, looking sexy as hell in her underwear. So he left.

Frustration fueled his every movement and it wasn't until he was back in his apartment that he realized he still didn't get his computer.

MAGGIE WATCHED SHANE LEAVE, AND SHE WANTED TO CRY. Beyond the anger, he looked so down, like she'd crushed him. What the hell was he thinking? She supposed it was her own fault by asking him to have sex with her, but how could he think they should risk their entire friendship based on one night in bed?

It was more than that, the annoying little voice in her head said. It couldn't be. He was just a guy thinking with his dick. Once he found some other girl to sleep with, he'd forget all about sex with her. This made the most sense, and she knew it. She'd done plenty of impulsive things in her life, and maybe asking Shane to sleep with her was one of them, but she tried to learn from her mistakes.

She couldn't imagine her life without Shane. Part of her could imagine life without sex. She'd been living that life. But life without Shane was unfathomable.

She glanced down at her scantily clad body and sighed. She set his laptop on the kitchen counter. Time for another beer. What the hell was wrong with her?

As she popped the top on her last bottle, she decided she'd see Shane tomorrow and apologize for trying to jump him. If he could forget they ever slept together, so could she. She couldn't risk losing her best friend.

With her beer bottle as company, she wobbled to her bed and collapsed. She would regret this tomorrow, but for the moment, she enjoyed a little oblivion.

When Maggie woke the following morning, her tongue felt glued to the roof of her mouth. This was one side effect of drinking she hadn't missed. Not one iota. In the bathroom, she drank a glass of water and swallowed a couple aspirin. After brushing her teeth twice, she still felt gross, but staying in the bathroom all day wasn't an option.

She needed to meet Moira for a working lunch. That made her smile. People with real careers had working lunches. Made her sound kind of grown-up. Getting rid of the hangover would probably help with that feeling. She made herself an awful cup of coffee and groaned at the time. She'd missed catching Shane by hours.

Maybe that was a blessing. She could shake her crappy

feeling, get her head on straight, and ask Moira for advice. Flying by the seat of her pants hadn't been working out too well, so this plan sounded better. Since she had some time until lunch, she eased onto the couch with her coffee and relaxed.

Then she remembered Shane had asked for his computer back, but he'd left without it. She should feel bad, but she needed it for her meeting with Moira. She had all of her work saved in cloud storage, but she didn't know if Moira would bring her laptop. She sighed again and grabbed her phone to text Shane. Hopefully, he would answer.

You forgot your computer last night. Do you need it right now?

She held her phone and waited for his response. In a way, she felt silly. If he really needed it, he would've come back for it last night or pounded on her door this morning. But she couldn't help making this slight contact to make sure they were still going to be okay. Her phone buzzed in her hand.

I'll go to my parents' house and use theirs after work.

Now she did feel bad.

I can drop it off to you.

She paused, stomach in a knot, and then added: Or you can come by tonight. I promise to stay fully clothed.

In her head, she heard his quiet chuckle, the one where he couldn't stop it, even though he knew he shouldn't laugh. However, when his response came through, her chest tightened.

It's fine. I don't need it.

There was no laughter. Not even a smiley face emoji. The fear that she'd completely damaged their friendship became real and painful. She needed more help than she thought. She finished her coffee, took a shower, packed the laptop, and headed to lunch. Moira would know what to do. She hoped.

. . .

MAGGIE AND MOIRA WORKED FOR A COUPLE OF HOURS, creating content for the magazine. She was having fun in spite of the hangover that lingered. Moira knew something was up but surprisingly didn't ask until they finished for the day.

"I'm worried about you."

Damn. Was she so transparent that she didn't even need to tell Moira?

"You haven't touched alcohol in five years. Is it a problem?"

Maggie giggled. Moira thought she was turning into a drunk. "I had a beer on Saint Paddy's Day at the bar. Last night, I had a beer with Eli, and when things went south with him, I continued to drink by myself. I'm not a drunk. I knew I'd be safe in my apartment, drinking my beer, and I really wanted a bit of oblivion last night."

"What happened?"

She summarized the whole situation with Eli and then debated telling her about Shane.

"You're hiding something."

"I think I did something stupid."

"Like what?"

"Shane came over for his laptop, and I practically jumped him. First, I asked if he wanted to fuck, then I said he probably couldn't get it right." She cut into the brownie in front of her. Moira was convinced that chocolate could solve most problems. Maggie wasn't sold on the idea.

"Ouch!"

"Yeah. I don't know what I was thinking."

"What did he say?"

"He said he wouldn't sleep with me, and he hadn't been trying to manipulate me the other day when he said we should be a couple. He wants to date."

Moira let out a whoop. "It's about damn time."

"What?"

"Oh, come on. Everyone can see how much that man loves you."

"Of course he loves me. We're friends. And before he left last night—left me standing in my underwear, by the way—he said it was all or nothing: friends or a couple."

Moira's face fell. "God, did you actually slap him back into the friend zone?"

"*I* didn't do anything. He left."

Moira studied her face, and Maggie felt self-conscious. "I say you go jump him again. Go out with him. Be a couple. Have fun."

Moira's urging caused a fresh flood of fear. "What if it doesn't work out?"

"What if it does?"

"I'm serious. He's my best friend. I don't want to fuck that up."

Moira patted her hand. "So don't."

As far as sisterly advice went, it wasn't very helpful. Maggie needed to stop this. She had to tell Shane that they could only be friends. She never should've slept with him. She drove home trying to find the words to give to Shane.

The last thing she wanted to do was hurt him. She replayed the end of the night in her head. Then it hit her.

Holy crap! He said he was in love with her. How had that not been front and center in her brain? That was the kind of declaration that changed lives. He had to be wrong. He was confusing sex with love.

She parked behind the bar and looked for Shane's truck. It wasn't in sight, so she sent him a text asking him to come over when he got home. That gave her some time to think about how to approach this.

Inside her apartment, she began to clean her mess from the night before. Empty beer bottles littered the table, so she gathered them in her arms and tossed them in the trash. The stale beer smell caught her, and she swallowed hard to prevent herself from getting sick. Although she no longer felt the need to completely avoid alcohol, she definitely had no desire to get drunk again.

After the room was clean, she settled on the couch to wait for Shane. It didn't take long before there was a knock on her door. When she opened it, Shane stood there with a scowl on his face but didn't come in.

She stepped back from the door and waved her arm out. "Please come in."

He took two steps, which barely put him over the threshold.

Fine. If this was where he wanted to do it, whatever. "I'm sorry about last night. I was out of line and I wasn't being fair to you. I treated you like an object. Like you didn't matter."

"Yeah, I was feeling a little used. I did a lot of thinking last night and today. Now that you're sober, I'm going to say it again so there are no misunderstandings. I think we should give us a shot."

"A shot? For what?"

"To be a couple. We're good together, Maggie."

"Yeah. We're good because we're friends. By definition, best friends are good together. But as a couple…that's such a risk. What if we screw it up? I would lose you." Her breathing sped up as nerves attacked.

"So we don't screw it up."

"Ha!" She stepped away, suddenly feeling cramped in the entryway. She paced between the two walls, barely two steps before needing to turn. "You're as naïve as Moira."

"What's that supposed to mean?"

"It means that people screw shit up all the time. No matter how much they love each other."

He grabbed her arms to stop her pacing. "And lots of people don't screw it up."

"Is it worth taking that kind of chance?"

He stared at her. "I don't know."

"I don't want to lose you."

"You won't."

"You don't know that. Look at how you reacted to my being with Eli. If we had a boyfriend/girlfriend relationship that went south, how much worse would you be seeing me with another guy?"

Although he didn't speak, his face said plenty. "See? It'd be bad. And then I would lose my best friend."

She reached up and stroked his jaw. "I will always be grateful for what you did."

"Anything for you, Maggie." He leaned like he might try to kiss her, so she needed to get this out.

"But I think we can only be friends."

He held her hand against his jaw. "Why?"

"Because I don't think it's worth the risk."

He pulled her hand away but continued to hold it. "What if I can't go back?"

"What are you saying?" The nerves turned to ice-cold fear.

"I'm sorry, Mags, but I don't think I can go back to being just friends. I've loved you for a long time, and I've been patient. I've waited while you dated other guys, while you traveled around the world, while you put your life back together. I'm done waiting."

He released her hand, and she felt like he was letting go of a lot more. She had no words. Her worst fear came crashing down on her. Shane shook his head and walked out the door.

CHAPTER 27

Shane walked back to his apartment in a daze. He hadn't planned to say that to Maggie. In fact, he didn't have a plan at all when he went to her place. But seeing her, holding her hand, feeling her touch his face, made him realize he wanted more. What he'd said carried his truth. He'd thought he could go back to being friends with Maggie, had tried to prepare for that as an option, but it didn't work.

He opened his refrigerator to grab a beer and remembered it was empty. He was moving out, which meant he had nothing. He stared at his door, willing Maggie to come to him. She was scared. So was he, but he knew they would work. Maybe with a little time, she would come to the same realization.

Staring at his empty apartment, he began to question every choice he'd made. He had no place to live, he almost ruined his chance to become a cop, and now the woman he loved most in the world had turned him away.

Fuck this. He grabbed some clean clothes and his keys and left. He couldn't sit in this apartment surrounded by

O'Learys and not reach out to Maggie again. He was done reaching out for her. It was time for him to get his life in order and go after what he wanted. Right now, all he wanted was a stiff drink, so he headed back to Alyson's place.

The thought sent another message about his sad life. He needed more guy friends. Since leaving college, he hadn't built many new friendships. He relied on his family and Maggie to fill that part of his life. It wasn't normal. He hadn't given it much thought before now, but he needed a drink and he didn't have someone to call other than his little sister.

His life wasn't just sad, it was pitiful.

FOR THE NEXT FEW DAYS, MAGGIE THREW HERSELF INTO HER work. She took on additional shifts at the bar, and during every free moment beyond that she walked the city, taking pictures. The freedom she felt as she captured images was almost swallowed by the deep pain burrowing in her chest.

Shane hadn't made any attempt to contact her since he walked out of her apartment. She'd tried to accidentally bump into him as he left for work or came home, but he must've changed his schedule to avoid her. Ultimately, she felt lost. She made an appointment to see Dr. Janzen, because talking it through with someone who was objective usually worked for her.

Her family, especially Moira, couldn't be objective. They all loved Shane. They would think his overprotective nature was normal, endearing even. Lying to protect her was a good thing in their eyes.

They all made her want to scream. And knowing that made her want to run away, because yelling never seemed to get her too far.

She waited outside Dr. Janzen's office, unable to sit still.

The restlessness had been an issue since her fight with Shane. Was it even classified as a fight? They hadn't argued, but they definitely disagreed.

Dr. Janzen opened her door and greeted Maggie with a smile. Today she wore a black suit and a coral top. Maggie couldn't remember ever seeing this blouse. She smiled. Even Dr. Janzen managed to change things.

Once they sat, Dr. Janzen asked, "How are you?"

"I think I screwed up."

"Screwed up what?"

Maggie sat on the comfortably squishy couch and rambled, filling Dr. Janzen in on everything. The letter from Todd, sex with Shane, her disastrous conversation with Eli. When she was done, the restlessness disappeared.

Tears pricked the back of her eyes.

Dr. Janzen had said nothing until now. "Why do you think you'd lose Shane if you altered your relationship?"

"Because people screw things up all the time."

"That would be true of any relationship. You're not avoiding having a relationship, just having one with Shane. Why?"

"Shane sees me as fragile, someone he needs to take care of. I'm not. I need to be with someone who can see me as his equal. And Shane…" She needed to continue. She knew she needed to tell Dr. Janzen everything, but some things she'd never mentioned before. Giving them voice proved harder than expected.

As usual, Dr. Janzen didn't move, didn't speak. She simply sat and waited until Maggie knew what she wanted to say.

Maggie bit down on her now trembling lip. Her words were barely a whisper. "I'm afraid that when he sees all of me, he'll realize he was wrong and leave."

"I thought you said Shane knew everything."

"Not about the locked doors and not…"

When she didn't say anything for a minute, Dr. Janzen added, "Feeling the need to be behind a locked door is not a deal breaker for most people."

"But it would reinforce the idea that I'm still broken, that he needs to protect me." The sun shone brightly through the window, and if she didn't know that it was barely fifty degrees outside, someone could convince her it was summer. She clasped her hands and focused there.

"Many men feel a strong urge to protect those they care about. Letting Shane know that you need the door locked probably won't faze him. What else doesn't he know about?"

Still looking out the window, Maggie said, "He doesn't know how fucked up I am. The whole time we worked toward having sex, he kept telling me we were going to do things *his* way."

"Did that make you uncomfortable?"

She huffed a sad laugh. "Just the opposite. It was a total turn-on. But then, he put me in charge. He was so worried about me freaking out that he wanted me in control."

"He sounds thoughtful."

"He is. Don't you see? That's what makes me fucked up." She spun and faced her therapist. "I want a man to come to me and take charge. I want a guy to do things *his* way. How fucked up is that? I was raped and I fantasize about some guy taking my control away."

Maggie buried her face in her hands. Confusion swirled through every ounce of her being. But she no longer wanted to cry. Minutes passed.

Finally, Dr. Janzen called her. "Maggie."

Then she waited until Maggie's gaze met hers.

"Having fantasies makes you normal. The fact that you want to explore your sexuality should be celebrated. What makes you think Shane would leave you because of this?"

"Because I'm a fraud. Don't you see that? He will always

think I'm weak, and in some ways, I am. I can't go to sleep unless I check and then double-check my bedroom door to make sure it's locked. And then I want a guy to be forceful in bed. I feel like a hypocrite."

"Let's put Shane out of this for a moment. Let's assume you continue to date and you find someone you care about. You talk to him about your past, including the rape. Would you include him in your sexual fantasies?"

She didn't even have to really think about it. "Probably."

"Why do you assume this new man would be able to handle your feelings and fantasies better than Shane?"

Huh. Maggie slumped back against the cushions. "I guess it's because Shane already thinks he knows everything about me. And this…this would ruin that image for him."

"Are you saying his image of you is wrong?"

"Not wrong, but skewed. He always treats me like I'm special."

By the time Maggie left Dr. Janzen's office, she was wrung out. Although she hadn't shed a tear, she felt like she'd run the gamut of emotions. And she still didn't have any answers. There were things she could count on Dr. Janzen for. Giving her solutions to her problems was not one of them.

She had, however, given Maggie lots to think about.

Maggie needed to reevaluate her relationship with Shane and what she really wanted from it. And what was she willing to do for it.

THIS WAS IT. SHANE STOOD OUTSIDE THE POLICE ACADEMY AND stared at the sign: CHICAGO POLICE EDUCATION AND TRAINING ACADEMY. If all went well today, he'd breeze through this interview and be placed in the next class of recruits. He was so nervous, he didn't even tell anyone that he had his interview today.

If he blew it, he planned to forget he ever got this far. He wouldn't be able to stand hearing everyone ask how it went. It was bad enough that his entire family kept asking him what had happened with Maggie. Alyson and her big mouth.

He shoved all of that aside and focused. This interview was the last hurdle he needed to clear to become a cop. Well, he had to make it out of the academy, but he knew he'd be successful given the chance.

After patting his pockets one last time to make sure he had his newly signed lease, he strode through the front door and checked in for his appointment. Detective Carroll sat in front of him, reading from a file.

"You played football in college?"

That was not the kind of question Shane had expected. "Yeah."

"What position?"

"Defensive end."

"What do you think about the Bears going into next year?"

Shane knew this had to be a trap. Carroll was looking for something, but Shane had no idea what as they chatted about football for the next ten minutes. Then it hit him.

"Why did you stop playing? You were on a scholarship, right?"

Shane leaned forward slightly. "No disrespect, Detective Carroll, but I'm sure it's all right there in my file. I quit after blowing the whistle on teammates who were doping. My allegations proved true, but I couldn't stay on the team after that. Everyone thought I had betrayed the team."

"Do you regret your decision?"

"No. It was the right thing to do."

"Do you always do the right thing?"

"I try, but I'm not perfect."

"What if the right thing is against the law?"

Shit was getting real now. He thought of Maggie, and he knew to a certain degree there were times when he could break the law. But he also knew he couldn't admit it. "I'm a law-abiding citizen. I was taught to believe in the system. I know it's not perfect, but it's the best we've got."

"Tell me about Todd McCann."

How the hell did Carroll get there? Shane had never been officially charged. "He's my friend Maggie's ex-boyfriend."

"You were brought in, but not charged, for beating him up."

Shane's jaw tightened. This hadn't come up in any of his previous tests. He'd believed he was in the clear. "Yes."

"Did you beat him up?"

"I plead the fifth."

Detective Carroll finally cracked a smile. "I thought you wanted to be a cop, not a lawyer."

"I do. So in this instance, keeping my mouth shut is in my best interest."

"He broke her heart, so you broke his nose?"

Anger filled Shane, but he fought not to react. Of course, Carroll would think he flew off the handle over something silly. He unclenched his jaw and answered, "No. He raped her."

Carroll inhaled deeply, and took a moment before saying anything else. Shane continued to stare at the man. Shane had no regrets about that either. Todd deserved much worse than what Shane had doled out.

"Why didn't you let the system handle that?"

"We did. But my temper got the better of me."

"So you decided to play vigilante."

"No. I went to speak to him to make sure he knew to stay away from my friend. He threw a punch and I defended myself, which is why no charges were formally filed."

Carroll seemed satisfied and changed the subject again. He jumped around from topic to topic. Shane assumed the man wanted to trip him up.

When Shane left the academy every muscle in his body had tightened and felt like they would snap. He climbed into his truck, barely resisting the strong urge to kick in the side.

Carroll had left him with a handshake and no promise of employment, just like every other step in this god-awful process. The man gave nothing away. Shane had no way to gauge if he'd screwed up. He drove to his parents' house, his temporary residence until he could move into his new apartment.

He parked down the street from the house, reluctant to go in. They would ask where he'd been and he'd attempt to lie. Then his mom would wheedle it out of him and try to make him feel better about the whole thing. No, he didn't want someone to pat him on the back and tell him he'd done the best he could. He already knew that.

He pulled out his phone and stared at Maggie's number. Over the last week, he'd gotten as far as looking at her name. He'd wanted to call her up about a million times, but each time he made himself stop. She hadn't tried to contact him once. He wondered if she was even aware he'd moved out of his apartment.

Things would be so much better if he could stop thinking about her. Beyond having extremely vivid dreams about her naked body, he missed his best friend. They'd always shared everything, so it would've been natural for him to call her about his interview. And to show her his new apartment. And just about anything else that could happen.

Silence between them was weird.

While he debated the merits of dealing with his family

versus finding somewhere else to eat dinner, his phone rang. Maggie's smiling face stared at him, and he did a double take before realizing that she was, in fact, calling him.

Without thinking, he answered and immediately regretted it. He had no idea where they stood or what he should say.

"Shane? You there?"

"Yeah. I'm here."

"You moved."

So she had noticed. "I told you I had to move fast."

"But you left without telling me." Hurt vibrated through every syllable.

"I didn't know what to say."

"How about 'Hey, Maggie, I'm moving.'" Anger quickly replaced the hurt.

He shifted in his seat. "I needed to move, and things between us have been…strained."

"So I tell you I want to be friends and you just walk away? That's it? Ten years of friendship gone?"

He thumped his head on the steering wheel. This was why he hadn't called. He didn't know how to walk away from her. But he also didn't know how to be with her and not want her completely. "I don't know what to say to you, Maggie. I don't think I can be your friend. It won't be enough."

"Why not? It was enough for all this time." Her voice had quieted like she begged for an answer.

"It was never enough. I pretended it was because I thought that was all I could have. I've been in love with you for a long time. So long that I can't remember not being in love with you, Maggie. You opened the door to us being more, having more. You can't just shut it again."

When she didn't say anything, he thought she'd hung up.

"I'm afraid," she whispered.

"We do it together. Nothing to be scared of."

"I wish it were that easy." She sighed and then said, "Good-bye."

He had no idea if it was a talk to you later good-bye or a good-bye forever.

CHAPTER 28

Maggie disconnected and curled on her couch, gripping her phone. Her day felt as if it had been forty hours long and all she'd wanted was to hear Shane's voice. She had no idea why she'd started yelling at him. If she'd told him she'd had a hard day, he would've talked to her and made her feel better. He might've even come over and let her lean on him while they watched TV together.

In her heart, she knew it wouldn't be fair to him. She wanted him back in her life even though it had only been a week since they'd fought. But he wanted all of her and she still wasn't sure what she could offer him.

She hadn't thought about that when she considered falling in love with a new boyfriend. She'd assumed things would develop in their natural course. Starting something with Shane would definitely take a different route. As much as she would have to reevaluate how she thought about him, he'd have to be willing to do the same.

A huge part of her feared that Shane would never be able to see her as his equal and he'd never let go of the guilt he felt over her rape. They never talked about it, but she knew how he felt. It was a shadow that followed them everywhere.

What if they could never get past that?

She snickered sadly. Dr. Janzen would point out that every *what if* could be spun on its head. What if they needed each other to free themselves of the shadow? What if Shane gave her the safe life she'd been seeking? One where she could explore and experiment without fear.

What if he thought she was a freak?

"Ahhh!" She stood and tossed her phone against the cushions. Her biggest problem was that when she needed to work through something, she'd always talked to Shane. How was she supposed to do this without him?

Maybe she shouldn't. This mess was as much his fault as hers. If he was so sure about how good they would be, he should convince her. She pulled her phone from between the pillows on the couch and sent a text.

We need to talk in person. I can't figure things out without you. Where are you living?

She went to her room to change and put on makeup. Regardless of how things went, she wanted to look good doing it.

My parents' house.

She almost poked her eye with her eyeliner when she saw his response. He'd hated living at home and couldn't wait to move out. You moved back home?

For now.

She sighed. Doing this in front of his parents and possibly one or more of his sisters didn't appeal to her, but she couldn't keep going on like this. Can I come over?

Sure.

Not a resounding welcome, but it was better than him telling her no.

She changed into her comfort wear: a snug tank top with

her faded flannel over it and her favorite pair of jeans. She wouldn't win any fashion contests, and it certainly wasn't let's-get-laid attire, but the clothes made her feel like herself.

Now more than anything, she needed to be confident in herself.

After parking in front of Shane's house, Maggie took a deep breath. The first time she'd walked into this house, she'd been sixteen. Shane needed a tutor and she needed to prove to her mom that she could handle being at a public school after being not-so-kindly asked to leave the all-girl Catholic school she had attended. She figured tutoring a star football player would earn her bonus points on the good scale.

From the first moment she stepped foot in the Callahan house, she'd been treated like part of the family. Shane's mom buzzed around offering them snacks and drinks and always profusely thanking her for her help when she left. Over time, Shane didn't need her help, but they'd developed a friendship.

His family was as much hers as hers was his.

Now she was going to have to have a serious discussion with his family around. His dad's truck and his mom's car sat in the driveway. She didn't know which of his sisters might be around. What were the chances they'd encounter anything resembling privacy?

She should've asked him to come to her apartment. Once again, her lack of forethought was biting her in the ass.

Stepping from the car, she filled her lungs with fresh springtime air, and then walked up the front stairs.

Shane's mom opened the door and greeted her with a hug. "Maggie, it's so good to see you. I've been telling Shane to bring you around."

"Hi, Theresa. Things have been busy, you know, adjusting to life back here, looking for new jobs, and stuff." *Stuff like having sex with your son.* Maggie quickly clamped her jaw shut for fear of saying something ridiculous. "Is Shane here?"

"Yeah. He's in his old room. You know the way." She disappeared back into the kitchen, and Maggie followed the sounds of rock blaring from a radio.

So much hadn't changed in ten years. Every time Shane was pissed off or struggled with something, it was always rock and roll behind his locked bedroom door. She knocked with a tight fist before trying the knob. Surprisingly, it was unlocked.

Sticking just her head through the door, she called, "Is it safe to come in?"

Shane lay on his bed, arms behind his head, legs stretched out, crossed at the ankle. He opened one eye when she talked. Like she wasn't worthy of his full attention and both eyes being open. "Sure."

She slid through the door and locked it behind her. Before approaching him on the bed, she turned the music down a few notches but didn't turn it off. She hoped the sounds might drown out their conversation.

Before she launched into what she needed to say—which of course she still wasn't totally sure of—she knew something was off with Shane. "What's wrong?" she asked as she sat at the foot of the bed, being careful not to come into contact with him.

He raised an eyebrow.

"I mean, yeah, there's stuff we need to talk about, but is there something else?"

He eyed the door as if to make sure she'd closed it. "I had my interview for the police department."

"And?"

"And what?"

"How'd it go? Was it bad? Is that why you're so mopey?"

He swung his legs over the side of the bed and sat. "I'm not mopey. I'm thinking. I'm not sure how it went."

"Come on. You have to have some idea."

He shook his head. "No. This detective, he's like a stone wall. No reading him."

"Then your chances are equally good that the interview was a success."

"Except for the questions he asked."

Maggie couldn't think of anything that would rattle Shane. He was honest and believed in doing the right thing. It was why she knew he'd be a good cop. "Like what?"

"He asked why I stopped playing football." He rubbed his hands on his thighs. Without looking at her, he added, "He asked about me beating up Todd."

"What?" Maggie jumped up from her spot. In both instances, Shane had been doing what was fair and right and just. "How could that be a bad thing and work against you?"

Anger bubbled up on his behalf. Shane deserved to have what he wanted, and if Todd took that from him, she'd never forgive herself.

SHANE LOOKED UP FROM WHERE HE'D BEEN STARING AT THE pattern of the carpet. Just like Maggie to get mad. "In general, they don't want cops who take the law into their own hands."

"But he raped me."

The pain in her voice pierced through him. He had no regrets about what he'd done. If given the chance to do it again, he would, police department be damned. "I explained that. On a personal level, I'm pretty sure he understood. But the hiring process isn't personal."

He'd replayed the interview in his head hundreds of times

already, trying to figure out how he could've made it better. He came up empty every time.

"Would it help if I talked to this detective again?"

"No. There's nothing you can do, but thanks." There wasn't anything anyone could do at this point, which was why he'd spent so much time lying in bed thinking about his options.

He'd been counting on the police department to hire him. He'd been biding his time, waiting for something to happen.

Maggie sank back down onto the bed. The springs squeaked like they had his entire life. He firmly believed his parents liked him having a squeaky bed so they knew he wasn't getting lucky in his room. She sat close enough that he could smell her perfume.

She wore her favorite flannel shirt, one that had been worn thin. It was a comfort thing for her, which he understood because it looked soft. He wanted to reach out and touch it but held back.

Since she didn't seem to be moving the conversation forward, he did. "Why are you here?"

"We need to talk."

"So talk."

She picked at the bottom button of her shirt. "I'm afraid I really messed things up between us, and I never meant to. I'm sorry I ever asked you to sleep with me."

"I'm not."

Her gaze flicked up and immediately shot back down.

Shane touched her jaw and lifted her face. "I don't regret a damn thing about it, Maggie. I've wanted you for a long time, and because I spent so much time wanting you, I started to believe I'd built it up in my head. But it was real. What we shared was real. That's why I can't pretend it didn't happen."

Staring into her blue eyes, he saw her uncertainty, but he couldn't understand. They belonged together.

She stared back, not shying away from his touch on her chin. "I know. I'm not sure I could pretend it didn't happen either, but that doesn't mean I wouldn't take it back if I could. There's too much potential for this to ruin our friendship." Her lip wobbled. "And now you're making it sound like if I don't become your girlfriend, I'll lose you anyway."

Crap. He didn't want to make her cry, and he definitely didn't want to push her away, but he couldn't go back. "Christ, Maggie, you'll never lose me. Not totally. But I can't pretend."

She pulled out of his grasp now, shaking her head. "But what if we do this and you find out I'm not who you thought I was?"

"I know everything about you."

"No, you don't. You think you do, but…"

"What is it? I can't imagine anything about you being such a problem I wouldn't want to be with you."

Her hands twisted in her lap. "In addition to the triggers, I have some other glitches."

"Glitches? You're not a machine."

She rolled her eyes. "Glitches—problems—things that are wrong with me."

He stifled his laugh. "Like what?"

She turned her head and stared at the door. Then it hit him. He grabbed her hand. "The door locking. I noticed."

Her breath hitched as she sucked it in.

"When you knew I was following right behind you to watch TV, you locked me out of your apartment. When I spent the night, you got out of bed to check the door."

She nodded. "I need it locked. It's not as bad now as it used to be, but sometimes, especially if it's been a bad day, I check and double-check out of necessity."

"And the morning I surprised you with coffee?"

"I saw the open door and panicked. Hearing the sounds from the kitchen exacerbated it."

"Why didn't you just tell me?"

She pulled away again. "Because I didn't want you to see how messed up I am. I'm dying to be normal. I needed you of all people to see me as normal."

She fell silent again. Was that it? She thought he'd lose interest because she needed locked doors?

"I do."

She shook her head. "No, you don't. You see me as damaged, something that's so fragile that I might break."

"You're the strongest person I know. Your strength amazes me."

Her head whipped up. He knew that look. She was about to call him a liar.

"I don't know anyone who fights as hard as you do to prove herself every day." He reached for her hand again and sandwiched it between his. "The thing is, Maggie, you don't have anything to prove to anyone."

"I need to prove it to myself."

"Maybe you should cut yourself some slack."

She tugged her hand away and slapped her thigh. "You just don't get it. When I look at a guy I'm in love with, I need for him to see me as a woman. That's it. Just a woman he wants to get naked. Not a woman who's been raped. Not a woman who might break. Not a woman he needs to take care of."

She stood and walked around the bed and toward the door. No way was she going to leave until they had this settled.

"Every time I look at you, I imagine you naked. I don't think about the rape, because it destroys me to do so." He stood behind her and brushed her hair off her neck. He lowered himself and whispered in her ear, "I want to take care of you, not because you might break, but because I love you and that's what you do when you care about someone."

He brushed his fingers across the skin on her shoulder where her shirt had slipped. "Tell me you don't feel it every time we touch."

"I can't."

Being this close to her, breathing in her scent, feeling her soft skin under his fingers, and not kissing her took every ounce of control he had. "What do you expect to happen?"

"I don't know."

"Then why are you here?" When she popped into his room, he'd thought she'd come to her senses and was ready to listen to him.

"I was hoping for answers."

They belonged together. If he spun her around and kissed her, he could prove it. But in the back of his mind, her triggers were always present. He never wanted to be the cause of an episode. So he waited for her to make a move.

Unfortunately, it wasn't the one he wanted. She turned the doorknob and walked out.

CHAPTER 29

Maggie walked out of the bedroom and then the house without speaking to anyone. She kept walking until she was next to her car. Why had she come here? What answers had she been hoping for?

No, not answers. That was a convenient lie. She'd wanted to see what Shane would do. How he would react to her being in his house. Talking about sex and being his girl-friend. Opening up and sharing a piece of herself she'd thought he hadn't known.

The entire time, all she'd wanted him to do was kiss her. She was a hypocrite. She told him she wanted to be friends, but as she admitted, she couldn't get him out of her head. And she wasn't thinking about him as her friend either.

She leaned against her car and stared at Shane's house. No one had made her feel more alive and safe as Shane always had. If there was no going back, maybe it was time to take that leap. Maybe she'd been looking for him to convince her. But why? She knew him, knew what she was getting in him, knew he loved her.

The last thought rocked her. Of course she'd known he

loved her. They loved each other. You aren't friends with someone for ten years and *not* love them. They'd opened a door that led to something she'd never considered, but Shane obviously had. She began to consider it, too.

What held her back? They were good together and the chemistry between them definitely hit the mark. Suddenly, she had no idea what she was doing standing by her car.

She jogged back up the walk and took the steps two at a time. Turning the knob, she was happy to find the door unlocked. *Ironic.* As she swung the door open, she smacked it into Shane. He was bent over putting his shoes on and the door clunked against his head and knocked him back.

"What the fuck?" He grabbed his head.

"Oh, my God. I'm so sorry. Are you okay?"

He straightened. "What are you doing here?"

She closed the door behind her. "I was coming back. Why are you standing in front of the door?"

"I was coming after you." He rubbed the spot on his head.

Her heart went all warm and squishy. She'd never had a guy run after her before. Of course, it would've been more romantic if he'd moved faster and didn't almost get knocked out. "I ran outside and had no idea what I was running from. I like the way I feel when I'm with you."

The words tumbled out easily. She'd expected to feel nervous or anxious, but her blood pumped steadily through her body, only warming when he looked at her. Lust was in his eyes.

He took a step closer, close enough that she felt the heat from his skin. "The feeling's mutual."

Her breath quickened and her gaze darted all over his body, making her want to touch everywhere. More important, she wanted him to touch her, but he didn't.

She looked up into his eyes. "I'm in. I want to give us a shot."

Another step and his body brushed hers. "Thank God." He lowered his head and she grabbed a fistful of his T-shirt as his mouth met hers.

The kiss was heady and warm, but still so cautious. He was holding back and she wanted him to push, take, maybe even manhandle. His tongue stroked her languidly and she sighed. There was something to this slow and gentle approach.

A gasp behind them caught their attention, and they both opened their eyes and eased away from each other. She released his shirt and smoothed it out. His face was filled with a ridiculously happy grin. When he turned around, his mother stood there with a matching smile and a plate of cookies.

"Hi again," Maggie said lamely with a slight wave of her fingers.

Theresa pointed back and forth. "Does this mean... you two...?"

"Yeah, Mom, Maggie and I are a couple."

Maggie took a step forward. Shane came up behind her and stuck his hand in her back pocket. She tried to slap it away.

Shane wiggled his fingers in her pocket. He picked up a cookie with his free hand and said, "Hey, Mom, you don't care if I feel up my girlfriend, do you?"

Maggie's mouth dropped open. He shoved a cookie past her lips.

Theresa crossed her arms. "I don't want to see anything you wouldn't want to see me doing."

Shane chuckled and looked at Maggie. "You're in trouble. My dad is always trying to molest my mom."

Maggie chewed the cookie Shane had put in her mouth. Warm and gooey center with huge chunks of chocolate and slightly crispy edges. Perfection. These were Theresa's specialty, broken cookies. Every time she made them, they were a little different because she broke up whatever snacks or candies she had around and added them to the dough. She reached for another cookie.

She had no response for his comment. He spoke the truth. His parents had always been openly affectionate in front of everyone. Not that they had been gross or anything, but they were clearly in love.

Theresa went back to the kitchen. Maggie spoke quietly to Shane. "I feel strange. I've never felt awkward in your house before, but it's happening now."

Shane smoothed her hair off her shoulder. His fingers against her neck sent a ripple of luscious sensation through her. "How?"

"This." She waved her hand between them. "I said I wanted to give us a shot, but what does that mean? We just sleep together and that's it?"

"That'd work for me."

"Shane Callahan." His mom's sharp tone had them both looking up. "I raised you better than to treat a woman like a piece of meat."

Maggie thought Theresa hadn't been listening. She should've known better.

"It's not like that, Mom."

Theresa continued to yell from the next room. "Oh, really? Have you taken her out on a date?"

"We go out all the time."

"You *hang out*, whatever that means. If she were any other woman you wanted to impress, you'd take her out. Make her fall for you."

Maggie snickered. "Yeah, Shane. Woo me."

His shoulders dropped with his sigh.

"Don't you sigh at me. Would you want some man to talk to one of your sisters like that?"

Shane tensed.

This was getting better by the minute.

With a pointed finger, Theresa added, "I thought not."

She picked up a towel and dried the pan she'd cleaned. "A woman needs to know she's worth your time and effort. Otherwise, there's no incentive."

Maggie started to feel sorry for Shane. She knew he wasn't really treating her like a piece of meat, and he'd always given her plenty of attention and effort. "It's okay, Theresa. I think Shane and I need to discuss some things." She winked at Shane. "Let's go to your room and talk."

He grabbed her hand and pulled her down the hall. Once out of the living room, the giggle bubbled up in her throat. "Well, that was fun."

"For you, maybe." He pulled her through his bedroom door and kicked it shut. His eyes coasted over her entire body.

She wished she'd worn something sexy instead of her comfort clothes.

He put his cookies on his dresser and stepped closer. "So you want to be wooed."

"I was kidding. And for the record, your mom was wrong. You always give me your time and attention."

"It would've been nice if you defended me out there."

"I can't make your life too easy."

"Uh-huh." His hand grazed her neck as it made its way around the back to hold on. "I'll woo you, Maggie. I'll woo you so hard, you won't be able to resist me."

"That won't take too much effort." She licked her lips and hoped he'd take the hint.

With his fingers gently caressing her neck, he lowered his mouth and pressed a kiss to her cheek. She turned her head for more, but he pulled away.

"Will you have dinner with me, Maggie?"

"Of course."

"I mean like a real date. Not takeout on your couch."

She ran her fingers over his chest. "But my couch is close to the bedroom." She looked over her shoulder at his twin-sized bed. "My bed is bigger, and there's no audience at my apartment."

He groaned. "Are you trying to kill me?"

With a smile, she responded, "Torment you a little, maybe. I'm not looking for you to woo me, but I need to know where we go from here. What's different? Do we continue the way we've always been but screw on occasion?"

"If I have anything to say about it, it'll be a whole lot more than on occasion. But otherwise, what else would change?"

"I don't know." In truth, standing this close to him, she couldn't think about anything. She stepped away. "Maybe we need to think about this."

"God, Maggie, stop playing games. You said you were in. Don't toy with me."

"No, I don't mean reconsider us. I mean think about what we expect. We know so much about each other and there are some things we might overlook in each other as friends, but as a couple, we wouldn't."

"Like what?"

She sat on the edge of the bed, still holding a cookie in her hand, the chocolate melting in her palm. "Like I expect my boyfriend to call if he's going to be late. But as friends, it didn't matter too much."

Shane laughed.

"What's funny about that?"

"You're the one who's always late, not me."

"Well, then, maybe you expect me to call you."

He shook his head and sat beside her. "Nope. I know you'll be late, and I plan for it." He took her hand in his. "No other men."

She snorted. As if that were a possibility. "No other women."

"There has never been anyone else for me."

She melted a little more and sighed. "You're really good at this wooing thing."

"It's a gift."

She stood, needing some space. Things felt too right, and she couldn't wrap her head around that. "Are we on for dinner?"

"Yeah. I'll pick you up at six. Where do you want to go?"

"You pick." She headed back to the door. As she turned the knob, she added, "And Shane? Plan to spend the night."

CHAPTER 30

Shane's world was about as perfect as it could get. He was settled in his new apartment, grateful to have privacy once again. And Maggie was his.

Although that would've been enough to keep him happy forever, as he was leaving work, he checked his e-mails and saw one from the police department. His thumb hovered over the message. It was probably another confirmation of the last step he'd completed, but no offer of employment, *they'll be in touch.*

But what if it was a rejection?

He turned the phone off and started the engine. He drove to O'Leary's because Maggie worked the day shift. He wanted to be with her when he read the e-mail. She would be his reminder that life was still good even without the police department.

He walked into the bar and his eyes found her immediately. She had her hair pulled back in a messy ponytail and he wanted to kiss her exposed neck. She'd smell fresh from a shower right there, and her pulse would kick up against his tongue.

She must've felt his stare, because she turned from where she was taking an order. She winked at him but continued to talk to her customers. When they were done, she turned to the register and waved him over. "What are you doing here?"

"I got an e-mail from the department."

Her fingers froze on the screen where she was inputting an order. "And?"

"I didn't read it yet."

She flicked him a look and finished entering her order. Then she turned and held out her hand. "Give me your phone."

He handed it to her and was a little surprised when she keyed in his passcode. Her having that information didn't bother him, but he wondered.

As if she read his mind, she said, "It's not like you hide your screen when you put it in. Plus, it's the year we graduated."

She scrolled and clicked. His stomach churned as he tried to read her face. Her forehead wrinkled as she read, but she said nothing.

"Well?"

She looked up at him and bit her lip. "You're in. You report to the academy next week."

"What?" He was sure he hadn't heard her right. He grabbed the phone and read. Then he let out a whoop and scooped Maggie up in a tight hug. Tonight, they'd celebrate.

She shoved his shoulder. "I'm at work."

"I know. I'm sure your boss would understand." But people were starting to stare.

"Congratulations."

He kept a hand on her hip for a minute, knowing she had to pull away to go back to work. He needed that connection for just a moment. "You are okay with this, right?"

They'd talked about it, but being accepted made it real.

"Yeah."

"You don't sound so sure."

"What am I gonna say? Give up your dream?"

She wouldn't and he knew it, but since he just convinced her to be his girlfriend, he also didn't want to jeopardize that.

"I have to get back to work. People are waiting for drinks."

"Pick you up at seven to celebrate?"

"Sounds good." She rose on tiptoe and kissed his cheek.

He watched her return to work, chatting with customers and passing out drinks. He needed to share the news with his family, but he enjoyed watching Maggie, so he did. Over the last week or so, they'd fallen into a routine. They spent their free time together, and now that he had his own apartment, she spent the night. He wanted her to move in but hadn't yet brought it up because he didn't want her to feel rushed.

Getting her out of the apartment upstairs would make him feel better. She'd told him Todd had sent a letter to the bar for her. He didn't like that Todd knew where to find her. Besides, he loved the idea of coming home to her. Or her coming home to him.

On her next pass to the bar she bumped her hip into his. "Are you going to stand there all night watching me, or are you going to get ready for our date?"

He kissed the top of her head. "I'm going to see my parents to tell them. Then I'll get ready."

"See you later."

MAGGIE WORKED LIKE A SPY FOR DAYS. FROM THE MOMENT Shane had gotten the e-mail about the academy, she'd been planning a surprise party. Once again, having a big family proved beneficial because not only did she get extra help,

Ryan let her use the back room of the bar for the party. Theresa had been fabulous by inviting all of Shane's friends and family.

Both of their families would be there, and she hoped Shane wouldn't mind it being at the bar. Over the last couple of weeks, he'd been getting more vocal about wanting her to quit working at O'Leary's. When she thought about having a take-charge kind of guy, his telling her what to do with her life hadn't crossed her mind.

It was the only way he was bossy, though. She'd hinted at wanting more of that in the bedroom, and while having sex with Shane had been pretty damn phenomenal, he was still holding back, being careful with her. No matter how many times she tried to convince him she was okay, it was like he still expected her to have a freak-out.

She hadn't had any problems at all in that department, which was why she wanted more from him. If they were ever going to make it as a couple, they needed to not hold back. When she was drunk that night he'd come to get his computer, she'd told him what she was looking for in a guy, but he never commented. He probably dismissed it because she was drunk. The problem was, she wasn't sure she could say it sober.

Shane wasn't the only one holding back.

But today was all about the party. His first day at the academy would be Monday, and their lives would change after that. She didn't even know in what ways; she just knew things would be different. So she wanted them to have tonight.

Mary came over to help her hang the banner and the streamers. Moira was bringing the balloons. She knew it was a little childish to have streamers and balloons, but she liked Shane most when he wasn't too serious. Who could be serious when they had helium at their fingertips and an endless supply of alcohol?

They'd just finished with the decorations when people started to arrive. She'd lied to Shane and told him she was working late and asked him to pick her up at eight to hang out. By the time he showed, beer was flowing and guests were laughing. He'd forgotten to text when he was on his way, so he strode into the back looking for her and saw the party before anyone could yell, "Surprise!"

He stood looking shell-shocked as she pushed her way through the crowd and said, "Surprise." She smiled and wrapped her arms around his shoulders.

With one arm around her, he said, "What is this?"

"A party, of course. Did you think we'd let your acceptance to the academy go uncelebrated?"

Then there was tapping on the microphone, and Theresa was on the stage to get everyone's attention. "Hey, everyone. Attention, please. In case you haven't noticed, the guest of honor, my son, Shane, is here. As usual, he didn't follow directions and text Maggie when he was on his way, so he snuck in."

A few people laughed. Maggie turned to look at Theresa but stayed in Shane's embrace.

"Before you all get drunk, I want to say a couple of things. First, Shane, congratulations." Her eyes met his and he waved.

The crowd echoed her congratulations.

"I'm proud of you, baby, but I will worry every day." Her eyes teared up and Glen held out his hand to help her off the stage.

As Theresa stepped down, someone started to chant, "Speech. Speech."

Maggie stepped away from him. "You need to say something."

He climbed up on the stage and someone handed him a beer. He nodded his thanks and took a huge gulp before saying anything. "I have no idea what to say. I didn't expect this. Umm…First, thank you all for coming. And where's Maggie?" He held a hand over his eyes to look for her, but his gaze immediately landed on her, just like it always did. He pointed at her. "I'll get you back for this."

"You can try, babe. But I'm like a ninja," she called out.

"Thanks to the O'Learys for letting us party here tonight." He raised his beer and said, "I'll do my best to be a great cop and make you all proud."

"How about getting us out of tickets?" someone yelled.

"You're on your own there." He waved and hopped off the stage.

Maggie sipped from a bottle of beer. She had no intention of getting drunk tonight, but she wanted to be part of the crowd. From where she stood, she saw Shane making his way to her, but he got waylaid by people wanting to talk and congratulate him. He smiled and nodded and spoke a few words. Before he made it another couple of feet, someone else grabbed him, so she waited patiently.

Moira came up next to her and bumped her shoulder. "Looks like a success."

"Yeah. Thanks for the help."

"No problem. I love a good party." She tilted her chin toward Shane. "He looks a bit like a deer in headlights. You should worry about his threat."

Maggie snickered. "He doesn't scare me."

"Better watch it. He might pull out his cuffs and lock you up."

"I should be so lucky."

Moira laughed. "Word of warning. Don't use the department-issued ones. They hurt. Get the padded ones."

Maggie smirked. "Spoken from experience?"

"Of course. The pain and red marks were totally worth it, though."

Maggie sighed. Now was not the time for her disappointment. She had a plan. Shane finally broke through the crowd and reached for her. He set his empty bottle on the table beside her.

Moira said, "I'll get you a fresh one."

"Thanks," he replied without looking at Moira. His gaze remained on Maggie. "You are like a ninja. How did you manage to get this done? I had no idea."

"As much as I'd like to take credit for all of it, I had help. A lot. Are you happy?"

"I couldn't be happier." He pulled her close and gave her a searing kiss. It was the kind of kiss that usually led to the bedroom, but they couldn't run off now, not with a room full of guests.

When he pulled away, she patted his chest. "Go enjoy your friends." She reached in his pocket and took his keys. "I'll drive you home tonight. I have a special gift for you."

"Yeah? What's that?"

"I'll tell you later."

He groaned and kissed her neck. She enjoyed the rush for a second before shoving him away. "Go party."

HOURS LATER, SHANE WAS STILL LAUGHING AND DRINKING with his friends, but he wasn't drunk. She knew him so well that she could tell his level of drunkenness by just watching him interact with people. Shane was buzzed but still clear-headed.

Throughout the night, he'd introduced her to college friends and coworkers as if he wanted to show her off.

Every now and then, she'd break away, but he'd sought her out, if for nothing else than a quick kiss. On this stop, he whispered in her ear, "Are you going to tell me what my present is?"

"Remember when we talked about fantasies the other night?"

His eyes got hot. "Yeah."

"Well, like I said, I don't have one of my old uniform skirts, but Moira does. I have it in my bag."

When he'd brought up the idea of the schoolgirl skirt, she'd rolled her eyes. Guys were pretty typical that way. But it definitely got her thinking. If she supplied one of his fantasies, he might feel obliged to fulfill one of hers. And she had only one, really.

More than anything, she wanted him to see her as whole, to take everything she had to offer without fear of hurting her.

"How fast can we leave here?"

"It's your party. You have to stay until everyone leaves."

"You really know how to torture a guy."

"I gotta be good at something. We have all night. Neither of us is working tomorrow."

He pressed a hard kiss to her lips and went back to his party. Overall, the night seemed to be a huge success. She only hoped she had as much success in the bedroom later.

CHAPTER 31

Shane walked through the party with a smile so big, his cheeks hurt. He loved having his family surrounding him as well as friends he hadn't seen in a long time. The fact that Maggie had pulled this off for him made him love her even more. He drank from a beer that pushed him from tipsy to buzzed and he watched Maggie work the room. She talked to everyone, made them smile, handed out drinks.

He needed to slow down on the drinking if he planned to enjoy his present from her. As much as he said he didn't like surprises, her offering up a Catholic school skirt was one he'd enjoy. This party was well worth the surprise as well. Maybe it was time for him to deliver a shock of his own. He sought Maggie out, wanting to hold her and keep her by his side.

She was in a corner, talking to his cousin Dave, and not looking like she was having fun. Not surprising since Dave couldn't handle his liquor. Dave threw his arm around Maggie's shoulders and she ducked away. Dave put up his hands, and Shane worked to control his irritation.

Maggie nodded and the line in her shoulders eased a fraction. Shane slid from his stool, ready to pull her away, but she continued to talk to Dave.

Dave let out a huge laugh at something she said, then he made another move. In a blink, he was all over Maggie, arms wrapped around her, face too close for comfort. Shane's blood boiled, and he stormed across the room.

In the seconds it took him to reach the couple, Maggie stomped on Dave's foot and twisted his arm at an awkward angle.

"I asked you politely to stop touching me. Even if that wasn't enough to dissuade you, Shane would kick your ass if he saw."

Shane swelled with pride at the way she handled herself, but he forged on. "I did see."

Startled by his voice, she released Dave's wrist and spun around. Dave rubbed his hand.

Shane grabbed him by the shirt and tossed him up against the wall. "Keep your goddamn hands to yourself."

"I was just being friendly."

Shane smelled the alcohol on his breath. He could only imagine what the smell did to Maggie. Shane cocked his fist back, but Maggie pulled on him.

"Shane. Shane!" She squeezed between his fist and Dave's face. "It's okay. I'm fine."

"Doesn't matter. He had no right to touch you."

"And I think he knows that now." She tugged his arm down. "Don't make a scene. Let's go dance."

He let go of Dave's shirt and looked at her. Really looked at her. No freak-out evident. She was clear-eyed and strong.

Dave slid away faster than any drunk Shane had ever seen.

Maggie smiled and ran a hand down his chest. "My hero."

Her eyes went from clear to lust hazy. Adrenaline and lust

pounded through him. He pushed her against the wall with the length of his body and captured her mouth with his. He held her tightly and tasted her. His fingers wrapped in her hair and pulled her head to the side to have access to her neck. God, he loved every inch of her.

He wanted the world to know she was his. Only his. No other man would ever lay a hand on her.

She held on to his shirt and whispered, "Shane."

He snapped to attention. She was breathing heavily, and he had her pinned to the wall. Regret speared through him. He was no better than Dave. "Shit. I'm sorry, Mags."

"Hey, it's okay. I just didn't think we wanted to put on a show for your entire family."

He licked his lips, her taste lingering. "You wanted to dance." He pulled her to the small dance floor and into his arms. He held her gently as she wrapped her arms around his neck.

They swayed to the music that he wasn't hearing because she filled his entire head. "I love you, Magpie."

"I love you, too."

"Move in with me." The words were out without thought. He just knew he needed her to be with him always.

"What?" She pulled back a little and stared into his eyes.

"It makes no sense for us to travel back and forth. Move into my apartment. I want to come home to you every day. I want to wake up with you every morning."

"I don't know what to say."

"Yes."

"This is all so new. Don't you think it's rushing things?"

"No. I've been in love with you for years. No one knows me as well as you do. We're best friends. All the rest is little shit. We'll figure it out as we go."

She didn't say anything, and fear gnawed at him. Maybe this wasn't as real to her.

"Let's talk later, you know, when you're sober and not blinded by jealousy."

He choked out a laugh. "I wasn't jealous. I was pissed."

"Whatever you say. Either way, it was really hot."

Shane kept Maggie by his side for the rest of the party. The crowd thinned out and wound down. He said his good-byes to friends and family and couldn't wait to get Maggie home. He let her drive his truck, even though he'd stopped drinking and had sobered up. He couldn't lose control with her like he had at the bar because of Dave. If anyone could make him crazy, it was Maggie.

Before he knew it, they were at his new apartment. He was mostly unpacked, in large part due to Maggie's help. She'd carried a backpack with her when they left the bar. He tried not to think about what was in the bag. They walked up the stairs to his apartment on the second floor of the two-flat. She unlocked the front door and pulled him through.

"Are you tired?"

"Not so tired that I want to miss out on my present. I don't want you to lose your courage."

"Not a possibility." She pressed a quick kiss to his lips and disappeared into the bathroom.

MAGGIE CHANGED QUICKLY, DONNING THE RIDICULOUS PLAID skirt. She rolled the top to shorten it, just as she has as a freshman, which upset the nuns to no end. Instead of buttoning up the white blouse, she tied it à la Britney Spears. Her hope was that what she lacked in cup size she would make up for by being commando under the stupid uniform. This thing had been one of the many reasons she'd wanted to get kicked out of the Catholic school Moira attended.

If she hadn't, she probably would've never met Shane, so

things worked out all around. She left the bathroom determined to catch more than a glimpse of the Shane she had at the bar tonight. When she got to his bedroom, he was sprawled on the bed, mostly naked, hand in his boxer briefs, stroking himself.

"I know I didn't take that long changing. You couldn't wait?"

He sat and shrugged. "I get bored easily."

She walked closer and did a twirl. "Am I every man's fantasy?"

"I don't know about every man, but you hit it for me." He pulled her close to him, but she pushed back.

She planted her foot on the bed beside his thigh and bent at the waist to adjust her shoelace, giving him full view of everything under the skirt. He groaned and rubbed his hands up her legs. His eyes were filled with hunger.

He kissed her stomach just below the knot in her blouse. Her nipples hardened. He knocked her leg off the bed, then stroked up the outside of her thighs and reached around to grab her ass. His mouth went to her nipples, sucking them through the thin cotton.

While his tongue ravaged her nipples, his fingers moved back and stroked her pussy, which was now wet. Her hips followed his rhythm. God, he was good at this.

"Come here." He tugged her hand and turned her gently toward the bed. "I want to taste you."

She snickered. "You already know what I taste like. I thought I was fulfilling your fantasy."

"Having my way with you is always the fantasy."

She bit back her sigh. He never really had his way with her. He was too busy being cautious. But then his lips and tongue found her center and flicked at her clit, and she couldn't think about anything.

After she came with her skirt flipped up on her stomach,

and her nerves were buzzing with need, Shane slid beside her body.

"You know, if you moved in with me, we could do this more often."

Christ. He was going to bring this up now? She shoved his shoulder to get him to lay back. "We agreed to talk when you're sober."

"I'm sober enough."

She climbed up and straddled him. She couldn't do this now. She wanted to have sex, not discuss it. His hard-on pressed against her and she shifted to create the friction she desperately needed. "Later."

Leaning over, she kissed him, but he pulled away.

"Wait." He sat up, pushing her back. "What's the problem?"

"Right now, the problem is you got me hot and horny and I want you inside me, but you insist on talking."

"As much as I want to be inside you, I feel like you're using sex as a way to avoid the conversation."

Busted.

MAGGIE'S EYES WIDENED AND HIS EARLIER FEAR RETURNED, curling through him, so he asked the one question he didn't want to. "Why don't you want to move in with me?"

She pulled completely away from him, smoothing her skirt as she stood. This was not going well. "I just...I don't know if we're ready for that."

"I'm ready. I wouldn't have asked if I wasn't. I love you."

She bit her lip and stared at the floor.

"What's going on, Maggie?"

"You're holding back."

What? He hadn't been expecting such a strange statement. "No, I'm not."

"When it comes to sex, you are. I feel like I've always known everything about you. You're open that way, at least with me. Except for when it comes to sex. You hold back."

He opened his mouth to rebut, but her hand flew up.

"You're afraid of hurting me. I get it. I've been telling you for a long time that I'm not fragile. But you can't see that."

"I don't think you're fragile."

"Yeah, you do. You're constantly checking to make sure I'm okay, that I'm not freaking out, that something isn't a trigger." Her face scrunched up. "It gets in the way."

He had no idea. She seemed to be enjoying sex. He didn't feel like he was holding back. He loved everything about being with her.

"The sex is good. Like crazy good. Better than anyone."

"I don't need you to stroke my ego. How can it be better than anyone if you're saying shit's in the way?" He scrubbed a hand over his head. "I'm not holding back, Maggie."

Her shoulders dropped, and she licked her lips before she paced in front of him. "Do you treat me like other girls you've slept with?"

Loaded question. "You're not like other girls."

"But I want to be."

How could she expect him to treat her like other women? They were never going to be a permanent part of his life.

She completed her circuit and stood in front of him. She swung a leg over his thighs and straddled him again. Wrapping her arms around his neck, she leaned in and whispered, "The hottest thing you ever said to me was when we first talked about sleeping together. You said, 'We do this my way.' I want to do it your way."

He held her hips to anchor her to him. There was no way he was letting her go again. "What do you want?"

Her lips brushed his ear as she spoke and his dick jumped in response. "The hottest thing you've ever done to me—hottest thing *anyone* has ever done—was when you pushed me up against the wall tonight to let the world know I'm yours."

His muscles stiffened at the memory, and not in a good way. He'd pushed her all right. He'd closed in on her and trapped her and forced his body on top of hers. His need to protect her compelled the action, but fuck, it had felt amazing. But the regret had hit him hard and fast.

Maggie leaned back and took his face in her hands. "When you came up on me and Dave, what did you see?"

"A man who wanted to die."

Her face brightened with a huge smile. "No, I mean me."

He thought back, and the image of her face remained lit in his brain. He recognized it in the moment. "You were okay."

"Yeah, I was. Even with him pawing at me. Even with his nasty whiskey breath filling the air. I took care of myself, and I was okay."

She snuggled her hips closer to his and his hard-on returned full force.

"I'm never going to stop needing to protect you."

"I know that. Part of me even likes it. Knowing that I have this big, strong dude at my back. But when it's you and me, you need to let it go. I know you won't ever hurt me."

Of course he wouldn't. He was glad she knew that. But he still had no idea what she was asking for. "What do you want?"

"I want you to let go of the fear of hurting me. I want more of what I got at the bar tonight."

He remembered her saying she wanted a guy who would take charge and make demands. He'd thought it was the alcohol talking. "You want me to slam you up against a wall and kiss you?"

"I want you to loosen your control enough that you don't worry about being careful with me."

"You were very clear when we talked. You said not fast and not rough. I'm okay with that." The way she had curled into herself that night almost crushed him. He'd never forgive himself if he had been the cause of such a reaction.

"I was wrong. It depends on who I'm with. It's different with you. It's right. I want all of you." She ground her hips down, and he felt how wet she still was.

"Does that mean I get all of you?"

"You got it."

His fingers flexed and dug into the flesh of her hips. God, he wanted to be inside her. He'd never wanted to take her as much as he did right now. He unclenched his jaw. "And you promise you'll tell me if I overstep?"

She giggled. "Have I ever held my tongue?"

"Good point." He lifted slightly off the bed and spun until she was flat on the mattress beneath his body. He pinned her in place with his hips and yanked at the blouse to spread it apart. Her tits pointed up at him and he sucked on a nipple while pinching the other. She moaned and wiggled.

She hiked her leg up and her damn gym shoes scraped against his side and his back. He hissed with the pain and spread her legs wide. She stared up at him with a cocked eyebrow. After tugging off her shoes, he stripped off his underwear and slid a condom on. Then he covered Maggie's body.

He stroked her clit while kissing her neck. She clawed at his head and his back. He brought her to the brink of orgasm and backed off. He'd show her all about losing control. He slid into her and paused, allowing her warm, silky smoothness to work its magic on him.

Barely pulling out, he bumped his pelvis into hers. Her muscles tightened around him. He wrapped his arms around her body, holding her close, as he pumped into her, driving as hard and deep as her body allowed.

He gripped her leg and pressed it toward her chest. The movement gave him the angle he wanted. Her body bowed, and she screamed her release. He slowed his movements until she came down. Her muscles contracted, pulling him in.

"Oh, God, Shane." Her breath came in little puffs. Her eyes barely opened to slits and her smile was weak.

He grinned. She thought they were done. He pulled out, grabbed her, and flipped her over. She landed on her stomach with an *oomph*. With his knees, he nudged her thighs apart and lowered himself to her. He smoothed her hair away from her face and neck. "Still good?" His voice was raspy with need. If he didn't get back inside her soon, he might explode right here, looking at her ass pointed up at him.

She raised her hips and nodded. He slid back into her wet pussy from behind. One hand held her shoulder and the other grasped her hip, his thumb pressing into her ass. He sank deep. As he began thrusting, her hands fisted in the blanket. He pumped wildly, flesh slapping, his release close.

Maggie screamed out. He growled and fell on top of her. They were both panting and sweaty and totally fucking wasted.

Her arm waved weakly. "Can't. Breathe," she huffed out.

He rolled off her. "Sorry."

She still didn't move. His hand had left a hint of a mark on her hip. Not enough to cause a bruise but enough to show that she was his. He tugged off the condom and tied it off. He struggled to sit up and toss it in the trash.

Maggie slowly rolled over. Red marks marred her chest, where his whiskers rubbed against her, and he'd left a bite mark on her collarbone. He didn't even remember doing that. Yeah, if anyone could make him lose control, it was this woman.

"Stop," she mumbled without opening her eyes.

"Stop what?" He lay next to her and tossed a leg over hers.

"You're worrying about this. All you need to know is that was the best freaking time I've had in my life. You're going to have a hard time topping that after I move in."

His brain was fuzzy, so he wasn't sure if he'd heard her right. He forced himself up, bracing on an elbow. He poked her side to get her attention. She opened one eye and smirked.

"Did you say you're moving in?"

"Yep."

"All I had to do was screw you blind to get you to agree?"

"You're a funny man, Shane." But her face grew serious as she opened her other eye and stared at him. She stroked his jaw. "You have to promise to stay open like this. To be your total self. I want it all."

"You got it." He echoed her words back to her. He kissed her with his last bit of energy. She was okay. He saw it in her eyes and in her smile. Not just now in the afterglow of great sex, but in working on her new jobs and dealing with her family. He held her close and breathed her in.

They would have it all.

Thank you so much for taking time to read my book. I hope you enjoyed hanging out with the O'Learys in Chicago. Although this is the last book of the series, I do have a spinoff series about the O'Malleys (Jimmy and his siblings). The series is called For Your Love and the other 4 O'Malleys each get a book.

Keep reading for the first chapter from *One Night with a Millionaire*, the first in my Daring Divorcees series.

If you could spare a moment, I would appreciate you leaving a review of this book.

If you'd like to stay up-to-date on my releases and have the chance to win some prizes, click here to join my newsletter.

Tess shimmied into her silk navy dress, knowing it wasn't quite as fancy or formal as some women would wear, but it would do. It was either this or the little black dress she'd had for almost a decade. Her life rarely called for formal wear. She checked the time and realized Nina would be arriving any minute. Trevor said he'd stop by to help as well. When William, her ex, bailed on taking the kids for the weekend, her friends that she'd made in divorce support group had stepped up.

The night was important to the hospital because it raised so much money every year, but for Tess, it was the only night of the year when she wasn't taking care of anyone. She wasn't a nurse or a mom, she was just a woman out for a good time. And with the kids home for the summer, she needed a real night off.

The doorbell chimed just as she slipped on her heels.

Opening her bedroom door, she heard the cacophony of her home. The boys fought over something in their room, and Zoe yelled from her position on the couch.

"Someone's at the door!" Zoe called for the second time.

Walking past, she tapped her daughter's head. "You could've answered it."

"You always taught me not to open the door for strangers."

Tess rolled her eyes. "Nina and Trevor aren't strangers."

"But they're babysitters. As if I need one."

She ignored Zoe and opened the door to see Nina standing on the porch with a huge smile.

"You look hot!" Nina told her.

"Eww," Zoe called from the couch.

"You should be thrilled your mom can pull this off. This is your future," Nina said and gave Tess a quick hug. She swept a hand down the length of Tess's body. "This is amazing. Don't listen to the cranky teenager."

"Thank you."

Nina narrowed her eyes. "But it needs something…" She pointed a finger at Tess's neck and then rummaged in her overnight bag. A moment later, she held a sparkly necklace in her hand. "I know you don't do much jewelry, so I brought this. It'll look fabulous."

"That's so thoughtful, but I can't wear that."

"Yes, you can. Turn around." She twirled her finger. "It looks incredible for an expensive fake."

She had no idea when Nina had become so bossy. They'd been friends for years, but it had taken Nina months of coffee dates with the group of divorcees before she'd even really engaged in conversation. Now she was telling Tess what to do.

Tess lifted her hair to let Nina clasp the necklace. As it dropped into place in the deep V neckline of her dress, Tess touched the cool stones. Adding glitter made her feel a little like a princess.

As if reading her mind, Nina said, "Okay, Cinderella, let me see."

The doorbell sounded again, and Billy and Andrew tore into the room screaming, "Trevor!"

It was like they had radar for finding a guy who was fun. They both ran to the door and fought over who would answer it. When they finally yanked it open, they launched themselves at Trevor.

"Hey, guys. Way to make *me* feel welcome," Nina said.

The boys pulled Trevor into the living room. He looked like the Jolly Green Giant being tugged by munchkins.

"Wow," Trevor said when he saw Tess.

She smiled. "I know that's a compliment, but I can't help but wonder what you think of me every other time I see you."

"Aww, you're always beautiful. But this…this is wow."

"Gross," Billy said. "That's my mom."

"I know. And she's my friend. Don't you know any girls at school who are pretty?"

"Yeah, but…" He looked at Tess with his whole face scrunched. "She's *Mom*."

"Yeah, I love you, too, buddy. Go to the kitchen and wash up. Pizza should be here soon."

Andrew started to follow Billy, but he turned back and whispered, "I think Trevor's right." Then he took off to the kitchen.

Tess turned to Zoe. "In bed by ten thirty."

"It's the weekend."

"You still need sleep, and you're not staying in bed until noon. Chores tomorrow."

"Gawd. Does it ever end?" Zoe shoved off the couch, tucking her phone in her pocket.

"Sure. As soon as you turn eighteen and move out."

Zoe heaved that teenager sigh Tess despised and walked to the kitchen. Tess focused on not grinding her teeth, which would cause tension to build, which would inevitably lead to a migraine.

"Go. Get out of here. Have an amazing time," Nina prompted.

Tess inhaled deeply and released the breath.

"Thanks. Thank you, too, Trevor. Don't spoil the boys or let them stay up too late."

"You mean no *Walking Dead* marathon fueled by greasy food and sugar? What the hell am I here for?"

Tess laughed. "You guys are awesome. I totally owe you."

"I'll stay until the boys are settled in bed and then head out," he said. "Have a great time."

Giving Nina another hug, she whispered, "My bed is made. Get comfortable there. I'm not sure when or if I'll be home."

"Stay out, have fun, get laid. We'll be fine."

She grabbed her clutch purse and shoved her lipstick and phone in beside two condoms. With her keys in hand, she rushed through the kitchen to give the kids a quick hug and kiss and a final warning to behave.

The pizza delivery guy pulled up as she walked toward her minivan. Nina stood in the doorway and waved her off. It was one night. They'd be fine. She knew it to be true, but even after all these years, she still got a sinking feeling every time she left the kids. Mom guilt sucked.

When she went to work, she usually took the train, but traveling on the El in a party dress didn't seem wise, so she drove into downtown Chicago. The city skyline was beautiful. At least that's what she told herself as she fought with the cabs on the road in the gridlock of the city.

By the time she turned the corner toward the Peninsula, she'd had enough. Even though it went against her nature, she forked over the exorbitant valet parking fee for the night. She didn't care how many extra hours she'd have to work to make it up. Not having to drive around on a Saturday night to look for parking was worth it.

She stepped from her mom-mobile and smiled at the valet, who was classy enough not to laugh at her and the picture she made—elegant dress, high heels, perfectly curled hair, and climbing from a minivan that reeked of French fries. Yeah, she was ready for a drink.

Inside the lobby, she texted her friend and coworker Angie to let her know she'd arrived. They'd made plans to have a drink together and scope out the crowd. Their boss thought they were there solely to help fill the coffers for their department. Tess usually put in her hours for the hospital and then went to the hotel bar to find company for the remainder of her night. If nothing else, she might be able to talk Angie into hitting another hotel or club.

***

Miles Prescott sat on the edge of his bed, careful not to wrinkle his tuxedo. The mere thought of listening to his mother nag about how he looked like he'd just rolled out of bed was enough to keep him neatly pressed. The St. Mark's Hospital gala would be his third event this week. His second black-tie of the month.

Normally, he didn't care about the fundraising and charity events he was expected to attend as the face of his family. While his siblings did the "real" work of running the family software company, he mostly dictated where they should send charitable contributions. But tonight, he was tired.

In fact, since his dad had died, this had begun to take its toll. When his father had been alive, Miles had been able to do his work in his office and at board meetings. His parents had been the face of the family. He'd attended only a handful of events. Now, the bulk of such affairs fell to him. And he hated it.

Of all the Prescotts, he was definitely the partygoer. Hell, everyone loved a good party. Except these weren't parties.

They were *events*. All polite conversation, shameless flirting with older women who always went home with their husbands, and superficial smiles with people he rarely wanted to see again, but often did.

Part of him would kill to go back to being in college. To drink beer at a party. To meet women who actually wanted to talk to him, not just to get a contribution.

Shoving off the bed, he smiled at the thought of his mother's reaction if he ordered a beer at the gala tonight. A knock let him know she was ready to go downstairs. At least with the gala being held at the Peninsula, he had an awesome view of the city and excellent food for the night. It was almost enough to make up for everything else.

Another sharp rap had him moving faster. He opened the door with an apology on his lips.

"What are you doing?" his mom asked before he had a chance to say anything.

"Getting ready. It's a big suite. Long walk from one end to the other." His sarcasm was lost on her.

"Are you ready?"

"Just about." He looked at her for a moment. Something was off. Stella Prescott was always formal, but tonight she looked stiff. "What's wrong?"

She swept into the room, lips pressed tightly. "It's the gala. I thought I could do it."

"What do you mean?"

"This one was always your father's favorite. I didn't make it last year…"

She didn't finish the thought. Miles knew she hated admitting how lost she'd been when Dad died. She was slowly coming back to herself. It was part of the reason why Miles kept agreeing to attend these things.

"It'll be fine, Mom." He walked across the room and gathered his wallet and key card. "Why did Dad like this one?"

Her face softened. "Because, like you, he hated formal high-society gatherings."

Miles laughed and pointed at the tuxedo he wore.

"Well, let's not get carried away, Miles. Of course, if you want to raise any real money, the event has to be black-tie, but this gala is open to so many more people. He loved talking to guests from all walks of life. Many of the hospital employees attend. Mostly, I think it's an attempt to draw in more funds. They plead their case directly to bene-factors."

Interesting. If his dad had liked this event, maybe Miles's night wouldn't be a total loss. He found it funny his mother managed to think doctors were of a different class. He highly doubted the maintenance staff would be joining them for the evening.

He held out his arm for her to take. "Shall we?"

She looped her hand through his crooked elbow. "Keep in mind not all of the guests will be who you're used to. Try not to comment on off-the-rack gowns and rented tuxedos. Not everyone is as privileged as we are."

"First, have I ever embarrassed you by looking down on anyone?"

"Well, I didn't mean that."

"Yes, you did. And second, do you think I would be able to tell an off-the-rack dress from a designer one? I'm too busy imagining the dress on my floor to think about something like that."

His joke had the desired effect. She lightly smacked his arm. "That is exactly the type of talk to which I'm referring. My friends find you simply scandalous."

He led her to the elevator.

"While my peers know you are playing games, not all the women here will understand."

His night was looking better by the minute. While it

wasn't a kegger, he might have the chance to actually enjoy himself.

The elevator arrived with a swish and a subtle ding. Inside, his mom rested her head against his shoulder as the doors closed. "Thank you for doing this, Miles. It means a lot to me."

Moments like these were exactly the reason he continued to agree. He could fight his brother and sister about always being the one to go. They could just as easily make appearances, but he couldn't fight his mom. He liked knowing she could lean on him.

Never one to show any kind of weakness for long, she straightened and put on her game face before they reached the ballroom.

###

Miles waded through the throngs of people to reach the bar. While his mother was content to sip champagne all night, he wanted something a little stronger. At least she'd been right about the crowd being different than the guests at the usual events they attended.

At the bar, he ordered a scotch, and while he waited, he eavesdropped on conversations happening behind him.

"Are you saying the work you do is more important than the cancer wing?"

"Of course not. We're all working our ass—really hard to save lives every day."

Hearing a woman nearly slip and swear at prospective donors made Miles turn to watch the interaction. The couple behind him he recognized. The Baldwins were generous but loved to make a recipient work for it.

Mrs. Baldwin reached out and laid a hand on the woman's arm. "Really, dear. How do you do it without becoming severely depressed every day?"

The woman stood with her back to Miles, so he couldn't

see her face, but her voice carried clearly. "Many days break my heart. I work with sick babies. When a newborn is so small she can fit into the palm of my hand"—she held her hand out, palm up to demonstrate—"and I hold and care for that baby daily, nothing in the world feels as satisfying as the day I get to see her go home."

Miles's gaze followed the line of her arm from her hand to her shoulder. Her brown hair fell in waves down her back. The dress she wore hugged her but wasn't tight. It also wasn't too revealing, which sucked for him. He didn't want to have to imagine her body. His eyes landed on the curve of her ass and down the length of her long legs, which were bare. The toned muscles made him ache to touch them.

Mr. Baldwin chimed in, "Why should we fund such a small department? Wouldn't our money have a greater effect at a hospital like Lurie's or even St. Jude's, where children are their sole focus?"

"Those hospitals are phenomenal, of course. But not every family can or will go to either of those places. Yes, St. Mark's is small, but we do amazing things in our tiny department. Our families come to us for help. We're close to home for them. They have extended family nearby for support. They don't have to disrupt the lives of their other children in order to save the newest member of the family. At St. Mark's, we care for the entire family, not just sick children."

"Are you sure you're a nurse, Theresa?" Mr. Baldwin asked.

"Absolutely. Why do you ask?"

"You talk like someone who has a lot of experience reaching into deep pockets and wringing them for all they're worth."

She chuckled, and the low sound shot straight through Miles. The bartender set his whiskey at his elbow, but Miles was afraid to turn away. He wanted to see the woman who had caught Carter Baldwin's attention so easily.

"I assure you, I work the floor every week. The only fundraising I do is attend this gala every year."

"If you're half as good at being a nurse as you are at talking about how good the hospital is, you should be running the gala."

Another gentle laugh. "Thank you for the high praise, Mr. Baldwin, but I love my job. I'm not looking to run anything. It was very nice to meet you."

Baldwin sipped his drink and nodded at her. "I'm sure we'll be meeting again."

She shook his hand, and Miles leaned forward, hoping she'd turn enough for him to see her face. As she moved, her long brown waves fell back from her shoulder, and Miles leaned to the side to see her. Then she turned completely around and faced him. Her eyes widened when she caught him staring at her. She inched her left eyebrow up a fraction as if to ask for an explanation, but she smiled.

"Can I help you?"

For a moment, Miles was dumbstruck. She was beautiful, with creamy skin sprinkled with freckles. But it was the smile that got him.

"Busted." He stepped forward with a hand extended. "Hi, I'm Miles Prescott. I'm sorry. I was eavesdropping on your conversation with the Baldwins."

"Why not join in?"

"I was intrigued by any woman who could capture Carter Baldwin's attention like that, but I prefer my conversations one-on-one."

She shook his hand. "So, you know the Baldwins?"

He nodded. "They're good friends with my parents." He released her hand. "Can I get you a drink…Theresa, was it?"

She nodded. "I'd love some champagne. Thank you."

Instead of stepping back to the bar, he waved a waiter over, snagged a glass from the tray, and handed it to her. She raised the glass, and Miles watched her lips settle on the edge as she sipped. Her head tilted back a little, allowing him to watch her throat work.

"So, tell me your secret. How did you captivate Mr. Baldwin so easily?"

She lifted a shoulder. "He asked what I do for a living. Personally, I don't think it's all that captivating."

"You might not think so, but I've been to functions with Baldwin, and I've been in board meetings with him. If he spares you more than a passing glance, you've caught him. Not an easy thing to do."

"Board meetings, huh? So what do you do, Mr. Prescott?"

He flinched. "Miles, please. I'm a numbers man."

"An accountant?"

"Not really. I help my family's business allocate funds." He retrieved his scotch from the edge of the bar and sipped.

"Well, now that is interesting."

"It's not like I save the lives of premature babies."

"No, but you're the man who can make my job easier. It seems as though you're the person I should've been using all my charm on instead of Mr. Baldwin." She took another drink of her champagne with a smile.

"I'm pretty sure that's unnecessary, but I would love to hear more about your work. Do you have a seat saved for dinner?"

"Are you asking if I'm here with a date?"

"That obvious?"

"A little." She finished her champagne.

"Does that mean you won't tell me?"

"I'm alone, except for my friend Angie."

"Excellent. Then the two of you can join me at my table."

She pursed her lips. "We'll see." She reached past him and

set her empty glass on the bar. "Pleasure to meet you, Miles. I'm off to mingle."

Miles knocked back the rest of his whiskey and stared at Theresa retreating through the crowd. She walked with confidence and the alluring sway of her hips wasn't lost on him. As she stopped to speak with various people, he kept an eye on her.

His gut told him that spending dinner with Theresa would be an excellent way to pass the night.

<h1 style="text-align:center">BROKEN COOKIES</h1>

When I had to decide what to make for a recipe for this book, I knew I wanted to go back to making cookies because that's my favorite to bake. I needed something that would fit who Maggie is—someone who seems broken but is really made of good stuff. The best thing about these cookies is that you can make them with whatever mix-ins you have on hand. My daughter and I made a batch of dough and then split it, each choosing what to add. Both batches came out great. Have fun with it.

Ingredients

    1 cup unsalted butter
    1 cup brown sugar
    ½ cup sugar
    2 teaspoons vanilla
    2 eggs
    ½ teaspoon salt
    1 teaspoon baking soda
    2¼ cups flour

Preheat oven to 350 degrees.

Melt butter on stovetop until golden brown. Let sit to cool.

In a medium bowl, sift together flour, baking soda, and salt.

In mixer, combine sugars. Mix melted butter into sugars. Add eggs and mix well. Add in flour mixture in thirds.

By hand, stir in your favorite combination of mix-ins. I used:

1 cup chopped pretzels (I used waffle ones—they chopped easily)
1 cup semi-sweet chocolate chips
1 cup toffee chips
Other options: pecans, walnuts, peanuts, white chocolate chips, dark chocolate chips…anything that sounds good to you.

Scoop ¼ cup of dough and place on cookie sheet, 2 inches apart from the next scoop. These are big cookies. Bake for 15 minutes until edges are golden brown. Cool on pan for a few minutes before moving to cooling rack.

ACKNOWLEDGMENTS

Wow! I can't believe that this is my last O'Leary book. When I started this journey years ago with the manuscript that would become *More Than This*, I never imagined a series. Back then, I hadn't given Maggie O'Leary's history a whole lot of thought. When I decided that the O'Learys should be a series, the reality of that history hit me, which is why Maggie's was the last book to be written.

I had a lot of help with this book. There were so many pieces that I was afraid of messing up. First, thank you to Beth Kery for reading the scenes with Maggie's therapist to make sure I didn't have her say or do anything egregious. Next, thanks to Remi Hunter, former Chicago Police, for helping me with all of the steps of becoming a Chicago cop. Any mistakes you find in the book are on me, not these extremely helpful ladies.

None of my books would be what they are without the help of my beta readers. Hanna Martine and Pamala Knight always push me to make the book better. Their advice is priceless.

And of course, my agent, Fran Black, and my editor, Peter Senftleben, who have always believed in me and my books. To my kids, who only look at me a little weird when I am deadline crazed and talk too much about characters and plot. Thanks for throwing out ideas, even if I don't use them.

Thank you to all of the readers, bloggers, and reviewers who are fans of the O'Learys. Your love of this fictional family has brightened more than one day for me. While I'll miss the O'Learys, there are new things on the horizon.

Finally, thank you to every rape survivor who has ever shared her story. I hope I got Maggie right.